A SNARE OF DECEIT

Tom Walsingham Mysteries
Book Five

C. P. Giuliani

SAPERE
BOOKS

A SNARE OF
DECEIT

Published by Sapere Books.

24 Trafalgar Road, Ilkley, LS29 8HH,
United Kingdom

saperebooks.com

ISBN: 978-0-85495-371-4

Aunt Rosa and Uncle Fortunato — this one is for you!

ACKNOWLEDGEMENTS

Several long-dead fencing masters appear in this book: in describing their world and their work I was fortunate enough to have a modern-day Provost-at-Arms and his Free-Scholar to endlessly question, and to watch in delight as they fenced in the different styles. Many, many thanks go to Fausto Lusetti and Giulia Pasini for sharing so generously with me their great skill, knowledge and enthusiasm — and to Barbara Pedrazzini for getting me in touch with Fausto and Giulia. All remaining mistakes and implausibilities are, of course, all mine.

I also owe many thanks to the lovely people at the Biblioteca Baratta — most of all Elena Montanari, who valiantly chased hard-to-get books for me through Italy and Europe, wading through all sorts of bureaucratic tangles and postal disservice with good humour and endless patience.

Last but not least, thank you to Amy Durant and everyone at Sapere Books: five books in and it's still a grand adventure!

PROLOGUE

New Year's Day 1587, Greenwich Palace

"A hayloft above the stables," Jack groused to himself as he searched around for his bells. "Ay, why not just shove us in a pigsty instead?" The players of Lord Leicester, the Queen's own favourite, and still they fared no better than this... Not that he was making the place any tidier, pushing about the pallets where they all would sleep that night. Cold, dusty, and stinking of horses — and where were the cursed bells?

After changing into their costumes, the players had carried their bundles downstairs from the hayloft and into the palace proper, where one of the boys would keep an eye on them — there being no lack of thieves in the Royal Palace. Perhaps one of those thieves had snatched the bells, a pretty toy, all silver tinkles and bright ribbons — and now there'd be a fine for losing it.

Jack gave the nearest pallet a half-hearted kick. Ah well — soon he'd have plenty of silver. His Lordship would be generous to a faithful servant bringing the sort of tidbits he had to bring. Let only this day's tumbling be done.

Still, it irked him to go back without the bells.

If only he'd had the wit to find himself a candle stump... He squinted in the pale light that filtered from the stables below, eyeing the shuttered window at the far end of the loft. A surly groom had told them to leave it alone, but a little daylight may be all he needed...

The only thing in the loft, apart from the pallets, was a three-legged stool. Jack dragged it under the window, and climbed up to reach the wooden bar that kept the heavy hinged boards in place. *Cursed rickety thing!* One knee braced against the narrow sill, he swatted at the bar with the heel of his hand until it flew free and clattered to the ground. At once the biting January wind tore the boards open to slam against the wall outside, and Jack was sent stumbling off the stool.

At least he hadn't toppled out into the yard below. He stepped back from the chill wind, laden with wet snow, and unthinkingly drew a sleeve across his face — his painted face, curse it! Now he'd stained his sleeve, the white ceruse showing grey on the lemon-coloured velvet.

Oh, was Kempe going to rap his knuckles over this!

Not that it was fair, mind you. Famous clowns like Will Kempe could be as careless as they pleased with their costumes, and not be fined for it, while hired men like himself jumped and leapt and tripped like trained frogs, to make the fine folks laugh. And soon Jack wouldn't have even that, for, at four-and-fifty, he was already too old to leap and trip.

It was a good thing that he had something else up his sleeve. Something that wouldn't make Lord Leicester laugh when he heard it — oh, no. If he played his hand well, he may never have to tumble again, with or without bells.

Jack looked around. Even with the window open, the winter light was so weak it made little difference. God's beard, if they were going to fine him for the soiled costume, then let them throw in the bells as well! His Lordship's silver would pay for both.

He stood on tiptoe and leant out to reach for the shutter's lower edge. Sleeping here was going to be no joy as it was, without having the wind whistling through the window, all of them catching their deaths after amusing the Queen... But then queens weren't thankful to common players. Were earls?

Kempe, who knew His Lordship better than most of the players, had little to say for the man's gratitude. Well, Jack had an inkling of who else might be less tight of fist — not for the words, but for the silence. But *that* would be a trickier matter. More dangerous, for there were more ways than one to keep quiet a man who knew too much.

Unease prickled at Jack. To know of young Stafford's design and to keep quiet — would it be treason? You went to the gallows for that. You went to Hell.

The Earl, then. Yes — the Earl.

Gritting his teeth, Jack snatched for the shutter again. The cursed thing had snagged open — Lord knew how. Jack righted the stool under the window and climbed back up, tottering as he leant across the sill. Another gust slapped at him, sending icy fingers down his neck. To think that, over in some passage by the Great Hall, the others would be calling him names! Teeth chattering he leant lower, groping for the shutter, numb fingers grabbing it for a heartbeat before the wind tore it away again. Panting, he leant back, holding on to the sill.

Across the loft, the ladder from the stable groaned under careful steps.

There — now they'd sent someone to hurry him. Fined for the bells, fined for the stained sleeve, and fined for being late.

"Oy, come and help!" Jack called over his shoulder. There — he'd scraped his fingers, too. The joys of being a hireling with Leicester's Men — and hear how the lazy dunce took his sweet time. That big fool Clarke, he'd wager, who lacked a sparrow's wits.

"Move your ass, you lurdane!" Jack squinted through the gloom. "Couldn't you have brought a candle?"

But when the shadow padded into sight, it was not Clarke who said, "There you are."

A shiver ran down Jack's back. "What are *you* doing here?" he asked.

And then there were hands on Jack's chest, and the sill digging in his kidneys, and the stool clattering away from under him, and the sudden bite of the cold.

When he opened his mouth to scream, the wind tore his voice away, and then there was the wind alone, and then nothing at all.

CHAPTER 1

New Year's Day, 1587

It seemed to Tom Walsingham that half of England was crammed inside the Great Hall of the Palace of Placentia – noisy, and glittering, and trying hard to be merry. The air was thick with the scent of roasted meats, crushed herbs and spices, sweat, and beeswax. Everywhere greenery and berries hung in garlands, and on a dais at the end of the huge room, Queen Elizabeth sat at the high table, gazing moodily upon the well-fed, well-drunk courtiers, whose festive chatter almost drowned out the musicians in the gallery at the far end.

Would the merriment stop, when the dire news was delivered?

Behind the dais, waiting in the stifling heat, Tom was perspiring in his rather faded burgundy grosgrain. He shifted his weight from foot to foot as he stood at the elbow of William Davison, Privy Councillor to Her Highness, and, in his Puritan heart, a great disapprover of gaiety and excess.

Not that there was much of that, at least not on the Queen's part. Even from where Tom and Davison stood, well behind the high table, a certain stiffness was plain to see in the sovereign's whale-boned back, a certain pinched look in the Royal profile.

Ah well. It was all about to get much worse.

Was there a tinge of bitter satisfaction in Davison's face, as the councillor leant close to speak in Tom's ear? Or shout, rather — in an attempt to be heard over the din.

"…Not quite herself…" was all that Tom caught. Davison had made this point about the Queen twice already, and they were not going to discuss their sovereign's spleen in any depth — not in this press that was all ears. After all, they both knew the cause of it: Mary Stuart, the imprisoned Queen of Scots, the intriguer, declared a traitor these past four weeks to much bell-ringing across the realm. But Queen Elizabeth hadn't rejoiced. She had balked at signing her cousin's death warrant. She'd shown no interest in her usual pastimes and, it was said, had been brusque to the French Ambassador. Right at this moment, she looked pensive even in the middle of festivities.

Not enough to sign the warrant, though — and not enough for Davison's taste.

"…With her kinswoman's fate weighing on her … some restraint…" the councillor groused, before catching himself, and pitching his voice beneath hearing.

Tom stifled a sigh. His cousin and master, Sir Francis Walsingham, Secretary of State and spymaster to the Queen, would never be caught discussing his sovereign in public — no matter how he disapproved her, which he sometimes did — but then, he'd also know all this for the Royal equivalent of restraint.

Restraint!

In certain things, Thomas, a prince is not allowed restraint — lest it be taken for weakness. Sir Francis's maxim echoed in Tom's mind as he let his gaze wander down the hall. In the light of countless candles, the long tables gleamed with gold and silver, plates of gilt marchpanes, and jellies in all the colours of the rainbow. The supper was advanced enough that food and wine had loosened all tongues, and much propriety —and a few gowns' necklines — and it took little imagination to fathom what Davison must be carrying on about.

But then, Davison didn't know.

Under his best lawn shirt, the sweat on Tom's back chilled with the though that he alone in this crowded place knew what was about to happen. He alone had to hide his impatience, wondering why the devil it hadn't happened yet.

Sparing a solemn nod for Davison, he turned back to the high table, where, at the Queen's side, sat Lord Leicester, another councillor, a Royal favourite, and a bird of very different plumage from Davison.

Oh, look at the man! Even in his restless wait, Tom had room in his heart for anger. Wasn't Leicester supposed to be in mourning for his nephew? Why, Philip Sidney had been dead two months, leaving a widow not yet twenty — Tom's own beloved cousin Frances — reeling and almost dying of a miscarriage, and here the Earl sat in attendance, making even his mourning an extravagance! Look at the tall, resplendent figure, wearing a king's ransom of grey pearls sewn into his black doublet. It took a man very secure in his favour — or very foolish — to nearly outshine the Queen. Tom had never quite made up his mind about which of the two was Robert Dudley, and either way it irked him a good deal that Sir Francis's plan — and his own — hinged so much on this particular nobleman's obliviousness. But then so it had to be — if Sir Francis's hand must not show, if the Queen must be swayed.

Jupiter — what the devil was that confounded player waiting for? Must Tom go back to Mr. Secretary at Barn Elms empty-handed? *I don't know what went wrong, Sir, and the plot is still uncovered.*

Always reason out all causes and all effects, Thomas, before you let yourself apprehend the worst, Sir Francis would say.

Tom drew a deep breath. The cause here was most likely that the player had decided to wait until after the tumbling, or even after the banquet — and then it would be hours still. The effect was much vexation on Tom's part — but the choice was sensible enough for the player.

A jab in the arm brought Tom back to Davison. The councillor was glowering at Tom, and bent close again to shout in his ear: "Do you not?"

Did he not what, now? "I do, Mr. Davison, most certainly," Tom shouted back, and it must have been the wrong answer, reckoning by the glare it earned.

"What, the Scots envoys?" Davison said, bushy eyebrows drawn together.

Oh yes — the envoys from Edinburgh, sent by King James to plead for his mother's life, and just arrived in London. Before Tom could think what he should have answered, a shout of merriment made them both turn to the high table, where everyone was roaring with laughter — everyone but the Queen, whose wit had no doubt caused the outburst, and who continued to eat suckets with ravenous ill-humour.

At her side, Leicester laughed the loudest. It was plain he hadn't heard any grave tidings yet.

Just as Tom wondered for the hundredth time about the player, a young page in Royal livery pushed his way to Davison's side, standing on tiptoe to whisper into the councillor's ear. At once Davison followed the boy towards the high table.

Good Lord. Tom's heart thudded. Could this be it? Leicester advised, and seeking his fellow councillor to pass on the news of a murderous plan against the Queen? Striving for impassiveness, Tom followed the progress of Davison, black as a raven among the many-coloured throng. He appeared more disapproving than alarmed, by the carriage of his shoulders.

"Why, Thomas!"

Oh Jupiter rain on all sociable idlers! With a hasty excuse ready, Tom turned around — and stopped short. There, with a sneer on his lips, thinner of hair and thicker of waist than when they'd last crossed paths, stood Tom's plague of an elder brother, Sir Edmund Walsingham of Scadbury.

"Ned," Tom greeted warily.

Edmund nodded, without the slightest pretence at friendliness. But then, they'd never been friends — not for all the years Ned had been the heir, with Scadbury as good as his, and Tom the third son and their father's least unfavourite, and not now that Sir Edmund was still unmarried at one-and-thirty, and Tom his only heir.

"Ever a visitor of Royal courts, are you, Tomkin?" Ned smirked, eyeing Tom's attire from head to foot.

Never had Tom wished so fervently that he'd had a new court suit made after all. One that wasn't five years out of fashion. Considering the state of his debts, what difference would a few more pounds do?

"I'm here —" *on Sir Francis's business,* Tom bit back. It was true, and it would annoy Edmund, so jealous of his brother's good standing with their powerful kinsman — but it wasn't prudent. Not with all that was at stake. Not even the safe half-lie of carrying letters to Davison. Tom glanced back over his shoulder. Amidst the sea of glittering heads and wheel-like ruffs, Leicester continued unmoved at the Queen's side, and there was no trace of Davison.

"Oh, you're here on most important business, I'm sure." Ned said, loud and flushed with too much wine — and let him think what he liked. He was unlikely to boast to anyone of his brother's work, and had no connections of the sort that could damage Sir Francis's work.

Or had he?

Over his brother's shoulder, Tom observed a thin-lipped gentleman with a grey forked beard, and a young lady in green on his arm.

"You know Sir Ralph Shelton, brother? No, of course you don't." Ned's eyes gleamed unpleasantly. "And Mistress Etheldreda, his daughter."

So this was what brought Sir Edmund to Court — wife-hunting?

Sir Ralph remained frosty in his stiff little nod — whether misliking Ned's proprietary manner, or the scapegrace brother, was not clear. As for the fair-headed Etheldreda — Lord, what a name for a girl! Such a pointed little chin, such measuring grey eyes. Tom disliked her at once.

But then, he'd have disliked the Queen herself for a sister-in-law, cutting him from Scadbury as she bore Ned's children—which Ned knew all too well, and enjoyed all too much. And, lest it showed too plainly on his face, Tom turned away, observing the high table — still quite undisturbed.

Ah, there Davison went, all but elbowing his way through the press — and dark-browed enough to have heard the direst tidings. To the devil with Ned's little games! With the hastiest apology, Tom turned his back on his brother and hurried after the councillor.

Calling was no use, much less when the musicians in the gallery struck up a new tune, all tambours and pipes, so it wasn't until Tom caught him by the sleeve that Davison turned around with the fiercest glare. He softened slightly when he saw who it was, tried to speak, and then, with a shake of his head, led the way to the large bay window halfway down the hall.

"I'll say he does it on purpose!" Davison hissed, as soon as he'd dragged Tom to the window. "My Lord Leicester, sitting at the table like a prince — and calling on me as though I were his chamberlain! Am I not a Councillor, just like His Lordship?"

Bless the man with hot water — here was petty rivalry, instead of dire news. Somewhat narrow-minded, Sir Francis called Davison — and of course the man wasn't privy to the game at play, but still it was an effort not to shake him.

"Mr. Davison, Sir!" Tom warned, with a pointed look at the courtiers and servants swarming all around.

"Yes — yes." Davison caught himself, white-lipped with fury. "But truly. Her Highness's patience is waning, he says. Begs of me to see what has become of his tumblers!"

"His tumblers!" Tom's heart skipped a beat. Leicester's Men, and the fellow who was to reveal. "What of them?"

Davison harrumphed, like one who bore many worries — but not this particular one. "They should be tumbling, and they're not — and he wants me to —"

This was where Tom Walsingham forgot his manners, and silenced a member of the Privy Council. "Don't be put out, Mr. Davison," he blurted. "I'll see to it."

And, waiting for no answer, he made his way through the press, to find Lord Leicester's Men.

A few of them he found in the screen passage under the gallery — a huddle of green and yellow popinjays, chattering aloud, tinkling with the bells they wore at wrists and ankles. They turned as one when Tom arrived, faces hard to read under the paint.

Was one of them Perkin? Tom had never met the man — but, even if he had, would he know him among these painted faces?

On being asked what they were doing, the players muttered of lost bells, of Will having gone to find Jack. There was much exchanging of glances — black-lined eyes gleaming yellow against the white ceruse — then one of the older men tilted his head past the kitchen and said: "Over at the stables, Your Honour."

A boy was dispatched to show Tom the way. Not that he needed it, for he'd been many times at Placentia, but perhaps he could glean something from the young player? He could not, it turned out. The lad, no more than thirteen or fourteen, led the way across the Outer Court and behind the tiltyard stables, hopping among the jumble of carts and fine carriages, shuddering in his gaudy player's apparel, and might as well have had no English — or no speech at all. Did he know what the matter was? A shake of the head. Who were Will and Jack? A shrug. Then a forefinger pointed at the half-timbered pile of the stables.

It was snowing again, and the cloud of Tom's breath hardly formed before the icy wind dissolved it — making him wish he'd thought to grab a cloak. It was a relief to step through the back door and into the dimly lit stables, warm with the breath of horses and the scent of hay. It wasn't peaceful, though, for the beasts were huffing and shifting in their stalls…

A groom with a lantern hastened out of the gloom to bar the way. "I'm sent by my Lord Leicester," Tom said — a tweaking of the truth, but not too much, which had the man's grim manner change to an awkward bow.

"'Tis the Earl's players that you seek. This way, Master." He pointed into the depths of the stables, a huge, long building with two wings. Old King Henry, by all accounts, had loved his horses. The groom showed Tom to the farthest wing, which had horse stalls on one side, and arrays of saddles, tack, and pieces of tilting armour on the other. Halfway down a ladder led through a hatch to the hayloft, and climbing down that ladder came a scarlet figure, booted feet feeling for each rung: a yeoman of the Royal Guard.

Holding his lantern high, the groom scurried close, eager to inform the guard of the gentleman from the Earl's retinue.

"Not from the retinue," Tom hastened to explain. "But His Lordship sent to hurry the tumblers."

The yeoman, a gangly, straw-haired young fellow wearing the everyday scarlet and black coat of his livery, studied Tom for a moment, sucking his teeth.

"Ay, there was some tumbling and no mistake," he said. "You'd better see, Master — before we move it."

The man took the lantern from the groom and, instead of climbing back up the ladder, walked along the aisle under the loft, towards the large doors. The horses blew their nostrils at their passage, big eyes rolling in the lantern's light.

"They feel it, Sergeant," the groom muttered behind them. "Just like Christian souls."

Stomach clenched, Tom followed in silence. No need to ask what it was that the brutes felt, was there? When they stepped out into the long walled court that led to the tiltyard, the sight was grimly unsurprising: a man's body lay sprawled face-down in the snow, a large stain around his head like a dark halo.

The lantern's light touched a group of men standing stiffly around the corpse — a dark sleeve here, a bright green cap there, a painted face. They parted for Tom and the yeoman. Even in the uncertain light of the afternoon, the dead man's attire was unmistakable: green hose, a yellow doublet trimmed with green ribbon.

Oh, Lord have mercy — on the fellow and on them all! "Who was he?" Tom asked — knowing all the time what he would hear.

"One of the tumblers," the yeoman said, which was plain enough, and turned a questioning look around the half-a-dozen watchers.

One of the players stepped forward. "Jack Perkin," he said. He wore the same sort of apparel as the dead man — only his doublet was of a blinding shade of green, trimmed with half a mile of ruffled ribbon. "One of our hired men."

Perkin. Tom's heart sank. And it was unchristian, surely, to contemplate a dead man and only have thought for the unravelling of Sir Francis's plan — but with Perkin dead, who was going to reveal the conspiracy to Lord Leicester? And then another, worse thought made itself known. "How did it happen?"

The yeoman pointed. "He fell from up there."

Up there, right under the peaked roof, a square window gaped open. It took some squinting to see that one shutter hung crookedly off its hinge, banging against the wall whenever the wind caught it.

"We sleep up there," the player in green said — talking more to the yeoman than Tom. "He'd gone back for his bells — and then that rapscallion..." He cast about, painted eyes narrowed as he looked around at the gaggle of stable-hands and players. "Where's he gone now? Marley!"

"Here," a voice called from inside the stables — one that wasn't unfamiliar.

Could it be, of all men…? Tom fought back a bitter laugh when a slight young fellow stepped through the door, rubbing at his arms.

Less hollow-cheeked than he'd been in Rheims two years earlier, less wild-haired — but, of all men, Christopher Marley!

"He's not one of ours," the player hastened to say. "He just found Jack."

Marley stepped closer, squinting through the light snow. And oh, the way he breathed in relief when he knew Tom, and then checked himself, and tried for blandness, and a sketchy bow — and then ruined it all by calling, "Why, Mr. Thomas!"

The dolt! Tom nodded back. "Marley."

It was small wonder that the head player eyed them both, thick lips twisting; and equally small wonder that, because yeomen of the Royal Guard saw many more tepidly-met claims of friendship than dead bodies, the sergeant wouldn't be strayed from his inquiries.

"You found him down here?" he asked of Marley.

The lad looked sideways at the body. "I spied him through the door, and…" He tailed off and shook his head.

Hard as it was to read faces in the thickening twilight, Tom remembered Marley's horrified excitement at the sight of death, back in France.

And then the yeoman asked the obvious question: "What were you doing in the stables?"

Lord let him have a good reason, Tom silently prayed. *Our man died before doing his duty, Sir, and another of our number was there by the corpse with little to say for himself.*

It was no great surprise when the prayer went unanswered. Kit Marley just shook his head. "I —"

"Seeking blows with Jack, he was — for they'd argued!" the head-player growled, shoving at Marley. And of course Marley shoved back.

"I trade no blows with the likes of you!" he seethed, and before they fell to fighting, Tom stepped in the middle, and so did the yeoman with his lantern. In the thin swirling of the snow, the dancing light made the group suddenly glow like a Flemish painting: the corpse's yellow doublet and crimson halo, the glint of far too many silver buttons on Marley's sleeve, the copper glints in the player's curly beard, the stares of the milling men.

And the yeoman, squinting in the wind, narrowing his eyes at Kit.

"If you're not with the players," he asked, "then who are you?"

Never be it said that the lad couldn't carry himself like a gentleman, when he chose. "Christopher Marley, of Corpus Christi, Cambridge. Poet."

It was possible that the yeoman didn't like poets any better than he did players, for he pursed his lips and cocked an eyebrow at Tom, thinking perhaps that a gentleman would know. Tom's nod satisfied him, but didn't pacify the players.

"A poet, ay!" one snorted. "Can't even make rhymes!"

Fighting words to a poet, no doubt. See how Marley reddened — and all the more when the head-player stamped forward. "Pestering us, he's been," the fellow cried. "Peddling a play of his own. Stuck with us all the way here — pestering us like we lack trouble!"

Because, of course, these men weren't where they were supposed to be, and an impatient Queen wouldn't like to have her pleasure disrupted over a dead player.

"The last I saw of His Lordship, he was fuming," Tom said — which hadn't been true at the time — but was bound to be now. "I'd hurry if I were you."

It was as though the men in green and yellow all startled awake at once. They looked at each other, then at the body in the snow.

Only their leader kept scowling at Marley. "What of Jack?" he asked.

"He'll be seen to until you come back," said the yeoman, and the players scurried away — one furtively crossing himself — for a dead friend was misfortune enough, without adding a displeased master.

They remained standing around the body — Tom, the yeoman, Kit blowing on his cupped hands, and a couple of grooms, the lantern throwing their black shadows on the snow.

When the guardsman ordered to move the body inside, the grooms shifted uneasily. "'Twill fright the horses, Sergeant Bray."

Sergeant Bray sighed. "So they'll be frighted," he said. "Or do you want this poor fellow left out here in the snow?"

Tom repaired inside the stables while the grooms found a board and rolled the dead man onto it. After some muttered conference, they informed the sergeant that the saddle-room, tucked away in a walled-off corner, would do for a charnel.

They had been right: the horses didn't like it. The passage of dead Jack Perkin was saluted by a dirge of nickerings and restless hoof-beats that sent a shiver up Tom's spine.

Fancies, he told himself, as he dragged his mind back to the catastrophe at hand. So now there was no hope that the plot would be discovered today. Time lost — a day at best, likely more, and that was hardly the worst.

Perkin had been meant to bring his knowledge to Lord Leicester, and now Perkin was dead. Who had known? Who had wanted to stop him? *Stafford himself?* William Stafford, their own faux-plotter, the pretend-regicide — either frightened of discovery after all, or — God forfend! — less faux and pretend than he'd appeared? Either way, disaster! Unless the player's death turned out to be ill-chance — which Tom wished he could believe. He found Marley, still hovering at his elbow, and watching him bright-eyed.

Oh yes, Marley who had found the body — this of all bodies! It was unreasonable to be vexed with him for this, surely. Why, he might even have observed something useful. "I never meet you without someone dying," Tom said.

There was the flash of a thin smile. "'Tis that you're always around when there's murder, Mr. Thomas."

But of course! Heart sinking, Tom made himself huff in surprise. "Now what put that into your head?"

And Lord forbid there should be even the slightest uncertainty in Marley's exclamation of "What else can it be?"

Well, the lad hadn't changed a whit in nigh on two years. "A good many things — an accident, for one. People do fall from windows. Unless you saw differently?"

"No." A frown. "He was there already when I arrived."

"Why did you seek him there?"

More frowning. "The door was half open, and I saw something in the snow, like a heap of..." He stopped, and raked none too steady fingers down his chin.

"You saw no one else?"

"Not a soul."

Would Kit Marley be the sort to have kept his head after stumbling upon a dead body? Tom went back to the door, and pushed it open enough to peer at the snow covering the ground outside. A fine notion, if only he'd thought of it earlier. Now it was near dark, and the fall had thickened enough to blanket the stain of blood, and fill the footprints of all the men who had trampled there in the last half-hour — never mind those of a fleeing murderer. Unless, of course…

Closing the door, Tom leant against it and narrowed his eyes at Marley. "What I meant, though, is why did you seek out Perkin at all. Did you truly have a quarrel with him?"

Marley looked away, scuffed a wet boot at a bit of straw. In the end he threw up both hands. "Have you ever thought of a truly good retort well after you needed it?"

The earnestness startled Tom into a chuckle. "Often enough, though I've never run after my opponent to let him have it when it was too late. I take it that you did quarrel with Perkin, then?"

Another memory from France: the way young Marley's humours changed like quicksilver. Now it was the turn of burning indignation. "A hired man calling my tragedy dross because I'll have no battles on the stage! I do it like the Ancients."

Peddling a play of his own, the red-bearded player had said. "Which explains how you come to be with Leicester's Men."

"I'm not *with* them!" Marley bristled. "But there's this tragedy I've written: *Tamburlaine the Great,* from shepherd-boy to emperor of Asia."

Trust Kit Marley to come up with such an outlandish notion. "And they won't buy it, so you fight with them."

"Do you fight swines for being swines?" A martyred sigh. "Perkin sneers because of the battles. Kempe hates it because there is no clown's part."

"Kempe?"

"Will Kempe, he of the ape's-laugh doublet." Marley sourly mimed the ruffled ribbons. "Leicester's clown. An ignoramus, a common player calling himself a gentleman."

Before he could truly warm to his subject, the yeoman returned, still holding his lantern. Sergeant Bray, the grooms had called him. If only he'd go away now, so Tom could observe the hayloft without raising too much curiosity.

That would have been too much to expect, surely — but, after all, Bray did the next best thing.

"You'll want to see upstairs, Master," he said, as though it were a matter of fact. "See for yourself — in case His Lordship asks about the accident."

Which, knowing Leicester, struck Tom as a most unlikely notion, but he didn't say so as he followed Bray: a figure of Inquiry having his way lighted by a scarlet-clad Philosophy. They were at the foot of the ladder when Inquiry noted Marley, tagging along and muttering to himself. *Accident?* the lad mouthed with both palms up and head tilted. Disbelief holding back — and weren't they turning into a whole allegory!

Tom beckoned the lad close enough to whisper. "Nick Skeres, my servant — you remember him from France, don't you?" One did remember the Minotaur — and besides, the Minotaur and the poet had irked each other too badly to forget. "Go find him in the kitchens — and tell him to seek out Master Lopes."

"The Queen's medicus?"

"His son. Tell Skeres to bring him here."

This was assuming that Ambrose would be at Court for New Year's Day. His father Dr. Roderigo Lopes — the Queen's physician — surely was — but... "Ha!" Marley perked up at once, eyes dancing. "I'm right, then —"

Oh, Lord give patience. "Begone, devil pinch you — and keep quiet!" With a grin far too bright for comfort, the lad trotted away — and Tom, shaking his head, climbed up the ladder after Sergeant Bray.

The hayloft held no hay — nor, in fact, much else. It was a low room, with a row of pallets pushed against the wall on each side, and looked as though it had been hastily boarded up to make it into a lodging for the players. It was also cold as Styx, with its one window thrown wide open, the broken shutter still banging in the wind. Snow had drifted inside, whitening a skewed circle on the floor, the corner of the nearest pallet, and an overturned stool a yard away from the sill.

It was to this item that Bray pointed. "See? I'll wager you the man mounted on it to close the window, and leant too far. The stool fell away, and…"

Tom nodded. It was so plausible. He looked around. "I see no lantern."

"Nor a candle," Bray said.

"So he opened the window to find his bells, and tried to close it before going back down." Oh yes, very plausible — and very convenient. That this could be all true, and still the work of a murderer, Tom wasn't going to share with this yeoman, so solemnly pleased with his notion. A false one, most likely, knowing what Tom knew — but, as long as Perkin's death could be ruled an accident, it needn't be the utter ruin of the plan. As long as Sir Francis's name could be kept out of it all. As long as Stafford himself wasn't the culprit.

"Indeed, Sergeant. I don't see that it could have been otherwise. Have His Lordship advised of this mishap — officially, I mean. And the coroner, I'll reckon?"

Not that there'll be much use, said the tilt of Bray's head. Which depended dangerously on the coroner's zeal and ability — but it was New Year's Day, after all. With any luck, even if the coroner saw the need for a jury, he would have trouble convening one before a few days — and even then, Bray's unknowing certainty would go a good way in smoothing things.

There was hope in the man's readiness to leave the window and the whole loft to their fate. "The players will sleep somewhere else tonight," he concluded, picking up his lantern — just as someone called from downstairs: "Oy, Master!"

It was more a bellow than a call — and there was no mistaking it, nor the stocky figure downstairs, bundled in an orange-coloured coat.

As he hurried down the ladder, Tom called back, "Here, Skeres. Be quiet. You'll frighten the horses." A most useless effort, the very notion of quiet being extraneous to Nick Skeres, who wasn't known as the Minotaur for nothing.

"I've brought you Master Lopes," the lad bellowed on, beaming as Tom jumped down the last three rungs.

"Master Lopes!" he greeted the slim, dark figure he glimpsed behind his servant. "Thank you — though I fear the poor man's past help."

Skeres glowered at Kit Marley — who, unsurprisingly, had tagged along.

"You said…" he began — and then, for a mercy, let it go, and moved away for the medicus.

Young Ambrose Lopes stepped forward in that marvellously grave manner that always made him seem older than his three-and-twenty years. "Are you quite sure?" he asked Tom, his face solemn. "Sometimes it's hard to tell, especially when the body has lain in the snow."

Bless the man for his sharp wit!

Upstairs, crouching by the open trapdoor, Bray had been observing with the most stolid calm. He shrugged, making the lantern dance.

"With a head cracked like a nut? Ah well, suit yourself, Master."

The saddle room was large, its walls hung with all sorts of fine bridles, halters, bits and stirrups, all wrought in curious fashions for the tilt, all polished to the merriest gleam — the strangest circumstance for the body that lay on the one hastily cleared table, under a piece of blood-stained sackcloth. Bray put his lantern at the table's end, and Ambrose lifted the cloth. The face was streaked with paint and blood that the snow had washed together — but the simplest observer would have known the sunken, rigid features and the staring eyes for the signs of death. Yet young Lopes gravely bent over the body, felt the chest, turned the head, poked at the broken skull. All the time Kit Marley observed him, wavering between disgust and fascination.

At length Lopes covered the body. "He's dead," was all he said.

Another thing that was admirable in a man of such young age was Ambrose's discretion. Only once they were out of the saddle-room, and Bray was busy bolting the door, did he explain. "The skull is dented, but I'd say he died of a broken neck. I wish he hadn't been moved, though. He fell from a window?"

Of course. Tom could have kicked himself — although how he could have kept Bray from moving the corpse without giving himself away, he didn't know.

After taking leave of the yeoman, he led the medicus back to the courtyard where Perkin had fallen to his death. The snow was still falling, and now the lantern's light showed a shallow depression in the white surface, not an inch deep, in the shape of a body. Only where the head had lain, the blood had melted a darker circle.

Lopes looked up at the open window, then down to the dark stain again.

"Could he have been pushed?" Tom asked.

"I suppose he could." Lopes looked up and down again. "Tipped over the sill, though, rather than shoved. But also he could have fallen under his own weight. I'm sorry, Mr. Walsingham. I cannot really tell."

Tom sighed. The yard was silent with the quietness of a snowy night, but the air carried a faint sound of music and laughter from the Great Hall.

The Court entertained itself, undisturbed and oblivious — the plot still undiscovered. The plot to kill the Queen that had been in truth a fabrication, but was it still? Was Stafford running with blood on his hands and ill intent in his heart? Or just hiding, cowering in fear? Had he been at Placentia at all? Tom cast about his mind a way to find out if the man was at Court. Of whom could he inquire, without giving himself away?

His mind ran in circles. Jack Perkin dead, the plan ground to a halt, and Sir Francis, ill, and grieving, waiting to be advised.

Staring at the faint trace of blood, Tom breathed in the scent of snow, let the cold burn all the way down to his lungs. He would have given much not to have to carry these tidings to Barn Elms.

CHAPTER 2

Unlike Scadbury, unlike Seething Lane, unlike even the Rue des Anglais back in Paris, Barn Elms had never truly felt like home. Nor, perhaps, should it, some might have pointed out — Tom being no more here than something halfway between a poor relation and a favourite servant.

These days the house was bleak with more than winter laying the beautiful grounds a-waste. The whole place, already reeling under the death of Sir Francis's beloved son-in-law Philip Sidney two months previously, had been shaken again when, not a week past, the widowed daughter of the house had nearly died miscarrying Sidney's child. All hopes gone; Frances wasting in her bereavement, Sir Francis ill with care and grief... A pall hung over Barn Elms, that it seemed no spring could ever lift.

Fancies. Tom would have shaken his head free of these cobwebs, but didn't want to seem impatient. Not that Sir Francis would even notice, as he sat hunched in his armchair by the fireplace, a thick vellum-bound book forgotten in his lap, watching the flames as he pondered the fate of Perkin.

Tom stood waiting, trying not to shiver in his snow-soaked clothes, trying not to dwell on how haggard his great cousin looked. He'd been as good as told by Sir Francis himself that the abscess was a convenient excuse to retire from court. Now he wasn't sure.

It was a while before Mr. Secretary dragged his gaze away from the fire. "Could the French have found out?" he wondered aloud.

Found out that there was no plot to kill the Queen, naught but the careful fabrication Sir Francis had devised and Tom set in motion — to drive home the dangers of keeping Mary Stuart alive.

Tom had had a whole sleepless night to consider this question.

"Ambassador Châteauneuf is not without resources. Or perhaps…" He hesitated a heartbeat. "Perhaps Stafford himself told him…"

"Stafford!" Sir Francis made it sound like the crack of a whip. "He seemed perfect, didn't he? A penniless, half-papist malcontent, so eager to repay a good turn. Eager enough to play the regicide, to hear him… And then he loses his head, and tries to stop it all — by doing murder. I should have known better than to trust Sir Edward's brother!"

Sir Edward Stafford, English Ambassador in Paris, was Lord Burleigh's man, and never an object of great trust in Seething Lane. On the other hand, his Catholic friendships and vast debts were part of what made his younger brother such a likely conspirator. A murderer, though?

"We don't know for sure that he killed Perkin, Sir." Another fruit born of Tom's restless hours — not that it offered much consolation. "He could just have lost heart and run."

Sir Francis clicked his tongue. "And run where? To Salisbury Court with Châteauneuf?"

"If he told the Ambassador, yes." Though Tom dearly hoped he hadn't — not that he knew quite what to hope when it came to Stafford.

Sir Francis shook his head and sighed. "At least we'd know where he is. Think of Babington and his cronies."

Or Father Ballard's cronies, rather. Tom didn't particularly want to think of them: a handful of traitors, hiding for weeks in woods and manor houses before they were run to earth. False intriguer that he was, young Stafford still knew far too much — and as a fugitive, there was no telling to whom he could unburden himself.

It gave Tom a pang to see the way Sir Francis lowered his chin on his chest. A few months ago he'd have been firing questions, discussing chances, probing. To see him so undone now, so forlorn... Tom went to kneel by the hearth, to stir a fire that didn't need it. When he turned back, Sir Francis had straightened.

"Young Stafford knew your player, I take it?" he asked.

These past few weeks, with Sir Francis retired to Barn Elms to mourn Sidney and worry about Frances, Tom had taken upon himself, together with the head-cypherer Phelippes, the execution of the plan in its minute detail — and still it made him uneasy to have his cousin unaware of so much.

"He knew of him," he explained, still on one knee by the hearth. "He had to be told of Perkin, so he'd know to let him hear what he must at the fencing hall."

It was not in question that Sir Francis said: "And you trust Rocco Bonetti."

"I do, Sir." Or did he? It had been Tom's notion to make use of the Italian, whose fashionable fencing hall Stafford haunted — not as a pupil, for he could never afford the immoderate fees, but to applaud wealthier friends. "He found Perkin — without fully knowing what was afoot. He asked precious few questions — for he hasn't forgotten what he owes to Mr. Secretary's kindness."

"Neither had Stafford, or so he swore — but I'll grant you that, of the two, Bonetti makes by far the steadier man." Sir Francis gave a small grunt as he shifted in the chair with a grimace, and the book slid from his knee to tumble in the rushes.

Tom hastened to pick it up, and his eyes went of their own accord to the title. Greek Polybius's *Histories* of Rome turned into Latin.

"The woes of old Hannibal." There was a pained look on Sir Francis's face as he took it back. "Just like Philip: never able to see a book but you must know what it is." He shook his head. "I used to hope that he and you could learn to be friends. Had you both had the time."

And what did one say to that? Always Tom had resented Sidney — even as he grudgingly admired the man's many perfections — for being Sir Francis's son of election, for having Frances and not loving her. And now that Sidney had died a hero, fighting the Spanish, Tom half regretted the friendship that hadn't been.

He'd waited too long to answer, and Sir Francis sighed, before he leant forward with some of his old sharpness.

"I will be plain, Thomas," he said, fingers tapping softly on the book's gilt fore-edge. "The Queen is out of charity with me as it is; if the false nature of Stafford's conspiracy becomes known, it will be the ruin of me and mine. However…" The finger paused its beat. "If I abandon this endeavour, Her Highness may never sign the warrant for Mary Stuart's death."

The Queen's sullen manner at the high table in Placentia came back to Tom's mind. "She has turned a deaf ear to all pleas for mercy, so far," he ventured. "She has sent the French envoy packing…"

"The French envoy!" A wave of the wizened hand. "Bellièvre irked her, made it sound as though England owed something to France. But now you say that King James's men are here. They may be subtler. They may see that Her Highness only wants a reason to belay the execution *sine die*. And then, how long before we have another Catholic plot — a true one? One that evades us? One that succeeds?" Knuckles white around the book, Sir Francis shook his head. "England will only be safe if Mary Stuart dies, Thomas — and she will only die if we frighten Her Highness into it!"

He sat back, breathing hard.

Forcing a Queen into sending another Queen to her death… There had been a time, not long ago, when Tom had recoiled from such a necessity. But then Anthony Babington and his fellow traitors had been hanged, drawn and quartered at Lincoln's Inn Fields. Among them had been Father Ballard, the traitorous priest, so broken on the rack they'd had to carry him to the scaffold, and his broken, bloodied smile still haunted Tom's nightmares. He still dreamt of Ballard, praying aloud in an ecstasy of pain, as his belly was sliced open, the intestines drawn out, praising the Lord that more like him would rise … The light in the priest's face had cured Tom of his qualms — or most of them.

But perhaps Sir Francis thought that some lingered.

"It is a narrow path that I walk," he said. "And slippery, and ruinous. If you want to leave my service, I won't blame you."

It was like being thrown out in the snow. All the cold of the ride came back to bite at Tom. What had he done that his cousin should think…? "I'll find another way to have the plot revealed, Sir." And, to his horror, Tom found he couldn't keep the breathless hurt out of his voice. "I'll unearth Stafford, uncover if he murdered Perkin, or who else did — and why. I…" *I'd never desert you.*

It seemed a long time before Sir Francis's searching gaze warmed.

"I should have known better, child. Forgive an old man's moment of weakness." Again he moved in discomfort. "Now have the kindness to send Davies to me. I'll need one of Dr. Lopes's powders, if I have to sit through dinner with my brother in law."

An old man's weakness — like Hannibal after Zama, betrayed by his peers, and forsaken by Carthage. Tom bowed deep, and was at the door when Sir Francis called to him again.

"Thomas, remember: courage needs not be rash." What had begun stern to the point of reproach, softened halfway. "We don't know how dangerous these people are. Do what you must — but take care."

It was a much disconcerted Tom that left his cousin's study, and, having sent Davies to his master, stopped at one of the windows in the gallery to sift through his thoughts. He leant against the embrasure, idly watching the snowy court below, and breathing in the scent of beeswax. It was a lovely place, the gallery — airy, and light, with its clear leaded glass and fine panelling. A gallery was what Scadbury needed — what Scadbury would have someday, if only Etheldreda Shelton failed to give Ned a son.

He should be ashamed of the thought, shouldn't he? His mother would have said so — but he was still wondering why (wasn't it natural for him to want the place?) when Sir Francis's wife emerged from a door halfway down the gallery and called to him.

A notion that she might have lain in wait did nothing to lessen Tom's worry at the sight of her. She had changed much, poor Lady Ursula, worn with care for her daughter: her black eyes had lost their brisk merriness, and her cheeks had hollowed. Still, she found a smile for him.

"Dear Tom, 'tis good to see you." She reached to take his arm, and frowned to find the sleeve cold and damp. "But you'll catch your death!" she chided. It was so motherly, the way she led him to her parlour, not content until she had him sitting by the fire, with a goblet of warm wine.

Huddling in the padded chair, Tom sipped and waited. He wanted so much to ask about Frances, and hesitated — seeking words that wouldn't sound more than cousinly, or less, which would be just as revealing. Before he found them, Lady Ursula spoke again.

"How did you find him, Tom?" she asked.

Weary, grieved, oppressed with care. "I do my best to spare him what worries I can, Madam."

A foolish answer for Sir Francis Walsingham's wife. And indeed, see what a sad tilt of the head.

"You won't shield him so much that he'll feel useless, will you?"

Useless! That Lady Walsingham should say this, that Sir Francis perhaps thought it. But how did one ask? Tom floundered until Lady Ursula sighed.

"Philip's death was such a blow — and now the baby. And I don't care if I go to the Tower for this, but the Queen behaves so dreadfully to him! He will say nothing, but..." She clicked her tongue. "You'll think me an unnatural wife, that I wish you'd brought some worry of the State to distract him from his black thoughts..." She tailed off, her gaze intent, questioning.

Oh Jove, but the world was going a-tumble! Never, in the years Tom had worked for her husband, had Lady Ursula unburdened herself so. Never had she tried to pry tidings from him — either this clumsily or in any other manner.

If ever he had been tempted to break his great cousin's confidence, this was the hour — not that the truth would have reassured her. He rose and bowed. "I won't shield him too much then, Madam. But you know Sir Francis will never be useless."

The flash of impatience was as soon come as gone, and Lady Ursula smiled as she tapped Tom's wrist. "As bad as my husband, that's what you are, Tom Walsingham!" She rose. "Now please fetch him for dinner, will you? Brother-in-law or not, I wish Sir Walter hadn't taken it into his head to visit at this of all times!"

And because he was to ride back to London at once, Tom had to ask or go away without knowing. "And my Cousin Frances, Madam?" He caught himself. "Or I should say —"

Lady Ursula waved it aside. "She'll never be Her Ladyship to you, Tom. The fever is gone, thank the Lord, but she's still weak and pale. Dr. Lopes says she needs much rest. I say she needs to weep, for sorrow festers otherwise. Lying there, dry-eyed, won't..." She broke off, shaking her head.

Ever since last summer the thought of Frances always brought with it a pang of regret, of happiness that could never be. To think of her so wretched, now... "Will you please tell her that she is in my prayers?" *And in my thoughts. And in my heart.* He had known what was seemly between cousins — until he'd come to love Frances most un-cousinly, and unlearnt it all. And perhaps he had betrayed himself, for Lady Ursula tilted her head to eye him.

"I hoped that having you here would cheer her," she said slowly. "And instead she won't see you, but..." she tapped a finger to her chin, "I trust that she will, Tom."

And, with her mouth set, she bustled away, leaving Tom lost and wishing that Frances would let him see her. Wishing it so much that it hurt.

Skeres was to be found sitting in the kitchen, busy sopping bread chunks in some sauce or other, and chatting with the maids. The women were cooing over his new coat, fingering the hideously-coloured mockado that was spread on a stool near the fire.

As had been the rule since the purchase of it, the coat's proud owner was bragging. "Real velvet, it is. Lion-hued. Cost me twelve shillings-eight!" And leave it to the Minotaur to be this loud and cheerful amidst the sadness of Barn Elms.

He jumped to his feet on seeing his master, brushing crumbs from his doublet, while the women scurried back to their work.

"I could hear you all the way from the hall," Tom groused, earning a frown that started half-repentant and turned appraising.

"You look bedevilled," was the appraisal — at which Tom gave a baleful glare.

Bedevilled! His careful plans all but undone, Sir Francis a shadow of himself, Frances buried in her grief — and he looked bedevilled! Reason said that Skeres knew little enough of it all — but Tom had little use for reason.

"I hope you've seen to the horses..." he began, only to be cut short when cries erupted in the hall. Someone shouting for Sir Francis.

Tom ran, glad he was already armed for riding, and burst into the hall with dagger drawn, Skeres on his heels, to see a burly fellow wrangling with two of Sir Francis's servants.

"I must see him!" the stranger howled. "I must!"

In his mad writhing, he sent one the servants tottering back against the long table at the room's centre. Old Gawton, Tom observed, as he closed in on the intruder.

The fellow swung around unsteadily, hands wide and empty, and gaped. "God's sake, Walsingham!" he cried. "Where's your uncle?"

And, Lord God above, it was William Stafford.

He hasn't run, part of Tom's mind sang in relief while, lowering his dagger, he grabbed Stafford by the arm. "You fool!" he hissed. "What are you doing —"

But Stafford wrenched free, shoving at Tom, and called: "Mr. Secretary!"

At the hall's far end a door had opened and more servants spilled in, as well as Sir Walter Mildmay and Sir Francis himself — and more people were running in from the kitchen and down the stairs, just as Tom and Skeres took hold of the bedlamite again — for all the good it did.

"There's murder afoot!" Stafford bellowed. "The Queen!"

Oh, devil take it!

For a heartbeat they were all frozen into silence, gentlefolk and servants, like figures in a painting, except for Stafford — who panted and strained in Tom's grip, stinking of sweat and wet wool — and Lady Ursula, peeking around the door-jamb.

Then Sir Francis spoke: "Bring that man in here, Thomas," he ordered, and retreated where he had come from.

It was no wonder that the hall buzzed with mutterings.

Well, at least it seemed that Stafford hadn't killed Jack Perkin.

There were four men gathered around the fire in the dining parlour. Sir Francis and Sir Walter Mildmay sat on either side of the hearth, and Tom waited by the table still laid for the disturbed dinner. In the middle William Stafford stood trembling, eyes darting from one man to another. He was unarmed, bare-headed, and soaked so thoroughly with snow that his bedraggled clothes smoked in the heat from the fire.

"So, Mr. Stafford?" Sir Francis inquired, with that formidable coldness he used to cover his anger. "What is this madness?"

Stafford's big shoulders rose and fell, a grimace on his coarsely handsome face.

Tom's hand went to his dagger's hilt — though more for show than anything. Had the madman been minded to run, Skeres and Davies were outside, each guarding a door.

"Mr. Stafford!" Sir Francis snapped, and the man's head whipped around, like that of a hound.

"Mr. Secretary — I swear —" he halted when Sir Francis interrupted him.

"Instead of swearing, which is a sin, you'd better explain your invasion of my house — and these rash claims of yours."

Stafford swallowed, and gave a long shudder, mastering himself enough to look at Mildmay, and then at Tom. "I don't…"

The arrant lackwit! Did he think he could barge in like this, shout of regicide in front of two Privy Councillors and a whole household, and then take it back?

Mildmay must have thought the same. His long face, mournful at the best of times, was grim as midwinter as he spoke: "*There's murder afoot*, you said. And you mentioned Her Majesty."

And each word might have been a blow, to see the way Stafford gasped and wavered. Dolt!

A glance from Sir Francis was all the order Tom needed to turn a chair away from the table, and push Stafford into it. He poured a glass of wine, and thrust it into the trembling hands — wishing he'd been more sparing with it when the man drained it in one gulp. All they lacked now, was for him to get drunk!

"This conspiracy…" Sir Francis prodded.

There was a shuddering breath. "They want to kill the Queen," Stafford choked out, and put his head in his hands. "*Monsieur* de Châteauneuf —"

"The French Ambassador?" Mildmay half rose in his seat.

Stafford nodded, without raising his head. The wine, if nothing else, had loosened his tongue. "And his man d'Estrapes, and one Moody, who is a prisoner at Newgate…"

"You say these men, the Ambassador…?" It was not often that one saw Sir Walter Mildmay thunderstruck. "But this … this is…"

It was a struggle not to fidget. There went the uncovering of the plot, Tom grimly thought — the uncovering that should have had nothing to do with Mr. Secretary Walsingham. And, disaster though it was, it still wasn't enough.

Or it wasn't until Sir Francis hummed in austere disbelief. "I must ask you, Mr. Stafford: how did you come to know of this?"

"Because I — *I* brought them to Moody! You don't believe —" voice rising, Stafford sprang to his feet like one stung, and Tom pushed him back into the seat.

"Soft and fair, now!" he ordered.

Had the dunce seemed bewildered that Sir Francis should ask him? There was nothing for it but hope that Mildmay was too turmoiled to notice. See how he leant forward to scowl, gripping the chair's arms.

"And this man at Newgate?" Sir Francis asked.

At least, Stafford wasn't howling anymore. "There's nothing Michael Moody wouldn't do, as long as he's bought out of prison."

The same words, to a syllable, the fellow had used a month back, when he'd been brought into the plan, and sworn he knew the means of feigning a plot against the Queen — why, he knew the very man!

It was working on Mildmay; would it work on the rest of the Council? Much as they'd known Will Stafford's unsteadiness… Tom had been wrong: the man hadn't lost heart, he'd lost his head! Was this because of Perkin's death? That he'd still denounced the supposed plot cleared him of murder. How he'd learnt of it, though… Tom kept his eyes on Mildmay as the councillor rained contempt on Stafford.

"And knowing this Moody for a desperate character, you led the French to him. Not only did you not uncover this evil design, in fact, you —"

Mildmay stopped at a gesture from his brother-in-law.

"But now he has uncovered it," Sir Francis said, and, as he turned to the confessed plotter, the conciliation changed to command. "You'd do well to tell us all, Mr. Stafford."

Stafford stared at the two older men in turn — one a statue of Disdain, one of the sternest Inscrutability, each limned by firelight — and swallowed hard, most likely thinking of the rack and the gallows.

Now just let this fool not betray himself — and them all!

He'd gone to Châteauneuf, Stafford said in a hoarse whisper, and asked for help in going to France.

"And you had to go to the French for this!" Mildmay scoffed. "Not to your brother, who is Ambassador in Paris!"

And must Stafford gape at that — as though Tom hadn't rehearsed him through it all again and again. Oh, to be able to hit the man over the head!

In the end he bowed his head. "My Lord Leicester loathes my brother, and since he cannot touch him, likes to make my life a misery. And Edward," he said bitterly, "he'd never risk more of the Earl's enmity for my sake."

Châteauneuf, Stafford said, had been full of understanding, but made few promises. This Tom believed in full: he'd only met the man once, and formed the impression that Guillaume de l'Aubespine, Baron de Châteauneuf, wouldn't go out of his wary way for the sake of any Englishman, much less one as useless as young Will Stafford. As for taking advantage of him, though...

"*Monsieur l'Ambassadeur* was very gracious. We talked of many things, and his secretary also showed me much friendship. They were grieved that, with this Queen's favourite sitting at the throne's foot, there's little hope for the likes of me in England. I didn't understand their meaning at first, and I fear that..." his breath hitched, and when it seemed that he would go no farther, Sir Francis finished his sentence for him.

"You fear that, in your mistempered humour, you agreed with that?"

To anyone who didn't know better, to Mildmay hopefully, it would sound like cold irony rather than the order it was.

Stafford hung his head. "Oh God," he gasped.

"Do not swear, Mr. Stafford," Sir Francis chided.

"Swear!" Mildmay cried, quivering with disbelieving rage. "Swearing is the least of his sins! Swearing pales to nothing before rank treason."

This startled Stafford to his feet and, again, Tom pushed him roughly back. Either the man was a better player than he'd seemed, or he lacked a maggot's wit. When he squirmed on the seat's edge, sweating and biting his knuckles, it all had the semblance of the truest fear — but then, what had he thought his actions would be called? Yet it couldn't be feigned, the desperation with which he clung to Sir Francis's words. Yes, it had been his mistempered humour, he vowed, to make him blind and reckless. The misery of his state, the cruelty of Leicester, the deaf ear of the Queen, the torments of his faith.

"By the time they spoke of freeing England, I was in a frenzy! I said I knew how it could be done — why, I knew the very man —" And, burying his head in his hands, he started sobbing, great wracking sobs that shook him where he slumped.

Idiot! Now Mildmay would see that he wasn't truly crying. At best, he would believe Stafford was making a show of great repentance — but the whole Council would never fall for such games.

"And when is this murderous plan to take place?" Mildmay asked.

Stafford's head shot up — and lo! He was weeping in earnest, though in fear, Tom thought, rather than repentance.

"I don't know!" he gasped, face reddened in blotches and streaked with tears. "I swear to God. We went to Newgate this morning, I and d'Estrapes —"

"Who is this?"

"The Ambassador's secretary. He wanted to see Moody, and wouldn't let it rest until I accompanied him to Newgate. They talked of poisons, or a trail of powder to make an explosion under the Queen's bed…" His voice rose to a howl and Tom hoped Skeres and Davies were keeping the household well away.

"But my mother, she's Mistress of the Robes, she sleeps in the Queen's room sometimes, I can't…" And again he collapsed in tears, drooping low in the chair.

Lost his heart *and* head indeed, but at least he hadn't run, and the plot was exposed now, and — whatever Lady Ursula thought — Fates be thanked for Mildmay's visit!

The old gentleman didn't disappoint. He slowly rose. "The Council must be advised," he declared, graver than ever. Tom at last let himself seek his great cousin's eye.

One who didn't know Sir Francis well wouldn't have seen it: ashen and spent, still Mr. Secretary seemed more clear eyed, and there was iron back in his words. "Yes, and Her Highness. And this man must be brought to the Tower."

Stafford stiffened in fear.

Sir Francis ignored him. "Thomas, you'll escort Sir Walter to London, and then to Greenwich. You'd better ride at once."

What with the snow on the road, and the lengthy affair of William Stafford's locking in the Tower, it was near dusk when Mildmay's cumbersome carriage rolled into the Outer Court at Placentia, with Tom and Skeres riding escort. Within half an hour, Sir Walter had gathered a handful of councillors in the Great Gallery. Vice-Chamberlain Sir Christopher Hatton, his jolly face scrunched in worry; Lord Burleigh, with his son at his side; Lord Leicester one head taller than the rest; and Mr. Davison in his Puritan black — together they stood in a circle that grew tighter as Mildmay spoke, in the light a signle branch of candles.

"See them, Dolius," Tom murmured. "The most powerful men in England."

"Saving 'Is Honour," Skeres grumbled — far too loud for comfort. "And you've seen 'em often enough, the lot of them. What's with you now, Mr. Tom?"

Tom shook his head, and waved for quiet. He couldn't very well tell his servant that it was the thought of having had a part in unleashing that great power, at the behest of the absent Sir Francis. The Queen would be apprised now, and orders would be drawn, and dispatched, and sent to the four corners of England. And Mary Stuart's fate would be sealed at last.

Only a few months back, he'd balked at forging a few lines of writing to force Mary Stuart's fate towards this end — and now here he was, light-headed, though heavy-hearted, at having done much worse. For weeks he'd worked on this false plot to kill the Queen, all the time fooling himself. There was nothing false to this: wasn't it a plot to kill the Queen of Scots?

Fancies, Thomas! Sir Francis would say. *This is war, and Mary Stuart the enemy, and England at stake.* Which was well and true, and had been back in July. If he was no murderer now, then Tom had been a hypocrite then. Perhaps Frances was right in wanting nothing to do with him. It always brought that little spasm of pain, the thought of Frances — ever since last summer. But together with the pain came a different certainty: rather than a hypocrite, that summertime Tom had been a fool. Father Ballard's arrogant faith on the scaffold — a faith that more like him would come, until one would slip through the web and succeed in overturning England. That had burnt away his foolishness.

A sudden sense of being observed pierced through Tom's musings, and he found Robert Cecil's gaze on him, dark and appraising. Or not quite on him. Lord Burleigh's son frowned at something beyond Tom's back. And sure enough, two ladies stood arm in arm at the gallery's far end, whispering to each other as they peered at half the Privy Council.

Maids of Honour, judging by their white garb, and the way they never batted an eyelash at being caught staring. When Tom turned back, the councillors were already moving as one down the gallery. Only Robert Cecil lingered behind, in the light of an ensconced candle, his velvet clothes so black they seemed to drink the glow. Tom followed slowly until he came abreast with him.

"We'll have to wait," Cecil said after a while — half an order, as though Tom might blunder his way on the Council. He had a light, cold voice, young Cecil, and the sort of sallow countenance not fashioned for smiling, as different as could be from his father. The unwary often fell for the twinkle in Lord Burleigh's blue eyes — not that the geniality was false, but it rarely meant what one thought it did; with young Robert, Tom suspected, only a fool would let himself be unwary. Not reckoning himself a fool, he just dipped his head in that nebulous degree between nod and bow that a gentleman's heir might owe a Baron's younger son, and disposed himself for a silent wait. Or as silent as could be, with Skeres shuffling and muttering a few steps away, scratching at mud stains on his coat, and bored to death already.

Tom was considering some errand to occupy the restless Minotaur when Cecil broke the silence.

"What an extraordinary affair," he said.

"Indeed," Tom said, finding himself observed sidelong through dark lashes. "Very." And let the little hunchback think him stolid, if he liked.

It was no great surprise that Robert Cecil wasn't done. "To barge in on Mr. Secretary like that! I wonder that he didn't come here instead?"

This time he turned to squarely study Tom, one thin eyebrow arched high.

Because William Stafford is frightened out of his wits — which weren't much in the first place. "I wonder."

The eyebrow went down. "Well, he went straight to Barn Elms, for all that Greenwich is closer to London — supposing he was in London at all."

Oh Jove rain on the man! "He didn't say, Sir Robert — not before me, at least. Perhaps he thought such tidings should be first heard by Mr. Secretary —"

"Master."

Tom was glad to drop the subject when Skeres sidled closer, jerking his chin towards the door at the gallery's end. The councillors were walking out of it in grim purposefulness. There was time to catch Cecil's cursed eyebrow rising again before Davison slowed down to join them. Davison, it was worth noting — and not Mildmay.

It was very much like him that he wasted no time in pleasantries. "Well, a warrant has been drawn," he announced.

A warrant! Tom gaped, dry-mouthed all of a sudden. Just like that? Mary Stuart's death warrant...?

But Davison went on: "For that Frenchman, d'Estrapes."

Of course. *Of course.* Tom found his voice again to answer Cecil's raised eyebrow: "Ambassador Châteauneuf's secretary."

"So Mildmay says," Davison grunted. "To be arrested in Dover, the moment he sets foot there."

And here was another surprise. "Has he left?" Tom blurted out. Had the man learnt of Stafford already? But most of all, how did the Council know he'd gone?

"Bound to run," Davison said. "Or so Stafford told Mildmay. For myself, I'd have sent to seize the scoundrel right now."

Only then did it occur to Tom that Stafford had ridden in the carriage with Mildmay, and between Barn Elms and London there was time for endless ill-advised remarks. What else had the fool babbled?

And perhaps Cecil took Tom's silence for agreement with Davison — which in part it was.

"But Mr. Davison," he protested. "It would be most improper to arrest a French subject in the Ambassador's residence!" And if the manner was one of respectful reproach, it was plain that young Robert was enjoying himself. "Besides, who can tell what letters he'll carry when he leaves?" And with that, he took his leave, hastening in the direction his father had taken, small, and black, and skew-shouldered. Did he nurse doubts? Well, it was plain that he did. Lord send it was about Stafford, and Stafford alone…

"Letters — just what my Lord Burleigh said," Davison rumbled under his breath. "Like father, like son — but I tell you this, young Walsingham: there are those in Council who drag their feet about this affair."

Which was perhaps small wonder: nobody wanted to be the one to tell the Queen of yet another plot, of yet more proof that Mary Stuart's intrigues would only end with her death. But at least it — together with the fact that they'd rather take d'Estrapes with what letters he carried — meant the Council was taking the matter seriously.

It could have been worse. "I'd better ride back," Tom said. "Mr. Secretary will be waiting to hear of this."

Davison scoffed. "In the dark? In the snow? You'll break your neck, and then what use will you be to Mr. Secretary? You can sleep in my rooms, if you don't mind a truckle bed, and leave in the morning."

Waving away Tom's thanks, Davison left to join his fellow councillors, with the air of one going to have a tooth pulled.

Skeres went to stand at Tom's shoulder, nodding knowingly at the departing councillor's back. "I'll wager you, 'e's cursin' 'is luck that 'Is Honour's sick at 'ome."

"They all are, Dolius." But Tom had a suspicion that Davison alone would end up braving the Queen's wrath — and knew it well.

"And you know, Master? The little 'unchback, I don't like 'im."

"Skeres!" Tom scolded, who had been thinking of young Cecil in the same terms himself. "Mind your tongue."

There was the squirming shrug that, with Nick Skeres, passed for a sign of abashment. "Ay, Master — though 'e 'as a 'ump, and I don't like 'im a whit — so what I've said wrong I don't know." And then, because the Minotaur never stayed contrite nor grudging for long, "Can't you find somewhere else to sleep? If you take the truckle, 'tis the floor for me."

And trust him to think of his own comfort!

"The place is crammed to the eaves. You'll have to make do and be thankful — unless you'd rather sleep in some hayloft." Speaking of which... "And you know, Dolius, while we're here, I might as well find the players."

Leicester's Men weren't in the stables anymore — nor anywhere else at Placentia.

"Gone back to London to bury their fellow," the clerk of the stables explained, rubbing at his chilled fingers. "Though they'll be back to tumble on Twelfth Night."

Tom frowned at this. "Does the coroner know they left?"

"'Tis him as gave them leave to go, Master, and good riddance. Not the dead man — rest his soul — but Lor', the others?" A sniff. "That clown of theirs misliked to have it ruled an accident. I saw him play, once. Thought my sides would split, I laughed so much. Another Dick Tarlton — and yet you wouldn't credit the mopish churl he is off the stage."

Somehow Tom could credit it only too well, and it was with a worried mind that he took leave of the clerk, and slowly made his way back through the stables. Good as it was that Perkin's death had been ruled an accident, it wouldn't do to have Will Kempe asking questions, and perhaps even go to Lord Leicester himself with his ill thoughts. At least the clown was in London for the moment, and the Earl in Greenwich.

"Master?" Skeres was bored by contemplation just as he was by waiting. "You brood all you like. I'm finding us a bit of supper, and where they put up Mr. Davison."

A most excellent notion. As Skeres scampered off on his quest, Tom lingered on the stables' threshold, watching the torches make red halos in the snowfall. Thick and fast as the flakes whirled in the wind, he couldn't help wishing he'd taken the road.

CHAPTER 3

"Well," said Phelippes, "at least we won't have to find another Perkin."

Tom almost choked on a sip of warm spiced ale. They were sitting by the fire in the deserted kitchen parlour in Seething Lane, as Tom thawed after the ride from Greenwich in the snow.

"It will be a great relief for the one we might have found, considering," he groused — which was a tad unfair, for the cypherer had no fault of Perkin's demise, and much less of Stafford's thunderbolt. In fact, when it came to that...

"Where have I gone wrong with that fool Stafford, Philippus? He had his instructions, he knew what to do — and most of all, he knew what *not* to do!"

Phelippes blinked in the way of the short-sighted, lips twisted in deeper consideration than the question truly deserved. But then, that was the fellow for you: a considerer by both nature and choice.

"A good, sound man wouldn't have accepted to do what we needed," he said at length. "Stafford's a braggart, I'm not surprised that he took fright when Perkin died."

Which was meant to be consolation, Tom supposed, as he stared into the murky depths of his ale. Except... "He took fright, yes — but I doubt he knows of Perkin's death."

Phelippes pursed his lips. "You were there, Mr. Thomas. Couldn't it have been truly an accident?"

Couldn't it, indeed? The body face down in the snow, the broken shutter, the stool under the window... *People do fall from windows.* "There's no telling for sure — but such a convenient accident!"

"Convenient to whom, though? And why?"

With the well-loved sense of coloured glass tiles shifting in his mind, Tom straightened in the chair, and bent to put the lukewarm pot back on the hearth.

"As to the why, I can see three possibilities, Philippus." He raised one finger. "Either someone wanted to avoid being exposed in his entanglement with Stafford's rigmarole." A second finger. "Someone, somehow, learnt of our plan and wanted it stopped." A third finger. "Or someone is pursuing some different and unconnected aim."

It was almost amusing how Phelippes ignored the third possibility altogether. "The French then — this d'Estrapes or some other man of the Ambassador's." He gave a mournful grimace. "Or anyone in Council who might want to make mischief for His Honour."

Robert Cecil's sallow face painted itself in Tom's mind. "The Cecils."

Phelippes tilted his head. "Lord Burleigh has changed his manner. I know you don't trust him, but truly, he's being a better friend to His Honour than my Lord Leicester, these days."

Not that this was saying much. Tom had never trusted Leicester, not when he was Sir Francis's ally in Council — much less now that he'd turned against him. That didn't mean, though, that he'd trust Burleigh and his cold-blooded son instead. Did Sir Francis? He shook his head. "Still, if anyone did murder for this, it must have been someone who knew what Perkin knew."

There was a thin groan from Phelippes. "I'd suspect Stafford himself, if he'd run."

"Oh, I suspected him very much — until he turned up at Barn Elms crying regicide. But of course there's no reason why Perkin couldn't have let something slip. Or tried to sell his tale to someone other than Leicester. As you said, it's not good decent men that we use."

The cypherer grunted a little in assent. It was something he wouldn't dream of doing — not to Tom, these days — unless he were distracted. "I wonder what Stafford the Elder knows of all this, over in Paris," he mused.

The huff of laughter, an especially cheerless one, was more than Tom could help. "A tad late for second thoughts, Philippus — though God knows young William gave you reason for them." He rose, stretching his arms, and bent to peer out of the leaded window. Through the diamonds of thick glass, the kitchen garden was an uneven whiteness. "But I think I'll have a word with Bonetti. He said he trusted Perkin to be greedy. Now I wonder what he *didn't* say."

Heaven forfend that one should call Rocco Bonetti's place in Blackfriars a fencing school or — worse! — a fencing hall. His was, the Italian maintained, a college, where only the best gentlemen learnt the finer points of the finest sort of swordsmanship. Of course, the finest sort was the Italian style; and, equally of course, seeing that he charged no less than twenty pounds for each lesson, and still managed to be crowded with pupils, Bonetti could call his school all he liked.

Tom had seen the huge paved hall — in fact, he'd nearly died there — when it was empty and dark and half-ruinous; now Bonetti had brought it back to life, with glass in the tall windows, panoplies gleaming on the walls, a fine gallery above, the extravagant luxury of a clock, and the air full of the merry, deadly ring of blades.

That he could keep shop there (though he'd have a seizure to hear it called that!) was in good part thanks to Sir Francis — which was why, on observing Tom in a corner, Bonetti went to meet him with a huge grin and a welcoming hand.

Brisk and nimble at forty years of age, swarthy of face, and dark of hair, he might have been the picture of the Italian in a ballad-sheet.

"Well, well, *signor mio!*" he greeted as he led the way to a quiet corner under the gallery — for, whether or not he'd truly been a captain in the Venetian armies, Rocco was most discerning in his use of names.

"Captain Rocco," Tom greeted in turn — smiling back, for it was hard not to like the man.

"Have you come for a bout? But no..." Bonetti shook a finger in mock outrage. "You fence with some rascal, one of the London Masters, eh? Do not deny it!"

All easy cheer, he was — even too much, perhaps. Did he know of Perkin?

"I'd deny it gladly, Mastro Rocco, if I could afford you instead."

Rapier under the arm, Bonetti half turned to study his hall. Only three pupils were there — one refreshing himself at the fine table at the far end, and two lunging at each other under the eye of the master's nephew — and a couple of observers sat in the gallery. "Most of my gentlemen are at Court for the festivities. What do you say to a bout, eh? I will not charge a penny: you fence with Gerolamo, and I watch. What do you say? I will wager your *affondo* needs work — the lunge, as you barbarians call it."

It was with nothing short of longing that Tom eyed the two pupils at work, their Italian lunges a thing of deathly, precise elegance, each in turn deflecting the other's blade with a bare flick of the wrist. There danced temptation — for never in his life would he be able to afford such fine instruction — and yet...

And yet there was a strain to Bonetti's smile, and more than laughter to the lines around the eyes. Jittery — and anxious to hide it. What was he trying to buy with a lesson worth almost as much as Tom's annuity, if he ever saw a farthing of it?

Whatever it was, there would be no trade. "Thank you, Captain — but I won't impose on your friendship. If ever I fence here, I'll pay for it."

"As you wish, *signor mio*." Bonetti sketched a salute with his hand. "When you —"

He was cut short by a thud against one of the windows. Something had splattered against the glass, and was sliding down in thick rivulets.

"*Dannazione!*" cried the Italian, and strode across the hall to the offended window, bracing both hands on the low sill to peer out. Tom followed, together with young Gerolamo Bonetti and the stocky Italian servant, while across the hall the fencers waited, rapiers lowered, to see what happened.

And what happened was that a pair of bullies outside ran up to the window, hooting and cackling, and making rude gestures. Rocco was white with rage.

"*Adesso vedono!*" Gerolamo exclaimed — and what the bullies should see it was easy to guess, but never happened, for Bonetti grabbed his nephew by the arm.

"Have you lost your wits?" he hissed in Italian. "Making a row before the gentlemen! Go back to your work!" He gave the boy a firm push, and Gerolamo stalked away, glowering like a thundercloud.

"Come, Bonifacio," he called, and the servant trotted behind him, obedient as a mastiff, and just as dour, while Bonetti raised an apologetic palm, and called across the hall to his disconcerted students — so bright-voiced it was painful.

"It is nothing, *signori miei*. Festivities make the rabble unruly, eh? Too much ale. Your Lordship, gentlemen, we ignore them — or, if they keep at it, I send for the constable."

No Londoner, no matter whether lord or scullion, would draw much assurance from a promise to call the constable — but still, as no more missiles reached the windows, the fencing bout resumed, and so did the chatter in the gallery. Only then did Bonetti turn away, and his face refolded to anger again as he glowered at the greasy streaks on the glass.

Tom wasn't half convinced. The fencing master's vexation spoke of a repeated nuisance, of some continuing grudge.

"Drunk wassailers, Captain?"

For a heartbeat Bonetti fixed his glare on Tom, and then changed it to a rueful grimace.

"Ah, *Signor* Walsingham! When I call the London Masters rascals…" He huffed. "They slander me. They try to disgust my gentlemen so they will leave my college. They hire rabble to…" he threw up a hand at the soiled window.

"And are they succeeding?"

A shrug. "It is not an easy thing to be a foreigner in this London of yours, *signor mio*. First the displeasure of my Lord of Oxford, and now these ruffians. And you know what is the worst?" Bonetti drew himself tall, the Italian accent thickening in his speech. "The worst is, they would kiss their elbows to have me. Why, they have begged me to join their halfpenny ranks — but I am a gentleman! I teach a style. Your masters, they do not understand that if it is beautiful, it works; if it is not, it doesn't. Do you know that they teach *players*?"

Which must be the extreme indignity for a fencing master. But Tom was pursuing another thought. The whole of London knew of this rivalry between the English masters and the Italians — why, the beggar-boys played at it in the streets, and Tom's own English master was full of jeers for Rocco Bonetti. It all had seemed a matter of insults and taunts, and perhaps a challenge now and then — but was it truly?

"Then I have to wonder, Captain. Your servant Perkin…"

"He is not —" Bonetti stopped short, brows knitting, and lowered his speech to a harsh murmur. "*Signor* Walsingham, I did what you told me, put him in *Signor* Stafford's way, where he could see, and where he could hear. I would say that it worked, since Perkin ran — and I told you the moment he did, and where. More than that, I neither know, nor want to. You think I do not have trouble enough, without borrowing more?"

Could it be honest aggravation? When the Italian made to turn away, Tom grabbed him by the elbow, and eyed him squarely as he said under his breath, "I wouldn't borrow Perkin's, if I were you. Death is hard to give back."

"Death?" A bewildered shake of the head. "You never mean…?"

"I mean that he was at Placentia to tumble with Leicester's Men, and fell from a window — perhaps of his own clumsiness, perhaps not."

As he slowly sat down on the sill, Bonetti crossed himself, never bothering to hide it. "*Gesù santo…*" he rasped, with a reproachful glare for Tom. "*Signor Tommaso*, what have you dragged me into?"

"Perhaps it's nothing more than you already had on your doorstep." Tom tilted his chin at the window. "This rivalry you say —"

Bonetti gaped. "But no!" He checked himself, paused to throw a glance at the hall over Tom's shoulder, and resumed softly, "I have little that is good to say of the London Masters

— but this one thing I will say: I cannot think they would do murder over this. And besides, Jack Perkin!"

"I'm not saying they meant to have him killed. But if some man of the masters had met your servant by chance, if they'd fought…?" *At Placentia? In the hayloft over the stables?* Tom himself saw the weakness of it well before the Italian shook his head.

"I told you, *signore*: he was no servant of mine. He used to be, back when I had my first college, but that was long ago. These days he does … he *did* some work here now and then, when he was not with the players, and it is like this that I could serve you. But the masters — how would they even know? Besides, Perkin would not fight over my honour."

Not that violence didn't have a way of erupting out of the flimsiest pretext. "You called him greedy —"

Of a sudden, Bonetti stiffened, his face again a picture of professional cheer as he turned to the door, where the servant, Bonifacio, was ushering in a gentleman in severe black garb.

"And see who happens to visit!" the master murmured through a brittle smile. "The French Ambassador's secretary!"

Tom frowned, observing the man. "You must be wrong — that's never d'Estrapes."

"D'Estrapes!" the Italian huffed. "D'Estrapes is a fussy pup, throwing money all around London, to make up for his lack of blood. He fences well, though. Better footwork than many of your lords. This one…" He rose to bow at the newcomer, who was striding close with the mastiff Bonifacio on his heels. "This is the one who comes to pay for the Ambassador's guests." And then, loudly, he greeted: "*Signor* Cordaillot!"

It could all have ended there, but Bonifacio shuffled at his master's elbow, his domed brow creased in unease. "*Padrone*, I told *Signor* Cordaillot that you were busy," he muttered in Italian. "But…"

But indeed! Bless the fool Bonifacio with hot water — couldn't he have kept the Frenchman away? So this was Pierre de Cordaillot — the name known among many from Salisbury Court, the thin face never seen before. Or was it? Châteauneuf's confounded secretary did little to disguise his curiosity. He talked to Bonetti of accounts to settle in a cold, stiff voice, and the wide-set brown eyes never ceased straying towards the window — and Tom.

Could it be they'd crossed paths before? Or had Bonifacio let slip names?

It was a good thing that Bonetti turned back to point the nearest panoply to Tom. "Well, then, *signor mio*, choose a dagger you like, and see: Gerolamo is ready for you. And I'll attend to *Signor* Cordaillot"

He ushered the Frenchman across the hall, to the door of his office under the gallery. *The one who pays for the Ambassador's guests.* Or perhaps, this time, it was D'Estrapes's account that he must settle. Surely Châteauneuf would never let his other secretary cross Bonetti's threshold again?

"*Signore*, if you like?" Tom turned to find young Gerolamo, rapier under his arm, dagger in hand, waiting with a touch of impatience and, perhaps, also a knowing smile.

If Tom liked! Twenty pounds he didn't have — and, after his pretty speech earlier, twenty pounds he must pay in full! More money he'd have to borrow from Skeres. Oh Jove. Was there a way to pass this off as Service expenses? *…And to cover my clumsiness, Sir, I took an hour of the costliest fencing instruction in the realm!* But there was no retreating with discretion, either — for Cordaillot, curse his suspecting soul, had stopped right under the gallery to observe. Trying, no doubt, to gauge whether this man in plain plumage could truly be a student here. And curse Bonetti, too: couldn't he have said that Tom had just finished his instruction?

But no — not if he must truly appear like yet another of the college gentlemen. Tom snatched the closest dagger, and threw his hat and cape on the bench.

"Let's make the best of it, shall we?" he groused — and see how young Gerolamo's smile broadened into a grin.

To make it all worse, there was half a dozen people in the gallery now — men and women, all very finely dressed...

Gerolamo saluted with his blade. "*In guardia, signore.*" And, when Tom obeyed, shook his head. "No English lazy guard, now. Up with your point. Let's see how you do the *affondo!*"

And, blushing to the roots of his hair, and feeling clumsy as a pup, Tom began his cursed instruction in the Italian style of fencing, under Pierre de Cordaillot's watchful eye.

As he made his way back to Seething Lane — twenty pounds the poorer, Lord help him! — Tom could have found some consolation in that he hadn't entirely disgraced himself with what little he knew of the Italian style — had he been of such a mind.

But he was not. All things weighed, he would have done well to stay away from the college, for Bonetti had been little help, and Châteauneuf's man had seen him in conference with the fencing master, and he was going to pay twenty pounds for it! It didn't help that his horse kept shying in the stained snow that concealed the accidents of the street, and the chill breeze clawed through cloak and doublet, all the chillier after sweating for a whole hour. Oh, for a swift wherry on the river — but the ice floats on the Thames made it too dangerous, and so one either walked or rode.

Rode, and near stumbled into obstacles! Tom drew the reins just in time to avoid a barrow upturned in the runnel. Curse whoever had left it lying there, wheel and one handle broken, amidst a ruin of trampled snow and scraps of dirty rags. The rag-seller had run with what could be salvaged of the load, most likely, and let riders mind for themselves!

"It won't bite you, you witless nag!" Tom muttered as he kneed the skittish sorrel around the wreck — much to the amusement of a gaggle of street-children. Sir Francis's groom would hear about this doltish horse.

And that was when Tom noticed. It was an impression, mostly, of being watched. Of being followed. Under cover of glowering at the boys, he peered around. Budge Row was no pleasant place. Skinners lived there, and even the coldest winter couldn't entirely rid the air of the stench of their piss vats, although it wasn't half as bad as it would be in summer. Dark, foul-smelling passages gaped on both sides between house and house — so narrow that snow didn't drift much past their mouths. In one of those the watcher must be hiding — of this Tom was sure. Once clear of the ruined barrel, he nudged the sorrel into a wary pace, sitting as though hunched against the cold, but alert, and thankful that the January chill kept a good deal of Londoners at home.

And there he was. A movement, a flash of colour — red, of all things? With thoughts of Cordaillot's measuring gaze in mind, Tom took Dowgate, that was larger and more populated, and led away from Seething Lane, down towards the river — and then, for good measure, dove into the winter-quiet warren of the Vintry, down sloping alleys and through yards so narrow, nobody could follow unobserved. He didn't much like the dead silence, so unlike London, nor the gaunt stray dogs scavenging for food — but soon enough he thought he'd shaken his red shadow. Unless, of course, he was lingering back, following by ear the horse's steps. He half turned in the saddle, watching over his shoulder when, of a sudden the nag skidded, nearly unsaddling him. He reined in hard, finding himself where the houses ended on a strip of frozen mud, not five feet from the river. The horse stumbled, hooves scrabbling down a set of ruined water-stairs, cracking holes through the crust of ice — and then, Lord be thanked, stopped.

Panting hard, Tom slid off the saddle, clumsily climbing back up the stairs, dragging the trembling horse.

The moat at Scadbury, frozen and gleaming. The shrill laughter of children. The wolfhound Mary called Silver. The sudden crack. Black water. Mary's scream. Silver's whine. The burning bite of cold on limbs, down throat and lungs —

"Oy, you!"

Hades and Hell! Tom wrenched himself out of the memories, to cold water seeping through his boots.

Across the alley a man leant out of a door, with a knitted cap on his head. "'Ave a care, Master," he called. "Ye'll drown yerself!"

"Indeed!" Tom found himself more winded than he liked. "Someone should see to these stairs!"

Ay, and pigs fly with their tails forward, said the man's sniff. "Were ye wanting aught, Master?" he asked.

And how did he explain he'd been evading pursuit, and had mistaken his way. "I'm lost, I —"

The man just jerked his head towards another alley that ran parallel to the river. "Three Cranes quay's that-a-way, and the Painted Tavern."

While he'd no use a quay, and less for a tavern, Tom thanked the fellow and led his horse on foot, away from the water and up the way he'd been directed — and on second thoughts, considering he'd made enough noise to alert any following ruffian, he did ensconce himself in the tavern, ordered a dinner of bad stew and worse ale, and sat there for an hour, thinking bleak thoughts before he hied himself home, with good hopes that nobody was following.

"Master! Where 'ave you been?"

Tom startled to a halt on the threshold of the passage to his writing room — irked to find himself still so discomposed by his river adventure that his candle's light danced. In the flickering glow Skeres jumped up from the bench.

The long absence had, it seemed, worried the household, and Skeres had no qualms in saying so, or in plying his master with reproachful questions, soon joined by a quieter but no less fretful Phelippes.

To think Tom was five-and-twenty, and eight years in the Service! When they began to observe the mud on his boots, he irritably plunked to sit on the bench Skeres had vacated, and told them of the red shadow. The mud was forgotten at once.

"Trounced 'im, that's what I'd 'ave done!" was Skeres's pronouncement in the end.

"You would not!" Tom snapped. "Not that I did much better."

And see how cheerily the lad perked up. "You tried to trounce 'im?"

Oh save and deliver!

It was a good thing that Phelippes put himself, metaphorically speaking, in the middle.

"No, Skeres, he did not. Mr. Thomas fears that he gave himself away to the fellow."

"Ay well, 'e didn't lead 'im 'ere, did 'e?" And let nobody ever call Nick Skeres a disloyal servant: see how he glared at the cypherer's worried face.

Hiding his amusement, Tom had learnt through the years, was mostly useless with the Minotaur, and pointless with Phelippes. "Thank you, Dolius — I hope I didn't, but I wish I knew who thought it their business to have me followed."

"*Who*, says 'e!" Skeres snorted. "Runs into the Ambassador's fellow, and says *who*?"

There was a hum of agreement from Phelippes. "Then we'd have to think that Cordaillot didn't like the sight of you at the fencing school — but…"

"But couldn't quite place me," Tom finished, whose first thought had been much the same. "And, if I did lose his hound, he still can't." But still something nagged at the edge of his mind.

Skeres was always damnably quick to catch his master's uncertainty. "Not that 'e's convinced, mind you," he grumbled. "Then who was it, the murtherer?"

And, even in jest, it wasn't an entirely witless thought — although a very unpleasant one, and not without its own difficulties. "And he's been following me ever since Placentia?"

"He wouldn't need to, if he somehow knows," Phelippes said — and, in the bleak silence that met his words, there came the sound of voices from the hall.

"See what it is, Skeres," Tom ordered — and, when the servant had marched off, went back to considering.

"If the murderer somehow knows where Perkin picked up his tidings, wouldn't he want to make sure just what Bonetti knows, and whom he tells? Now the French come to mind —"

He stopped when the Minotaur barged in without a by-your-leave, and proclaimed: "There's Corpus Christi as wants to see you, Master, and 'e won't go away."

It was a speech to make a man stare — and both Tom and Phelippes did, before another voice was heard.

"No, I won't go away, you oaf. Let me in!"

And why he should be surprised when Kit Marley pushed past Skeres and through the door, Tom truly didn't know. But Marley wasn't done with making an impression: he planted himself in the middle of the passage, short-winded and glittering with silver buttons, and all but shouted: "Mr. Thomas, you must look into Perkin's death!"

There! Tom couldn't help a glance at Phelippes, who was gaping a little — and small blame to him.

"Phelippes, this is Christopher Marley. You've heard of —" Tom began, and went no further, for the other three all spoke together.

"Of Corpus Christi, Cambridge. Poet," said Marley — just as he'd done at Placentia.

"Ah yes — Rheims," said Phelippes.

And Skeres said nothing in words, but his snort was very loud.

Oh, Jupiter. "In my room," Tom ordered. "All of you."

Once that was done, and the four of them crowed in the small place, Tom perched against the writing table, right in front of Marley.

"And now, if you don't mind, what is it that I *must* do?"

Even poets from Corpus Christi, it seemed, saw when it was better to get hold of their fiery humours; they just did it with more flair than most. Marley exhaled loudly, and rearranged himself less like a terrier poised for a fight, and a tad more like a reasonable man reporting. "Jack Perkin. You must find out who killed him."

"Killed him," Phelippes echoed, and Marley nodded fiercely enough to make his buttons tinkle.

A chill, grey church in Rheims, the smell of cold frankincense… Tom huffed. "Kit Marley — always crying murder!"

"And wasn't I right, the other time?"

Which was true enough, but still the other time hadn't been half as fraught with danger.

"I thought the coroner had ruled it an accident," Tom tried — not that he expected it to work.

And indeed, all Marley had for the notion was a contemptuous wave. "The coroner would have ruled it a blessing, just so he wouldn't bother Leicester."

There was a guffaw, but, when Tom glared at Skeres, the Minotaur's countenance was unconvincingly grave, as he leant against the door as though they needed guarding.

Not that Marley was wrong, when it came to the coroner — but still… Tom raised an eyebrow. "And this offends your noble sense of justice?"

"Justice!" The lad gave a little bark of laughter. "What offends me is that Kempe thinks I offed Perkin!"

Tom ignored the grunt from the door, as well as Phelippes's question of "Kempe?".

"Jove, Marley," he groaned. "How do you get yourself into these tangles?"

Which Marley didn't consider a real question, so he answered the cypherer instead: "Will Kempe. The clown with Leicester's Men — though, to hear him, you'd think he must be a god from Mount Olympus."

That Phelippes made to speak and then didn't was a matter for later — so Tom put it aside and asked the obvious question.

"Why is he so set on having you hanged for a murderer?"

"Because he's a half-wit." The lad sniffed, and the implication was plain that anyone not dismissing in contempt the clown's suspicions must be similarly afflicted.

"And what of that squabble you had with Perkin?" A hired man calling his tragedy dross didn't strike Tom as a killing matter, but then he was no poet.

This particular poet snorted, and perhaps meant to sound derisive, although it came out petulant. "I squabbled worse with Kempe himself, and he's alive, isn't he?"

"Hardly the strongest of arguments, in truth — but does it matter very much, what Kempe thinks? The coroner's ruling holds." Which was perhaps a mistake, thinking back to Rheims, and Marley's high-browed conviction that justice should be served.

"Ay, but Kempe won't have it, for Perkin was his friend. He says he'll find the murderer, and go to Lord Leicester to see justice done." Marley threw up both hands, disgusted with high-browed notions, now that he sat on the wrong side of them.

"But you can't be his one suspect, surely?" Phelippes asked. He blinked when Marley exclaimed and started to pace, milling his arms around — something of a feat in the small room.

"Why, yes — I am! And mind, Perkin had plenty of ill-wishers: he had words with some musician or other the day he died, and the other players teased him about a woman who wanted his bollocks on an Italian fork — and that's just two I know of, and I'd known him three days!" He spun around to face them, palms raised in a gesture out of university disputations, so wide that he upset a pile of quartos and broadsheets, and sent them skidding across the table.

"Mind what you do!" With a grimace, Phelippes rushed to gather the things. As he stacked them neatly again, he glared at the blushing Marley. "And, if you don't mind my asking, why should Mr. Thomas clear you?"

Was it honest disconcert, when the lad's eyes went round? Was it even hurt? *Because, back in Rheims, I saved him from capture when I could have run to save my hide.*

"Because I'm innocent!" he cried. "And I've no one else to help me. Even if he had no stakes of his own in it…"

Stakes! Tom's stomach clenched, most of his thankful sympathy gone. "How do you mean, stakes of my own?"

"I mean," Marley shook his head, taken aback. "You appeared at once at Placentia, Mr. Thomas, and…" He darted a peek at Phelippes. "And your men here haven't once asked who Perkin was. I thought…" He raised both shoulders.

Oh Jove, this one! Tom wanted to laugh. "Yes, I remember this from Rheims, Marley," he said instead, with all the coldness he could summon. "You think yourself a good deal shrewder than you are."

Which was mostly unfair — but perhaps the lad had grown in these past years. The Kit Marley of Rheims would have talked back; this one swallowed whatever answer he'd been about to make, and just stood there, and bristled quietly, ignoring Skeres's mutters.

And, most of all, he never brought up Rheims.

In the end, it was a foregone decision. "You say you've no one to help you?" Tom asked.

"No one — *and* I'm innocent."

The emphasis was hard to miss — as was Nick Skeres's sniff from the door — though quite what it meant... That Tom hadn't been innocent at all of what the Catholic exiles held against him?

Ah well.

"Where are you staying?" When Marley hesitated, Tom at first thought him wrong-footed by the abrupt question. "Within or without walls?"

The answer, when it came, was wary. "Shoreditch."

Without walls, then, and the same was most likely true of Kempe... Oh. Staying in Shoreditch — *with Watson*, that was the meaning of the odd wariness. Watson, who had been Tom's friend, and then had betrayed his trust, and been kicked out of the Service for it. *I'm innocent* — as opposed to Watson, then. Not that it had been a matter of murder, back then, but still, here was one more reason to keep Marley in the dark — and out of harm's way, lest he blather what he shouldn't, either in spite, or to save himself.

Tom made no sign that he'd tied Shoreditch to anything but the nightly barring of the city gates. "'Tis too late now. Be here early tomorrow: we'll pay Kempe a visit."

Whether he'd expected to be thrown to the wolves for his own sake or as Watson's friend, Marley brightened at once. It was nothing less than cheerfully that he thanked Tom, and followed a much less cheery Skeres outside.

Tom closed the door behind them, and turned to lean his back against it. "Oh, devil pinch Kit Marley!" He exclaimed — and out of the corner of his eye caught Phelippes flinching. "Pardon, Philippus."

That Puritan soul tilted his head, with the mournful resignation of one living among heathens. "He's no complete fool, though," he said.

"He does his best to make one forget it — but no, he's not. Nor, I'm afraid, is Kempe. Not that Lord Leicester will bestir himself over a player's death, but we can't have a shrewd clown asking questions..." And there it was again, the cypherer pursing his lips at the mention. "You know something of Kempe."

"And so do you. William Kempe, of Leicester's Men. His Lordship's jesting player."

A thread of memory knotted itself in Tom's mind. "Carrying letters from the Low Countries, wasn't he? Only..."

"Only he delivered Sir Philip's letters to Lady Leicester, instead of Lady Sidney."

"Including the ones for Sir Francis! Oh Lord..." Tom dropped into the seat with a groan, leaning his forehead on his joined fists. "All the more reason to keep Kempe off Marley's back, *and* away from the truth — not that I know what the truth is, mind." And that was without wondering where the untrustworthy Watson stood in all this. Could it never be easy?

Phelippes looked worried – he always did, whether he was or not – and thoughtful. "A shame that Marley smelt a rat with Perkin's death. If he were a little less sharp, you could throw *him* at Kempe."

"Innocent or not?" Tom couldn't help but laugh. "Is swearing the only sin you fret about?"

The one-shouldered shrug, the fussing with the candle... And then, just as Tom thought he had offended him, the cypherer looked up with the faintest curl of lips.

"You're going to clear him now — innocent or not. I'm sure that's a sin too, after its own fashion, but then..."

But then, if Leicester ever learnt the truth of Stafford's plot, what of Mary Stuart's warrant, what of the Queen's trust — such as it was? What of England?

"*Concedo*, Philippus," Tom sighed in defeat. "And apologies."

And, when the cypherer had gone, he sat there by himself, listening to the snow-thick quiet, and the creak of the house's old beams. And all the time Sir Francis's Polybius kept coming back to his mind — and the woes of embattled, thankless old Hannibal.

CHAPTER 4

With his face unpainted and in the drabbest of clothes, Will Kempe seemed nothing like the peacock of New Year's Day at Placentia. This one was a round-cheeked fellow around Tom's own age, red of hair and beard, with porcine eyes and square shoulders. The distrustful manner was the same, though, as well as the apprentice boy trotting at his heels like a terrier.

He didn't much like the invasion of his one room in Cripplegate Without; when Kit Marley introduced Tom by name, he liked it even less.

"Walsingham," the clown chewed the name the way he would a crab. "The other day, that yeoman said you were from His Lordship's retinue."

"Did he? I don't know why he would. I certainly am no such thing."

The clown sniffed, and, as he sometimes did, Tom wished he could have been Sir Francis's kinsman on his mother's side. How much easier would life be for Tom Guildford?

All else apart, Kit Marley wouldn't have been half as keen to boast the acquaintance, would he? He wouldn't have proclaimed Tom a friend to poets and scholars, just like Mr. Secretary himself. Or perhaps he would — but to a much paler effect.

Then again, the effect wasn't so huge with the Walsingham name, either. Kempe perched himself on one of several trunks, and pulled a face that was just short of clownish. "So you've fine friends, Marley. So what of it?"

And that was when Tom decided he'd had enough of the player's blustering. "So, Master Kempe, Marley's fine great friends itch to know why you'd call him a murderer — and over a matter that has been ruled an accident."

It worked well enough that Kempe straightened to his feet. "Ay well, Master, 'tis that…" He hesitated, sucking his teeth, reckoning perhaps how far he could go. "I don't much trust the ruling."

Not very far, apparently — at least not yet.

"There are reasons why coroners hold inquests and players play," Tom said. "And laws to keep it so."

How many times had Will Kempe feigned anger on the stage? Did he always do it with nostrils flaring large, and bunching forehead? "And there are earls to have rulings undone!" he growled.

In the blink of an eye Skeres pushed past Marley at Tom's side, face knotted in a glower. "Do I trounce 'im, Master?"

"No, Nick — you don't. Not yet." Tom held the clown's gaze until the man turned away — and it was amusing that the terrier-like apprentice didn't.

When Kempe turned back, all arrogance was gone, replaced by earnestness.

"You're defending a friend, Master," he said, jerking his chin at Marley. "Perkin was mine. If this young pest were dead, and you thought they'd killed him, wouldn't you want to find out?"

Which had Marley sniff, and Skeres huffing, and was the sort of neat little speech a player's art could well pretend — and yet…

"'Tis fair enough. And in the interest of both your friend and mine, would you tell me what makes you call the young pest a murderer?"

Kempe blew out his cheeks, and looked about him. Half of the room was taken up with a two-poster bed, three trunks and a big basket — apparel of Leicester's Men, most likely. Clothes hung from several nails in the white-washed wall and, under the one window stood a chair and a stool. The clown dragged the chair to the middle of the room, and offered it to Tom.

"Sit down, Master, and we can talk."

Tom bit back a smile as Marley took the stool to sit by his side, finding it quite low, and squirming to adjust his legs in a dignified stance. With Skeres standing at Tom's back, ferociously cross-armed in his lion-hued coat, they must make quite a sight.

When Kempe sat at the foot of the bed, with the boy standing at his side, the ranks were, so to say, closed for battle. A battle where the enemy thought that Kit Marley's innocence was at stake — and must be kept thinking so.

"I'm listening," Tom said, the way he'd move a first pawn when playing chess with Frances. One thing he'd never do again. One thing to push out of his mind now, together with the flare of pain.

For his part — and perhaps to his credit — Kempe looked uneasy, rubbing at his head as though he could pick his words out of it. "Well, it is like this: I call Marley a murderer, because he had words with Jack Perkin right before he died."

And of course the lad had to leap up from the stool. "I didn't —"

"Peace, Marley." Tom dragged him to sit again. "He can be a nuisance, I'll grant you — but he doesn't go around killing people over a squabble."

"A squabble! That's what he called it?" Kempe exchanged glares with Marley. "Your poet here, he's been pestering us to buy a tragedy of his —"

"Which they're too hen-hearted to play!"

"Which —" another, darker glare — "would give the Master of Revels a calenture! Who's ever heard of Godless tyrants that don't die in the end?"

"Ha! So it's not that there's no clown, now?" Marley muttered, only to fall quiet again under Tom's glare.

"Well, I wasn't the only one to dislike Tamburlaine here. With me he squabbled — but with Perkin…" Kempe beckoned to his boy. "Tell the gentleman, Daniel."

Young Daniel, all ears and knobbly bones, stepped forward and pointed at the poet with the fervour of the stage and ill-will combined. He spoke beautifully, though. "He called Master Perkin a lurdane and a cocklorel!" he cried, in a silvery trill that he then pitched low to mimic Marley to perfection. "'The likes of you don't deserve the light of day,' that's what he said! All red in the face, he was. Angry as an adder. And he shoved Master Perkin. Hard." He motioned to his side. "And he put his hand on his knife — like this."

Some squabble! Even considering childish exaggerations. But if Marley felt any qualms over his understatement, they weren't enough to keep him quiet.

"He'd called me a paper-waster," he exclaimed. "A drivel-monger *and* a lackwit. And if he had a say, I'd never see a penny from Leicester's Men!"

Kempe sneered. "Well, he had no say — for he was just a hired man." He turned to Tom. "But poets out of Cambridge, what do they know? They see Perkin go away alone, and next we know, a groom comes a-running from the stables, crying of a dead body — and lo! this one's there!"

It was all flimsy enough that Tom was tempted to heed Phelippes's counsel, and let Kempe bark up the wrong tree. Would a magistrate even bother? But there Marley sat juggling his knee, seething on his too-low stool, ready to explode at the drop of a hat, and make things worse. And Rheims. Oh, devil take it! Tom raised an eyebrow at Kempe.

"And this is all you have?" he asked. "A child's word — and besides…" he turned to the boy. "Tell me… Daniel, is it? This fight you saw, when did it happen?"

Kempe answered. "He's told you —"

"I'm asking him. When, Daniel?"

Young Daniel's gaze slid towards his master — as sure a sign of guilt as one could wish for. "They… 'Twas in the yard with the carriages."

"The Outer Court? When?"

"Right before —"

"You ferret-faced liar!" Marley sprang to his feet ferociously enough to make the boy step back. "Right before nothing! It was in the morning, when we arrived!"

If Kempe wasn't caught off guard, he feigned it well. He grasped his apprentice by the shoulder and shook him. "Is that true, Daniel?" When the child just looked away, Kempe pushed him aside in disgust. "It still doesn't mean…"

It didn't, in fact, but Tom wasn't going to say so. "I hope you have someone else in mind, Kempe. Someone who didn't let half a day pass between hard words and murder — *if* murder it was."

Kempe sat there and ate gall, and perhaps he had no other notion formed. Why, he might have conceded defeat, if only Marley had kept quiet. But no, of course – he had to wrench free of Skeres like Innocence Vindicated, and bring up the angry musician and the still angrier woman, and see how Kempe perked up!

"Elias Warner? Is that the one you mean?"

"How would I know?" Marley scoffed. "Youngish, fair-headed, plays the recorder."

"Ay, that's him." The clown's lips twisted. "And I'll say he had little cause to be fond of Jack."

This earned a bitter laugh from Marley. "Fond! A fine row they had. A shame your ferret wasn't there to see it."

Pacing now, Kempe only had a glare to spare for the poet. Instead, he came to stand in front of Tom. "Not that it clears your friend, Master — but ay, there *is* Warner. As for the woman…" He snapped his fingers at the apprentice. "Go find Master Leveson, Daniel. Ask him where Jack Perkin's lass lives. Janet, she's called, or the like. He'll know."

"Wait," called Tom. "Skeres, go with the boy — and you too, Marley." Before he started another row with Kempe…

None of them looked overjoyed at the prospect, and young Daniel stopped on the threshold, eyeing his master warily — and Kempe eyed Tom.

"As long as you suspect my man, Kempe, I'm not letting you mouse about alone." *And as long as you dabble in things that you should not…*

Kempe's nostrils flared. A mopish churl, the clerk at Placentia had called him. A fire-breathing discontent was a more fitting description, and truly one wouldn't think him a clown to see him lower at them all. But common players, no matter how angry, didn't stand up to Walsinghams. Kempe blew out his cheeks and nodded at the boy. It was a trine of disgruntled fellows that walked out in search of the knowledgeable Leveson.

And it was a very sour clown who crushed a soft cap on his head.

"And now Your Honour'll want to come and find Warner with me," he groused, sketching a half bow — and waited for no answer before leading the way out.

They found Elias Warner piling firkins of butter at a stall in Newgate Market. The fellow — youngish and yellow-haired as Marley had described him — wasn't called Warner, after all.

"Werner," he said, as he ushered his visitors into the passage between two stalls, "Elias Werner, if only the English could be bothered."

He pronounced it *Eh-lee-as Ver-nah*, the surname little more than a guttural cough.

"From Lubeck — and wish to God I'd stayed there." There was a row of kegs against the wooden wall. He sat on one, and wiped a sleeve across his forehead, listening for a moment at the din of calls, peddling, laughter, lowing, bleating. "What do you want now, Master Kempe?"

Having heard the man's story on the way from Cripplegate, Tom thought it best to take the lead.

"You were playing at Court, on New Year's Day," he said, making it only half a question, in the way that made people want to fill the shapeless blank. He'd seen it work on earls and ambassadors; it worked on bitter foreigners as well.

Werner threw a half-hearted glare at Kempe. "It still happens, sometimes — no thanks to Leicester's Men. But I'm good, so when someone is desperate for a player..." He narrowed tired, calculating eyes at Tom. "Do you want someone to play the recorder, *mein Herr*? I can sing too, and if it is the lute that you want, that, too."

And all the time he kept kneading at his fingers — one hand and then the other — trying to keep them supple between firkins of butter.

"I'll keep it in mind," Tom said. "But I'd rather know how you came to fight with Perkin at Placentia. Jack Perkin, of Leicester's Men."

The German leant his head back against the wall. "*Oh Gott im Himmel*, that again!" He eyed Tom a little wildly. "What has Perkin told you, *mein Herr*? He's a very great liar. They all are." Another scowl at Kempe. "I played for them for two years, did they tell you? Then a necklace went missing — Venice pearls, very beautiful — and Perkin said it had to be the foreign lad. They searched me, searched my things — and there were no pearls. But Perkin, he said that I must be the thief, and not a soul believed me, and they kicked me out. And still he wasn't happy, your Perkin — not until all the playing companies knew me for a thief — though I was not! Well, I've stolen no pearls, *mein Herr*. And if Perkin told you —"

Kempe grabbed the German by the front of his tunic. "He's told him nothing, you dullard. He's dead!"

And there subtlety went! "Oh, finely done, Kempe!" Tom pushed the clown away from Werner, who plunked back down on the keg, slack-jawed.

"And now…" he gasped. "And now you think…?"

"And now I think — for you told me — that you had cause to hate him."

"And you fought with him at Court, the day he died!" growled Kempe.

With a groan, Werner dropped his head in his hands. "Even dead he does me harm!" he said through his fingers. "Now I drudge for my father-in-law, and thank my stars when some consort or a company find no one else to play the recorder. That is how I came to be at Court: the Queen's Men, their recorder player broke two fingers." He looked up at Tom. "And as soon as I get there, I must run into Jack Perkin — and he … he laughs like an *affe* — an ape. *Mind your knicks-knacks, lads!* he shouts to the other players. *Mind your purses with this one!* Ach, I grow very angry, and I go to follow him, and…" A shake of the head, and then a bitter chuckle. "*Ein feigling, mein Herr.* A weakling, that's what I am. A foreigner with a bad name: if I brawl at Court, who will call me to play again?"

One could be sorry for the man. "So you went back to play."

"To play?" Werner shook his head, all his fire gone. "Wish to God that I had. I walked away, for you do not play well when you are angry." He rubbed his fingers again. "I walked under the snow, past the Friars, past the armoury, and to that little church…"

"St Alfege?" Tom asked. "It's a good way."

Werner chuckled again. "A good way, ay. And when I came back, they even fined me for missing out three tunes! Ask the Queen's fellows, they'll tell you."

Someone unseen shouted for that good-for-naught, Elias. When the German pushed himself upright, the bitter smile was back in place.

"My father-in-law," he said. "He tells my wife I should not eat, if I don't work very hard. Please you, *mein Herr*, I must go."

It's no easy thing to be a foreigner in this London of yours, Bonetti had said. Yes, Tom was sorry for Elias Werner. "One last thing. When was that?"

"There were two tunes in a row without the recorder at one point." The German tapped a forefinger to his lips. "That's when I went to stretch my limbs. Downstairs, they were eating sweetmeats." And with that he was gone.

As they emerged back into the market crowd, and found themselves besieged by peddlers and beggars, the clown was quieter than he'd been.

It was more than Tom could help. "Did it leave a bad taste, Kempe?"

Kempe's harrumph was no more than half-hearted. "Jack never knew to leave a fellow be. The pearls were never found

— mind — but…" he grimaced at the poulterer's stall over his shoulder.

A phenomenon of nature observed: Will Kempe, jesting player and discontent, was possessed of a conscience, although he didn't wear it well.

A fact of policy: Kempe's conscience could not be allowed to needle him a way from the secure path.

"And none of it makes him innocent," Tom pointed out, swallowing a twinge of guilt. "That he trudged to St. Alfege we only have his word."

Kempe shook his head. "There's that, ay."

"He had all the time to go to the stables. And, most of all, his bitterness toward Perkin is a good deal stronger and older than Marley's."

All of it true, all rather solid. Had Tom not known what he did, Elias Werner would have made a good culprit, for all his sorry tale of lost music — or rather, most unfairly, just because of it.

At the tail-end of the market, on the corner of Ivy Lane a bevy of young women thronged around a ribbon-seller, chattering and laughing, red-cheeked in the cold. Kempe elbowed his way through without a by-your-leave.

"Does it irk you so, Kempe? That Marley didn't kill your friend?" Tom asked, and nearly walked into the man, when the clown stopped dead in the middle of the street to turn around, fists on his hips.

"You don't know that, Master!" he exclaimed. "It could have been Warner, ay; but that doesn't mean it wasn't Marley!"

What a plague of a man! "Nor that it wasn't an accident! People do fall from windows. Why are you so sure…" Tom let it trail, as he caught sight of something behind the clown's back. Or someone, rather, huddling in the shadow of a carriage gate ... had it been a flash of red?

"What is it?" Kempe turned around, following Tom's gaze as he squinted at the gate. A servant was pushing it half shut — and nothing red was in sight. And yet...

"Nothing," Tom said, resuming his way and the conversation both, so that Kempe would have to follow. "What makes you so sure it was murder?"

The clown hadn't much in the way of argument, but that Perkin had acted oddly for the last day of two: sly and jittery at once. Tom only half listened, keeping an eye out for a glimpse of the red shadow. He knew only too well what had troubled Perkin. If nothing else, it didn't seem he had confided in his fellow players — and thanks be for that.

"A man may be sly over a good many things," he said, after letting the clown ramble awhile. "And I don't see that it must have to do with Marley." *Or Werner, for that matter.*

There was a grunt from Kempe. "But it all happened about the same time: Marley turning up, Jack turning sly..."

Oh, Jove rain on the fellow! "And you all going out to Placentia, and the German being there, and God knows what else!" Which perhaps wasn't the best course of reasoning. Tom quickly veered away. "What of this woman, Janet? Could she have been at Court?"

More grunting. "Who knows?" Kempe shrugged. "She told Jack she'd find him, there or anywhere he ran. Whether she did, though, I don't know."

A tryst at Placentia didn't sound too promising. "But *is* there a way she could have been there?" Tom insisted.

"She's maid to a lady," the clown admitted through gritted teeth. "One who buys her ribbons at the shop of Leveson's wife in West Cheap."

And then the boy Daniel came running up and waving.

"Master!" he shrilled, skidding to a halt in the trodden snow. "Jack's lass, she hasn't been at the shop since before New Year," he panted. "Bought yards and yards of silk ribbon, and was off somewhere with her mistress, Mrs Leveson says."

Would *somewhere* and *yards of silk ribbon* be enough to give Will Kempe another bone to chew? *A woman who wanted Perkin's bollocks on an Italian fork*, Marley had said. Thinking of which...

"What have you done with my men, Daniel?" Tom asked.

Did this boy always seek his master's leave before answering a question?

When the leave came, "Waiting at the Angel Inn, Master," he said. "The small one said to say, they're checking something."

The small one being certainly Marley — which Kempe had the air of not much liking. Ah well, he didn't have to.

"Well, good day then, William Kempe. And have the sense to think well before you throw charges around."

And with that, he took off up Cheapside Street, bound for the Angel and for home. But, as he did, he could have sworn that something — someone — moved in the alley across from them.

Skeres alone was to be found at the Angel Inn, sitting by the fire, and none too upset that he was rid of Marley. When Tom asked a little testily where the young fool had gone, the lad shrugged.

"'Unting for the mother," he said, busy waving at a maid.

Tom grabbed him by the arm. "I don't want to drink — and nor do you. Whose mother, if you please — that woman Janet's?"

"Ay." Skeres subsided on his stool, sulking no worse than usual. "The player, what's 'is name, doesn't know where she is — the girl, not the mother."

Girl? Perkin had appeared well into his fifties ... how much of a girl could his lover be? "Off somewhere with her mistress, Kempe's boy told me. What's with the mother?"

Whatever it was, Marley hadn't seen fit to share with Skeres.

"'Orn-mad — that's what 'e is. That player said something of the mother, and off 'e scampered, the moment the clown's boy was gone. 'Orn-mad, I say — and why you don't let Kempe 'ave 'im, I don't know."

Tom refrained from asking whether Skeres had discussed Marley with Phelippes. "Even if he's innocent?" he asked instead, earning no more than an unconvinced huff.

Ah well — just let Marley not court more trouble than they all had already. Of the mother, Tom had a suspicion he'd hear soon enough. Meanwhile, there was the matter of the mysterious pursuer. Would it be too much to hope to have lost him twice in a row?

The Angel's taproom was becoming crowded as the morning ripened towards the dinner hour, what with the inn being wedged between two busy market streets. Merchants from the Exchange across the street flocked there, loud and brisk, and speaking many tongues — for commerce knew little of the holiday season in London. The moment Tom and Skeres moved, a pair of Flemings wedged themselves in their place by the fire. One of them wore a red doublet under his furred coat — but, with his round paunch and heavy writing case, didn't seem a likely red shadow ... nor seemed anyone else in view, which meant nothing at all. There were a dozen nooks and snugs and closed doors where a man could hide — or he could be waiting outside.

"Now, Skeres," Tom tilted his head towards the back door. "You get out in Lombard Street, and I in Cornhill."

And see the Minotaur with brow fierce and nostrils a-flare, all ready for the hunt! "Your lurker again? And if I catch 'im…"

For once, it was with some regret that Tom shook his head. "No trouncing — unless you want the Watch for company. You march him quietly into the inn-yard, and then we'll see."

They parted ways, and Tom took the door out into Cornhill. It had begun to snow again, and the thoroughfare was busy, the air chill after the warmth of the inn. Wrapping his cloak more tightly around himself, Tom stopped to make a show of squinting up at the white sky. When he'd made himself conspicuous enough, he started back the way he'd come, and turned around the Angel. The inn was a timbered building, shaped like a wedge where the two streets met at a narrow angle. And, sure enough, as he doubled back in Lombard Street, there he was again … or was he? The hair on Tom's neck stood on end — and yet, when he peered over his shoulder, he could see nothing. But no! There stood a church right at the end of Cornhill, and on the steps, among a clutch of beggars, a man half-crouched, wearing a cap of faded red. Tom crossed in haste, cleaving through the midday crowd, just as the man leapt to his feet, and scurried across the churchyard. Tom gave chase, pushing his way past the beggars just in time to see his quarry dive into one of the huge doors of the Stocks Market.

Tom dove after him, up the steps, through the threshold, into a reek of fish thick enough to swim in — and at once slipped in a puddle of fish-guts, barely catching himself against a blood-stained table. Hades and Hell! The hall was huge, filled with row after row of stalls, with countless fishmongers gutting and cutting and scaling at their counters, with women with their baskets, with servants haggling for sturgeons and pikes…

Where the devil had the man gone? But then, he needn't go anywhere, did he? Just conceal his red cap, and loose himself among the market-goers.

Tom cursed some more, wishing he'd had a proper look at the fellow's face. Still, in half-hearted haste he crossed the hall, amidst the ring of calls, and shouts, and laughter, and the dull thuds of cleavers, all the way to the entrance from Poultry — and there, still denser than inside the stocks, sat the throng of stalls that gave the place its name.

No use in searching further, and the cackling of the frightened birds in the cages seemed to mock the useless effort. The hope that Skeres might have had better luck was dashed when the lad joined Tom, stumbling to a halt, flailing, and crestfallen.

"Ah, but next time," he growled. "Next time."

All that Tom had for this was an impatient sigh. This fellow had been following him about for days, finding him all about London — which was most worrying — and less than half-careful of not showing himself. "By next time, Dolius, he may well know all he wants to know."

Skeres cursed and kicked a clump of frozen snow: the Minotaur disheartened.

Back in Seething Lane, Fisher announced a guest awaiting.

"'Tis Mr. Douglas, Master," the head-servant muttered, darting a glance over his shoulder as though he feared the Scot might hear him through walls and doors. "Mr. Phelippes said to put him in the old parlour upstairs."

Whether he should be surprised, Tom wasn't sure. With Archibald Douglas — intriguer, man of the Kirk of Scotland, consummate liar — one never knew.

"What does 'e want now, Parson Douglas?" Skeres growled, so ferociously that Tom couldn't help a huff of laughter.

"I'm about to find out," he said. "Tell Mr. Phelippes, will you?"

The old parlour upstairs was no idle choice — having a concealed door that would let a keen-eared cypherer listen from the adjoining closet — and, Douglas being what he was, Tom very much wanted Phelippes's cold, sharp mind at work. He also wished that he could spare the time to change out of his damp clothes — but Douglas practiced his own kind of pettiness: never one to hazard his own careful cobwebs, and yet able to add much malevolence to them.

So, cold to the marrow and very much hoping Fisher had lit a fire there, Tom asked for wine to be brought, and hied himself up to the old parlour, to find out what he could of Archibald Douglas's mind.

The fire was there, crackling and smoking a little as it always did in that fireplace, and by it sat the Scot, hunched in a tall-backed chair to hold his hands to the flame. He turned when Tom entered — smile askew in his gingery beard, deep-set eyes twinkling.

"Young Mr. Walsingham!" he greeted — and one who didn't know him could have thought it the pleasure of friends meeting again.

Knowing the old devil as he did, Tom had little friendliness to waste — and kept his surprise to himself when the request came of a meeting with Sir Francis.

"You weren't told, then, Mr. Douglas," he said — not that he believed it for a moment. "Mr. Secretary is away at Barn Elms. Ill."

And see how mournfully the Scot shook his head. "I've heard, aye, and believe me, I wouldnae intrude on his illness and his mourning without a reet good cause." He studied Tom for the briefest moment and, when no question came, he pressed on, "But it's of Sir Robert Melville and the Master of Gray that I would speak tae him."

The Scottish envoys, sent by King James to plead for his mother's life. Yes, Sir Francis would want to hear what Douglas had to say — but still Tom didn't want to show too much interest.

"They've been in London five days, haven't they?" he asked, and let Douglas wonder just how much Sir Francis knew already.

The reckoning was plain in the Scot's countenance, and the moment when he decided that he couldn't be sure.

"Five days, aye." He said, with the smallest twitch of the lips. "And it will be two more before the Queen deigns tae receive them — but I'm sure you ken that."

Tom hadn't known, but surely Sir Francis would have. Why, had he been at Court, he would have likely suggested the holiday himself. "Twelfth Day."

The Scot held up a finger. "Oh, they ken they'll hardly be heard with all the music and dancing. They're nae fools, dinna believe it — not even young Gray, no matter how much he fences and gambles tae while away the wait — and Melville is an old fox. They see very well that Her Highness is buying time."

Which in its own way sounded promising — a sign that the Queen was unwilling to listen to the Scots — but still... *Never be sated of knowledge, Thomas — and yet be wary of showing your hunger.* It was too little yet to show interest in Douglas's game — whatever it was.

"And if they didn't see, I'm sure you pointed it out to them, Mr. Douglas."

"Och, they'd nae need of me for that, I tell ye!" was the cheerful answer. "Ye said it, young Thomas: they've been five days in London, and not a soul has met them on the Queen's behalf. You wouldnae feel neglected in their place?"

Well, Queens hardly let foreign envoys slip from their minds, did they? "And so, out of your own charity, you ran to console them."

Jove fulminate the old devil, chuckling as amused as you please! Had this been some sort of trap — and Tom fallen in it?

But perhaps not. Perhaps the glee was not at Tom's expense after all. "Och no — *they* ran tae me! It galled them greatly, mind, for they neither like nor trust me, but there were orders, from the King himself, that they should take me intae their full confidence." How the dark eyes sparkled at that! "Melville made it very plain, and young Gray sulked and groused within an inch of lese-majesty."

"King James must value your counsel very highly, Mr. Douglas." That, or both Melville and Gray had displeased their master very much — and, indeed, to have been sent on such a doomed errand…

Douglas tilted his head in a show of great modesty. "King James is a man of generous judgment — but my advice… I had none tae give, ye understand, for I'm dependent on Her Highness's good will, and wouldnae displease her for the world."

And this was quite likely the message for Sir Francis.

"I'll wager you the envoys didn't like to hear this. Which, I'll also wager, they heard *after* unburdening themselves to you."

The Scot bent forward again toward the fire — so there was no reading his expression. The voice, though, was quite serious, and ever so slightly reproachful. "Being yer cousin's cousin, my lad, ye ken better than most the weight of a Royal order. It was my Christian duty, surely, tae spare those two gentlemen the temptation tae disobey." He turned, the fire limning half his face the red of copper. "Now I ken what I ken, and it is in my mind that Mr. Secretary would hear me."

One heard a good deal, in the Service and out of it, of how the Church of Rome trained her priests in the art of justifying sin. If Archibald Douglas was an example of the Kirk of Scotland's men, though... Tom shook his head.

"I can send word to Barn Elms first thing in the morning — although I can't promise that Sir Francis will be well enough to see anyone." Less than half the truth — for Sir Francis was much more despondent and angry with the Queen than anything else.

What Douglas thought of it, he never showed — but he half turned in his chair to squint through the window at the white afternoon sky, and though he said nothing, his meaning was plain: there was still day enough to send a man to Barn Elms, without waiting for morning.

There was a knock at the door, and Fisher entered, bringing the wine and two candles — whose light made the day outside darker at once. When the servant was gone, Tom poured the wine, sat and lifted his glass to toast Douglas's health, and they drank in silence, the Scot eyeing his host.

Then Douglas sat back with a small sigh.

"Melville fears what influence I hae at Court," he said. "He'd like tae fathom how far it goes." He let it hanging, half a question perhaps — though Tom wasn't sure just what it was. It had been easier back when the old devil felt that his freedom, and his safe continuation in England, were in Sir Francis's hands.

In doubt, Thomas, wait rather than speak in haste. An easy game — too easy for this Scottish fox — and yet...

Douglas's mouth worked — either a twitch of a smirk, or a bitter curl. "Gray and Melville asked me — with nae great grace, I'll say — tae solicit an audience with the Queen. I wrote tae Mr. Davison, and he answered that, since King James's envoys saw it fit tae hae dealings with the French Ambassador, Her Highness isn't sure whether they were sent out tae her or tae him."

"Not an unreasonable uncertainty," Tom said.

"Och, but ye see: they deny ever meeting *Monsieur* de Châteauneuf. Even Bellièvre, the King of France's envoy... Not that he obtained anything for the Queen of Scots — but still, it was unseemly that King James's men should offer nae thanks tae him before he travelled back tae Paris — empty-handed as he was. Yet, they didnae go and see him. They sent one of their gentlemen — and never met Bellièvre themselves. I myself advised this tae Gray, mind ye — so as tae give nae offence."

Now this was much better. Not for a moment Tom flattered himself that Douglas didn't see through him — and yet the Scot was showing his game to buy his visit at Barn Elms.

"Then you did your countrymen a great service, Mr. Douglas. The audience was granted, you say?"

"It was, aye — and not two hours ago Melville writes, begging me tae intercede again: young Gray fell ill, and asks tae delay the audience. I'm advising Mr. Davison in the morning, young Thomas, and my Lord Burleigh."

"But you'll discuss it with Mr. Secretary in person?"

"It — and something else." A pause. "For it came tae my ears that Châteauneuf might have suggested this delay."

Châteauneuf — but why would he? Hadn't his own King sent Bellièvre to the Queen, much on the same errand as Gray and Melville? Why would he try to hinder them now?

"Not that they ever met him," he slowly said. "But meeting is not the same as having intercourse, is it? This man of theirs who went to meet Bellièvre…"

Douglas beamed like a proud uncle. "Ye've grown, young Thomas. Now do ye think that Mr. Secretary will see me?"

The moment Douglas left with his deaf servant for company, Tom hastened past the scriveners' room, to the small pigeon-hole that Phelippes had claimed for himself. The place was so narrow that a trunk, a standing desk, and a stool — all strewn with papers — were enough to fill it. There was no window, and the good Lord knew how the cypherer stood to work endless hours in there. Phelippes was at the desk already, scribbling furiously — a letter for Sir Francis, no doubt. He looked up to blink at Tom. "Well…"

Well, indeed! "I wish I knew what game he's playing! Or Châteauneuf, for that matter."

"Or the Scots," Phelippes muttered.

"But Douglas most of all — advising Gray to avoid suspicion, and letting Sir Francis know that the suspicion is founded…"

"Keeping the Scots happy so His Honour can cook and season them for the Queen?"

Leaning against the trunk, Tom reckoned on light and miles. At least it wasn't snowing anymore. "We should have left it to Douglas, and never bothered with Stafford."

Phelippes hummed — or it might have been a chuckle — as he busied himself with wax and seal.

One thing was certain, they weren't waiting for morning to dispatch a messenger to Barn Elms.

CHAPTER 5

Douglas of course had known they wouldn't wait. He was back as soon as it was light, bundled and horsed for a long ride in the cold, with his servant for escort — the unnervingly silent, unnervingly alert deaf youth.

"I'd ask ye tae let my lad bring the horses in the yard," Douglas said. "But I dinnae reckon I'll have long tae wait."

Did the old devil see how tempted Tom was to keep him waiting, just as a reward for that piece of smugness? A very short-lived temptation, it was — and let Sir Francis never know what a petty fool he had for a kinsman. Douglas was let in and offered spiced ale against the biting cold, as well as the company of Skeres on the road for safety.

The ale was accepted and drunk, the Minotaur politely demurred at. Douglas would not impose.

Tom was equally polite. "'Tis no imposition, Mr. Douglas. The roads are not safe — and Skeres, if you remember, is a good man to have in a scrape."

Yes, Douglas did remember a flight under the rain through river and alleys, a bunch of hired ruffians. Skeres, who never liked to be sent off on what he called piddling errands, looked much reconciled in hearing the praise, and in seeing Parson Douglas swallow the plain lack of trust.

And still, never be it said that the Scot surrendered without biting back. "But aye — with all the rumours of the Duke of Guise landing in England with a force... Your man will mind us if we run intae some French cut-throat, eh?"

The Duke of Guise! *How did you come to hear of this? When? And where in England?* Tom was faintly proud of how he ignored

Skeres's scowl, and kept his voice even, and never missed a beat.

"I doubt that Monseigneur would haunt the roads — but Skeres is well armed, and willing, if it comes to that," he said, as bland as he knew. Let Douglas think he'd brought no news if he was truthful, that he was seen through if he was lying.

All through the work of seeing the Scot on his way in the chill morning, Tom remained bland; the moment it was done, he turned on his heel and ran to find Phelippes.

"The Duke of Guise has landed in England," he announced, leaning against the doorjamb to Phelippes's cupboard of a room.

The cypherer looked up from whatever he'd been cyphering or uncyphering. "Oh," he said.

Oh? Tom entered and closed the door in the face of Tobias Chandler — not quite sure that even Phelippes's pupil should hear this yet. Had there been room, he would have paced.

"I'm glad to see you don't believe it, Philippus — but Douglas heard it somewhere, unless he made it up just to make my life a misery because I foisted Skeres on him. I couldn't very well ask, but what *Monsieur le Duc* is supposed to be doing is plain. Now, who'd like the notion best, the French or the Scots, is what I —" Tom stopped short, taking in the way Phelippes leant both forearms on the desk's slope, and grimaced. "You knew already!"

The grimace deepened. "I'm sorry, Mr. Thomas — I thought you knew too. But then you've been so taken up with this matter of Stafford."

Oh, indeed. "Our doing?" *Sometimes you will convince with reason, Thomas; sometimes you must work on humours.*

A half-guilty nod. Misplaced guilt, for the most part, for Tom *had* been much taken up with Stafford.

Still he couldn't quite keep the sourness from his voice. "Good to know I needn't worry about it. It's come back to our ears already, I take it?"

"Well…" The way the cypherer was nibbling at the end of his quill did little to reassure. "The fact is, it hasn't."

And yet Douglas had heard it somehow. "Curse it!" Tom softly hit a fist on the trunk. "I should have asked how he knows."

"His Honour will — not that there's trusting a word of the Parson's. Still…" Phelippes sighed, rubbing at his eyes with thumb and forefinger. "We'd better find out whether they've heard of this at Burleigh House."

Tom met this with his stoniest silence. Lord Burleigh, once mentor to Sir Francis in the affairs of the State, then foe in Council when the pupil had surpassed the teacher, these days was changing back into something of an ally. An alliance of mutual wariness so far — and yet, when one thought back to Robert Cecil's calculating manner…

And of course Phelippes had known Tom long enough to recognise the colour of his silence.

"We've been working with His Lordship's men on this," he ventured. "I'd say they've orders to be helpful."

Thoughts of wolves circling close to their injured fellows crossed Tom's mind — but he kept them to himself. It seemed disloyal to think of his great cousin lowering his guard — nothing that he'd discuss aloud, not even with one as trustworthy as the cypherer, who seemed so unperturbed at working with Burleigh House.

"Mr. Thomas, the longer the Queen dithers on the warrant…" Phelippes hesitated, picking at his nails. "Lord

Burleigh wasn't going to believe that His Honour, ill or not, would just sit at Barn Elms and do nothing. But if they worked together on the false rumours, perhaps..."

"Perhaps it would blind the Cecils to the other game." So much for fearing that Sir Francis would trust Burleigh too much too soon. "Which still doesn't explain how Douglas heard about the Guise."

A faraway consideration came into the cypherer's eyes. "I pray it wasn't Sir Edward Stafford in Paris, telling the French —"

Oh Lord! "But how would *he* know? Surely not through his brother. Unless you think Burleigh knows, and told his man in Paris, so he could give it to Châteauneuf to spread here?"

"No, no — you're right. Then I hope it was from the Scots," Phelippes muttered, bending back to his work. "It would wrong-foot them well and truly, to go and plead for Mary Stuart's life just as a French force lands in Sussex to free her!"

To hear him, one would never think he'd been the one to plant the rumours.

"You know, Philippus," Tom said, less glum than he had been, "if you weren't so opposed to wagers, I'd wager you that's what ails the Master of Gray of a sudden: wrong-footing."

And, for a wonder, Phelippes forgot himself enough to smile.

It was a day for early callers. Kit Marley was waiting in the hall, stamping his feet and blowing on his fingers. That flea-ridden beggar Kempe, he said, hadn't given up his investigations. On the contrary.

"He still wants to peg it on me!" he fumed. "But I've found the mother."

Having just finished discussing the affairs of two Queens and two Kings — not to mention the fate of England, Tom paused, taken aback. "Whose mother?"

"But the girl's!" Marley's forced patience wasn't especially flattering. "That girl Janet, Perkin's lass. Isn't it strange that an old scarecrow like Perkin had a *girl*? Not a common woman, either, but a lady's maid?"

Tom had to admit it had occurred to him.

Players of fame, Marley said, had all sorts of fine mistresses — but the likes of Perkin? An old and penniless hireling? And to hear him, one'd think he'd been around the playing companies all his life!

"So I went to another of Leicester's Men," he said. "Not that Leveson, for he's Kempe's friend — and found that Janet's mother has had a to do with Perkin. And, say what you will, I'll wager all my books, she's the one who'd have gelded him!"

Oh, Lord have mercy — wasn't there trouble enough without this? Tom leant against the newel post. "You found the mother — good for you. Now go and talk to her —"

"But you must come too — you must help me!" Marley clutched at Tom's sleeve. "Mr. Thomas, why you won't have Kempe smell into Perkin's death is yours to know and I won't ask. Kempe will keep seeking, though, and so will I, for I killed no one, and I'm not going to hang for it. The trouble is, I don't want to lead Kempe where he must not go, either — and where that is, you know and I don't."

Master Corpus Christi, Skeres called the boy, with scant liking — all eyes and silver buttons. He could have hinted at what he knew, made it a threat, or he could have gone straight to Leicester with it, and he had not. He hadn't even mentioned Rheims. Only a plea for help, and the white-knuckled grip on Tom's sleeve, that vanished in a trice the moment it was noticed. And of course it *could* all be calculation — but the fact remained that the boy wasn't wrong about Kempe.

Tom blew out his cheeks. "Where do we find her, Janet's mother?"

Kit Marley grinned.

In the shade of the old cathedral, Paul's Cross churchyard was alive and cheerful. Frost had set in during the night, and London glimmered under a sky of the palest blue, streaked with the smoke from countless hearths. It was still early, and still cold, for those who bought books — but those who made and sold them had been at their work for hours by the time Tom and Marley strode through Paul's Gate at a brisk pace, the icy air stinging their cheeks and burning their lungs.

Bookshops lined the churchyard on the north side, and huddled dwarfed between the great buttresses around the transept door. Marley hadn't learnt just where Sarah White kept her shop, so they had to ask their way.

And of course, of all people, the lad had to ask Bishop at the sign of the Bell — who of course saw Tom, and leapt at the chance.

"Mr. Walsingham," the bookseller called. "Such a long time since we last saw you! I've a new fine Horace that you'd like, I'm sure. *The Odes*, a very fine print, and I've been telling myself: this I must set aside for Mr. Walsingham! If you'd just step inside, Master."

If you'd just step inside, and pay the five pounds or so that you owe me, was what the fellow meant — pinch him!

"Another day, Bishop." Tom smiled brightly. "Do keep *The Odes* aside for me — and would you know where I can find the Widow White's shop?"

The bookseller explained that the sign of the Gun was to be found by St. Paul's Little Door — a place for ballads, truly — and if his smile had lost all warmth, Marley failed to notice.

"A fine thing it must be," he grumbled, as they made their way around the transept. "A marvellous thing, to have all the books you want!"

Oh Jove! Tom didn't bother to swallow a cheerless chuckle. "You have no notion," he muttered, and pushed Marley past a walled triangle of garden and into a thin alley that ran between tall walls of grey stone. Only a couple of stationers plied their trade there — one being at the sign of the Gun.

Bishop had been right, and there was a reason why Tom had never visited the place before: Widow White confined her trade mostly to ballad-sheets. Of a finer quality than most, judging by what was displayed on counters and tables in the shop's front, but still nothing he liked to read. The bitter smell of ink hung in the air and, early as it was, a few customers were cheerfully perusing the wares. In the back, two men in ink-stained aprons were working a print-press, with much wooden clacking.

"Do you see her?" Tom asked — and found he was asking it of no one, for Marley had been lured away by the wares. On a smaller table, he'd found an array of slender, cheaply bound quartos and octavos. *Cambises*, Tom read over the lad's shoulder. *The Misfortunes of Arthur.*

Marley turned to smile brilliantly at Tom, holding up a copy of something called *Fedele and Fortunio.*

"Plays," he whispered, half-awed, half-hungering. "You think they'd print my *Tamburlaine*?"

Oh Jove — even as they strove to clear him of murder. "Shouldn't you have it staged, before?" Tom asked. "You'll still need players for that."

"Players, ay…" Marley's smile dimmed, and he dropped the play-book back where he'd found it, just as a woman — the book-seller surely — glided towards them like a Spanish galley in full sail.

"Good day, my masters," she called. "Is there anything you're looking for?"

To the shrewd joviality of all shopkeepers, most booksellers added this air of sharing precious knowledge; Widow White made no exception. She was a small woman well past her fortieth year, thick of waist, fresh of cheeks, with faded blue eyes.

"Would you want the *Ungratious Son*?" She picked up a ballad sheet, and waved it with a momentous air. "Most moving verse, my masters, scarce out of the press. Or else *The Lamentation of Folly*. See what elegant woodcuts."

A most notable and worthy example of an ungratious Sonne, Tom read, *who in the pride of his / hart denied his owne Father: and how God for his offence turned his meate into / loathsome Toades.* If only all ingrates could be so punished!

"I'm sure they're both very fine, Goodwife, but what we're looking for is a word with you, if you'd be so kind?"

And see how the bookseller's eye bore unerringly on Marley, with his worn mockado and ink-stained fingers.

"A writer," she pronounced — and struck home.

Oh, how she did! Of all things in this world, the lad blushed. Why, he even surged on tiptoe. "Christopher Marley, of Corpus Christi, Cambridge. Poet. And —"

And before the lad could bring up the printing of plays, Tom stepped in between.

"In truth, Goodwife, we've come to ask you about a player named Perkin," he said.

Another broadside hitting home: Goodwife White gathered her figurative sails, crossed her arms, and scowled.

"Is it Jack Perkin that you want? Well, then you're late."

"Late?" Marley had dragged his eagerness back to the matter at hand. "Then you —"

"Late?" Tom cut in, elbowing the fool quiet. Oh, for Skeres's company! Even the Minotaur knew better.

The bookseller tilted her head in such narrow-eyed suspicion, and small blame to her — Jove rain on Kit Marley's loose tongue!

"Does he owe you money, Master? If he does, I've naught to do with it."

Which, if nothing else, meant they'd come asking questions in the right place. "No," Tom said. "He doesn't."

What was Sarah White seeing, as she studied them both head to toe — the gentleman making inquiries, and the lad quivering at his elbow like a hound pup? Whatever it was, it decided her all at once. With a shake of her head, she turned to wave away a journeyman who had inched his way close enough to hover, and motioned Tom behind the counter, where a window gave light to the shop's front.

Once there, she took a deep breath, and spoke just loud enough to be heard over the clacking of the printing press.

"I'll tell you this, Master: I don't care what Jack Perkin has done. I don't know what you were told..."

"That he works here," Tom lied.

The bookseller gave a snort. "No, Master. What you've heard is that Perkin had attached himself to Widow White's skirts, and true it is — the more fool I. Oh, charming as you please, that's what he is. Ugly as an ape, but charming, and the greediest leech in London! A tenter-hooking liar who'd sell his grandmother for a farthing." She clicked her tongue. "Why, no

— I'm being unfair. Never for a farthing. He'd fleece you dry for it!"

Had she wept, had she protested her virtue, had she flustered, Tom might have doubted the widow. This plain-spoken bitterness, though, smacked of the truth, and painted Perkin in the most alarming colours. This was the man Bonetti had chosen for their ploy? What had the Italian been thinking? It sounded as though anyone could have bought Perkin's knowledge of a plot which, for all he knew, was true.

"And," Sarah White drew herself as tall as she could. "That's all I have to say, Master. I care naught if he's in trouble — why, I care naught if he's alive or dead!"

Well now… Tom threw a warning glance at Marley, who looked nothing short of triumphant. He might have done so at the door-jamb, for all the good it did.

"Strange that you should say this," the lad said, leaning forward most wolf-like. "Jack Perkin's dead, Goodwife. Has been these four days, didn't you know?"

Tom would have sworn she hadn't. The gasp, one hand to the partlet, the other braced against the counter, these were things that one could pretend; the chalky pallor, though, the reddening of the eyes…

For all her sour words earlier, there was a stammer to Sarah White's words as she asked: "How?"

This time Tom didn't let Marley charge ahead. "A mishap," he said. "He fell from a window."

Oh, how she tried to harden her face. "Drunk, wasn't he? Little wonder, with Jack's ways…" And then her voice wavered and she turned on her heel, and stalked away.

Only Tom's grip on his arm stopped Marley from following.

"You see?" The lad was bouncing on his toes. "You see — she broke weeping. As plain a sign of guilt as you please!"

Or a clear mark of innocent ignorance — not that Kit Marley would have conceded the point if it were argued. "Tears always equal guilt? Where did you read that?"

Marley was too busy gloating. "I was right! Perkin had an angry woman, not an angry girl."

There was that, yes — and hardly a great cause for celebration, for it meant that Kempe was blowing smoke in their eyes, knowing perhaps more than he should. Before Tom could speak his misgivings, one of the journeymen sidled up, tugging at his cuffs.

"Please you, Masters, is it right?" he asked, glancing over his shoulder where the bookseller had disappeared. "Perkin is dead?" He shook his head on hearing that he was. "Well, rest his soul." Precious little mourning showed in the skewed face. Worry was another matter, and there was some wincing before the man found the heart to hunch closer and murmur, "You must not mind what Mistress says. She's been mistempered since she found that Perkin had being dallying with her daughter — and then he dropped Janet just as he'd done with Mistress White."

So there *was* a girl. Tom raised an eyebrow at Marley — and there was a poet with his speculation unravelled. Still, the lad was quick enough in recovering his step.

"And where would she be, this daughter?" he asked.

Oh, how the journeyman was wishing he'd kept his counsel! " I don't know…" He squirmed, tugged again at his stained cuffs. "She'll be at Court, maybe."

"What?" Tom snapped — and so did Marley, a good deal louder, making a couple of the customers turn.

"She's maid to Sir John Coates's lady, is Janet," the man whined, gesturing for quiet. "Still at Court for Twelfth Night, Mistress says…"

Still at Court. "And for New Year's Day, also?"

"Ay, they would be…" He stopped short and gaped. "You never think…? Where did Perkin…? She's a meek little thing, poor Janet…"

And before Marley began to answer questions instead of asking them, Tom said, "You've been most helpful, Goodman," and, after flicking a penny at the discomfited journeyman, he pushed the poet through the door and out into the alley.

He was smiling that wolfish smile again as he rubbed his arms in the sudden cold. "God's nightshirt — there *is* a girl!"

What did one do, but laugh? "You are the one who said there wasn't."

This was shrugged off. "That Jack Perkin should have not one woman but two — and respectable into the bargain!"

Thinking of the ballads — and let alone Perkin as a lover! — Tom wondered just how respectable his mother would have called Sarah White. But still…

"Perhaps we misjudge him?"

Marley began to snort, and then the scorn changed to consideration. "Perhaps… One with so many who'd want him dead." He counted on his fingers. "Little meek Janet — jilted. The widow — also jilted, and angry over her daughter. And the journeyman: don't all journeymen want to marry their widowed mistresses? Perkin would have been in the way!"

"Neither the journeyman nor the widow would have been at Placentia," Tom reminded him.

Perhaps it was in the nature of poets that logic shouldn't warrant more than a toss of the head. "But weren't they? That we don't know. And Janet was there, at all events — jilted, perhaps ruined, perhaps even with child… Say what you will, Mr. Thomas: Kempe must hear it all!"

That they knew little enough of Janet's whereabouts on New Year's Day — never mind Janet's mother and the journeyman — and that a woman ruined would want a husband rather than revenge, that this was more play-making than sound arguing, all of this Tom was about to say — and didn't. All these wrong trees to bark up — why couldn't Kempe be welcome to them?

"Very well then, Marley. Go and find the clown."

And see how the young fool grinned.

"We're on the scent, now!" he said, and ran away, mightily pleased with his ill-reasoned tidings. Kempe was welcome to waste what time he liked on it — but it was just as well that Kit Marley had veered away from theology to poetry.

They'd walked all the way to old St. Paul, for Marley had no horse. Now, having had enough exercise for the day, Tom hired a horse at the Two Cups Inn, and turned towards home, half musing over Bonetti's choice of Perkin, half minding his mount's step on the treacherous muddy ice. He was picking his way along the narrower part of Tower Street when there was a sudden burst of shouting and cantering hooves.

"Make way! Make way for His Lordship!"

What crowd there was, surged in a wave of protesting heads and milling arms. Horsemen, and beggars, and women, and labourers, and even a lady's sedan chair, all squeezed themselves in great haste wherever they could hope to avoid being trampled, and all the voices merged into a shrill hubbub.

And still the forerunners bellowed to make way for His Lordship — devil pinch all cavalcades! Spying the mouth of Mincing Lane a few yards ahead, Tom pushed his horse into the shaded space, sparing little thought for the elbows he grazed. The horse was growing restive, so he dismounted and ran a hand down the creature's muzzle, clicking his tongue to soothe it.

There were more cries of "Make way for His Lordship!" in the street — and there they went, a chubby young fellow in a fur-lined cloak of the finest emerald-green velvet, and no less than two dozen liveried riders cantering along, splashing in the snow, crushing the unwary, and every man for himself!

At least, it was not long before His Lordship and his retinue were gone, leaving a trail of churned mud, trampled caps, and overturned baskets.

Cursing more or less cheerily, the crowd loosened again, and Tom patted his horse, ready to mount — when he caught sight of someone watching him from across the street, at the corner of St. Dunstan's church. A large, burly fellow, ruddy-cheeked, and bird-eyed, he wore his doublet open down the front, in spite of the cold — and a battered bag hat askew on his head.

A red bag hat.

Ah, but this time... Tom vaulted into the saddle, spurring the inn horse across the street — earning some leftover cursing — and into the passage, meaning to corner the spy at last.

Only, the spy didn't try to run. In fact, he stopped with his back against the churchyard wall, hands well away from his dagger and, of all things, had the gall to smile!

Feeling a little foolish, Tom dismounted, drawing his rapier. "Now, fellow, I'd know who sent you after me."

The man spared the rapier no more than a wary glance. "Mr. Skeres, ain't ye?" he asked, a dirty silver toothpick hanging from the corner of his mouth.

Tom hesitated. *Skeres?* What pickle had the Minotaur found? "I think you're mistaken," he tried, raising his chin in his haughtiest manner — and all he earned was a click of the tongue.

"No, no, no mistake. 'Tis Nick Skeres's cousin that ye are." The man had a slow Irish tilt, and grinned wide enough to show several rotting teeth. "Been following ye, I have. Following Nick, at first — and Nick, he don't troop together with too many gentlemen, eh?"

Oh good Lord! The glass pieces inside Tom's mind jangled into a most worrisome, most disgraceful shape. This was nothing to do with Perkin or Stafford. Devil pinch Nick Skeres! When the lad had offered to secure a bond of loan for Tom in an especially lean time, he'd said naught of loutish, stalking Irishmen. In fact, for all these people knew — or should have known — it was the lad himself borrowing their money.

Again, Tom tried his coldest glare. "Now, fellow, whatever truck you have with Nick Skeres —"

Again, the bully shook his head, reaching to pat the horse. "Faddigan," he offered, as pleasantly as though they'd met at a country inn. "Name's Cormac Faddigan — but never ye mind that. Now ye know Nick's ways, don't ye — all heart, he is. So maybe he'll want to spare ye. He won't be telling ye my master's minded to have back half of his money."

"Half!" And look at him: Mr. Secretary Walsingham's own kinsman, a keeper of secrets, fighting against murderers and traitors — struck speechless before a money-lending bully-rook! Tom wanted to laugh and to curse. "Your master must know, Faddigan, that if Skeres had that much money —"

But Faddigan seemed bent on never letting Tom finish a sentence. "Ay, ay," he waved the objection away. "My master wants that ye should know, though, and think on it. There's ways to raise coin in this world. Ye think on it." He reached again to pat Tom's horse — and see how the traitorous creature pushed his muzzle into the none-too-clean palm! "There, there. 'Tis a good boy that ye are, eh?"

And with another black-toothed smirk, Faddigan backed out of the alley.

Oh, Tartarus and Hell! At least it was no Service matter. But to pay back that much money! Skeres must know what this was about, for surely this wasn't the way of things? There must be terms in the bond of loan? Tom led the horse into the street, and cast about. People went placidly about their business, and there was no red cap in sight — which meant little enough, even though Faddigan hadn't gone out of his way to remain unseen.

If there was one consolation in all this, it was the lack of even the smallest hint at Tom's true name in the Irishman's conversation. Could he hope they didn't know? Just on the chance of it, there was no going back to Seething Lane yet.

It was easy enough to take a different direction, to ride up to Leadenhall Street, and ensconce himself in the most crowded inn he found, and have an early dinner of kidney pie and ale. Harder it was to keep one's thoughts from lingering on such disasters as debtors' prison — and, above all, Sir Francis's displeasure. It was a long, glum hour that Tom spent at the King's Arms — trying to sift through Douglas's devious words, rather than think of his own woes. When, having paid a stable-lad to take his horse back to the Two Cups (as though he needed more expenses!), he slipped out of a back door and took a long circuit back to Seething Lane — thinking, for the most part, that this must all be Skeres's fault.

Skeres rode back late in the afternoon, frozen to the marrow, full of black bile at Douglas, and carrying a packet from Sir Francis.

There was a letter for Lord Burleigh, and instructions for Tom to deliver it on the morrow, and warnings about Douglas. Much as he itched and burnt with his own questions, Tom dismissed the lad, and closeted himself with Phelippes in his own writing room that, though a small cabinet, and fire-less in the winter evening, felt commodious next to the cypherer's pigeon-hole. Over bread and cheese, they sat and read by the light of that luxury that all who worked for Sir Francis enjoyed: good beeswax candles.

Douglas was playing games, Sir Francis wrote. Douglas claimed to know not only of the Guise's supposed jaunt across the Channel — but of trouble in the Low Countries as well.

"And that's not of our doing, I take it?" Over the letter's edge Tom raised an eyebrow, and Phelippes's whole face wrinkled.

"Not that I know…" The cypherer's eyes slid to the sealed missive propped against the inkwell.

Nor Sir Francis, most likely — hence the letter to Lord Burleigh…

Tom couldn't help a measure of sourness. "I'm glad to know that you retain some doubts, Philippus." *And Sir Francis with you.* "The trouble is, of course, there's no believing Douglas."

Phelippes ignored the barb, and pretended he'd only heard about Douglas — for whom he had a glum nod. "On the Low Countries, and on Gray."

"*Young Gray promises news to Châteauneuf,*" Tom read aloud. "*Boasts that he'll succeed where Bellièvre failed.*" He looked up from the letter. "Gray — and not Melville. Do you think…?"

"That there's discord between them? That Gray dances to his own tune?"

"He dances a most fitting metaphor! Gray sounds like a fool and a braggart — but Douglas made a point to tell me that he's not…"

"I wish we knew where Douglas hears his rumours." There was a rind of cheese abandoned on the trencher. Phelippes took his knife, and started cutting it into small, precise squares. "I wish Nick Skeres had made conversation with the fellow on the way to Barn Elms and back."

The notion startled Tom into a laugh. "Nick's no fool, Philippus, but it would take a far subtler soul to fence-word with Parson Douglas."

The unsubtle soul was sleeping as a newborn babe — though one who snored — when Tom kicked at the foot of his truckle-bed a while later, and it took much groaning and rubbing of eyes before he dragged himself from sleep. Faddigan's name, though, had him shoot up with a mighty growl.

"'E never did — the filthy whoreson!"

"Quiet — you'll rouse the whole house!" Tom sat on his haunches at the foot of the truckle. "And ay — he did. It turns out his master never believed you borrowed the money for yourself. He spoke of some cousin of yours."

The Minotaur lowed, grinding the heels of his hands in his sockets — and it was hard to tell by the one candle stump — but was he colouring in blotches?

"Faddigan's master, devil take 'im, didn't like to loan so much to a servant. So I told 'im of this cousin of mine, who's 'is brother's 'eir."

Tom's breath rushed out of him. For one who thought himself so cunning! "One thing I told you — *one thing*: to keep my name out of it."

Skeres looked up like one stung — his brief abashment forgotten. "And why d'you think I made up my cousin?"

"And it never occurred to you that Faddigan would try to smell him out, this cousin?"

Of course it hadn't — reckoning by the shifting gaze, and the dark muttering. "'E 'ad no business doing that, following me about, and coming to bother you! But I'm trouncing 'im, Master. I'm teaching Faddigan 'ow things are done —"

"To Hades with Faddigan! What of his master? Who is he?"

A shrug, mighty enough to rattle the truckle. "Lund, 'e's called — or the like. I've never met 'im."

"You —" Tom caught himself, loud in disbelief, and lowered his voice. "You never met him! You don't know who he is?"

"'Tis through Faddigan that 'e does 'is business."

"But even if it were only Faddigan — what if he finds out? And what of the money? You said it would be a long time before I'd have to pay it back. What does the bond say?"

"You don't worry your 'ead, Mr. Tom — I'll see to it," he snarled. "I'll teach 'em to play tricks with Nick Skeres!"

Oh Lord above have mercy! Tom sat back against the trunk. "Why didn't you tell me, Dolius? Why didn't you say there were difficulties? I'd have…" Have what? Done without the money? Ended up in gaol? Begged from Edmund? Had their father been alive…

"You don't worry your 'ead, I say. I'll set it all to rights."

Don't worry! Tom shook his head. He'd trusted the lad — and see how well that had turned out. And now look at him, face knotted and chin jutting, all earnest and fierce — the Minotaur ready for battle.

"See that you do, Dolius — or I'll be in the briars." With a sigh, Tom pushed himself upright, and undressed to the music of Skeres's mutterings of what he'd do to the lousy Irishman.

He lay awake for a long time after he'd snuffed out the candle — thinking of Douglas, old fox that he was, of Scottish envoys and French ambassadors; thinking of Stafford; thinking of the dead Perkin, and Bonetti, and Bonetti's French pupils; thinking of Will Kempe, and of Elias Werner, and of Sarah White at the Gun with her journeyman and her maidservant daughter; and not thinking of Frances. And, between one thought and the next, the black-toothed grin of Cormac Faddigan would jump up, again and again, like a devil at the play.

CHAPTER 6

Lord Burleigh received the letter with that solicitous gravity he had for Sir Francis these days.

"I trust that Mr. Secretary is not too unwell?" he asked, grave and solicitous enough to set one's teeth on edge.

"He bears his misfortunes with great fortitude," Tom said, as curtly as one could to a Royal councillor and a baron. Sir Francis would shake his head. *It's in the nature of the human heart to like and dislike men, Thomas, to trust and distrust; it's wise to learn to show none of it.*

There would be much to learn from the Lord Treasurer, who thanked Tom so warmly. "I may have an answer later, Mr. Walsingham. I'm sure I can presume on your kindness to deliver it? Meanwhile, perhaps, you'll want to attend the function in the chapel. All too often the work we do forces us to neglect the care of our souls, doesn't it?"

Such a polite dismissal! And the work *we* do! Once it would have warmed Tom to receive such condescension; now, as he bowed himself out of Lord Burleigh's room, he wondered: did the Treasurer think him still this green and gullible? On the other hand, most of the Court would be gathered there to see the Queen present her Epiphany gifts of gold, frankincense and myrrh. More pious and less secure in his standing, Davison would be there — and Leicester too, whose mood it would be useful to observe. It was with thoughts of politics, rather than devotion, that Tom made his way to the Royal Chapel, on the river-side of the palace.

The yeomen at the chapel's door peered dubiously at his riding clothes, but didn't like to stop Mr. Secretary's man from seeking Mr. Davison, and let him pass — one even showing him where the councillor was to be found.

It was no surprise that the chapel was full to bursting, bright with a king's ransom's worth of beeswax candles, whose golden glow glanced off the vault's gilt and bright blue ribs, and made the day leaden outside the mullioned windows. The *Gloria in Excelsis* was being sung by a choir of voices so heavenly to move even Tom's indifferent ear. Was the Queen moved, too, or too deep in her brooding over her cousin's fate? Tom could see nothing of her past the wall of those standing in the chapel's back, nor of Lord Leicester. Davison, on the other hand, wasn't hard to spot: one of a very few black crows among the shimmering silken peacocks. Whether it must be a surprise to find the councillor in the company of Archibald Douglas, Tom was trying to decide when the Scot spotted him.

Davison's knitted brows rose a little, and lowered again as he beckoned.

Tom obeyed the summons, whispering apologies, and trying not to tread on hems and toes.

"Young Mr. Walsingham — here at his cousin's behest," Douglas breathed — and leave it to him to make the most obvious salutation so maliciously knowing.

Davison was less cheerful. "Are you for Barn Elms, young Thomas? Then you can reassure Mr. Secretary that King James's men are going home empty-handed — at least for today." He was looking across and a little down the nave, where two finely-dressed men occupied a pew all to themselves, the way they would a battlement.

"Sir Robert Melville," Douglas whispered. "And the dark-haired one is the Master of Gray — restored tae health."

And talk of crows and peacocks! Old Melville was as austerely garbed as Davison himself — although, even at a distance, his silks gleamed the richest black. At his side, young Gray had his own notions of how an envoy should dress to plead for an undertaking of life and death. Tom had heard of Patrick Gray — and who hadn't? He was a very handsome man (like many, it was said, who enjoyed the friendship of James of Scotland). Tall and long-shanked, clad in shot-silk of sage green and burgundy, he carried his head thrown back, much like one who, on surveying Elizabeth Tudor's court, found little to like or to admire.

"They are much nettled," Douglas explained, leaning close to murmur in Tom's ear. "Still hoping that Her Highness will find the time tae hear them."

Had they told Douglas so? Tom wondered. Perhaps what happened in London still fell under their orders to confide in the Parson, or perhaps Douglas was trying to make Davison believe it. Or else, Douglas read men's minds — and to see him smirk in his beard, one would be tempted to believe it.

Davison — there was a man not given to fancies — hummed. "Well, they have themselves to blame," he said. "Delaying the audience … what did they expect?"

Indeed, whoever had counselled such a step to them, must either wish them failure or greatly misread Queen Elizabeth.

And perhaps Douglas did read men's minds — for he shrugged and said: "*Monsieur* Châteauneuf will be nae gladder…"

"He wouldn't be," Davison murmured, so soft that Tom hardly caught it over the soaring music.

Whether Douglas was, there was no saying — not by the tilt of the head and the thin smile. "it's in my mind that King James will regret his choosing. Melville has changed his coat so often, he scarcely knows whose man he is — and young Gray..." he shook his head at the tall figure. "He doesnae lack wits, mind ye. But, at least now, ye'd think he'd use them for something other than gambling."

"Gambling!" Davison exclaimed, Puritanical contempt darkening his brow, and raising his voice enough that a white-haired gentleman turned to glare at him. Davison nodded in apology, and waited until the man had turned back before he glared at Douglas, and rasped under his breath: "He comes to plead for the life of his King's mother — and he gambles?"

Douglas raised a hand, palm up, in a what-will-you-have gesture. "And he fences. Ye don't know the Master of Gray, Mr. Davison," he said, all mild tolerance. "Not a day in London, and already he'd found himself some Italian fencing hall in Blackfriars."

But this was Archibald Douglas, and whatever he knew, or didn't know, or guessed, or angled for... *He fences!* There was but one Italian fencing hall in Blackfriars. *Not a day in London...* What did Bonetti think he was doing, keeping such tidings to himself? How much chance was it that Gray fenced just in D'Estrapes's haunt — and Stafford's? What was Douglas's game, dangling this piece of knowledge? And the bait — if bait it was — was dangled before Tom, surely? Never Davison, who knew naught ... or did he? And Gray himself, what game was he playing? For even strutting popinjays could weave nets — on their own or under orders. Supposing, of course, that Douglas wasn't lying through his teeth. Questions, whole and in scraps, clinked inside Tom's mind, like bits of coloured glass thrown all haphazard.

"Mr. Walsingham, Master."

Tom startled so hard, he nearly elbowed the page-boy in the face, and wondered just how servants were trained at Burleigh

House — for the lad, in the blue and white Cecil livery, hardly blinked.

"Please you, Master," he said, in one of those childish voices that are not made to whisper. "Sir Robert asks, would you spare him a while."

Lord Burleigh's letter, surely, and a politely couched command from Burleigh's son — for lowly messengers, no matter the name they bore, didn't rate a second audience with the Treasurer himself. The *Gloria* ended, the Queen's chaplain exhorted the Court to pray, and Gray was looking down his nose at it all as Tom, with a bow to Davison and Douglas, followed the page out of the chapel.

It was a small room, snug and cosy and well lit, with tapestried hangings against the cold, and a fire cracking merrily in the narrow fireplace — and still Robert Cecil huddled on himself. A thought crossed Tom's mind of cold-blooded lizards.

"For Mr. Secretary." Cecil turned between his fingers a thick sealed letter. "It is most kind of you, Mr. Walsingham. I regret that we have to add to your burden but I'm sure you understand, there are matters of some urgency that my father needs to impart to Mr. Secretary."

Unaccustomed courtesy — empty as it was, for they both knew Tom wasn't likely to linger at Placentia.

"I'm glad to be of service to His Lordship," was the equally empty answer. "It's no burden at all."

And perhaps Phelippes was right, and Tom was over-suspicious of the Cecils, but wasn't it strange that young Robert should smile?

"Oh, but I'm afraid it must be, what with all your worries." The narrow face changed when he smiled, making him look more like an unhealthy shadow of his father.

"Mr. Secretary bears his misfortunes with fortitude," Tom tried. It had worked with the father, hadn't it?

But the son tilted his head and went on smiling. "I'm glad to hear it. But it's of yourself that I was thinking, Mr. Walsingham. Many gentlemen go to debtors' prison at some time — but when one is close to a man of great importance as you and I are…" A pitying rise of the arched brows.

Tom faltered in the act of taking the letter, and tried to arrange his suddenly stiff face into polite incomprehension. "Debtors' prison…?" How the devil did he know?

"We're not always as wise as we could be — but then…" Cecil pushed the letter into Tom's hand. "I know only too well the unhappy plight of younger sons. I wonder if Sir Francis does."

How could Tom have thought of Robert Cecil as unsmiling? He did nothing else as he took Tom by the arm, and steered him out of the little warm room. Such a slow, knowing smile… As they walked arm in arm down the corridor, where the draughts ran like ghosts and the glass panes rattled in their casements, anyone who saw them would think them a pair of friends in conversation.

"Even if you stand to inherit now, your brother is sure to marry soon, to have sons of his own… Mr. Secretary always was his father's heir, wasn't he? He's bound to lack sympathy, I fear." Young Cecil shook his head most mournfully. "My father says Mr. Secretary speaks warmly of you. Such a pity, if this matter were to change that…"

And at last Tom's dazed wits made an attempt at responding. He stopped where he was, abruptly enough that it was just short of wrenching free his arm. "I'm not sure that I understand you, Sir Robert," he said, as coldly as he could manage.

Cecil tilted his head. "You said yourself glad to be of service to my father. I hope that you mean this. You could find a good friend and a support in His Lordship."

And then he walked away, unhurried and crab-shouldered, back up the long corridor — and it must be a foolish fancy that the flames in the sconces shuddered at his passage.

Oh Lord. *Debtors' prison… He speaks warmly… Bound to lack sympathy… Of service to my father…* Oh Lord! It all roiled like vinegar inside him. He must… He must what? Go quietly to gaol? Confess all to Sir Francis, face the end of his Service days? Sound as though he were begging for money? It bore no thinking — but Sir Francis must be told of the Cecils' duplicity, surely? And how the devil had they come to know? It wasn't hard to imagine that little hunchbacked imp chasing after men's weaknesses, buying them away from their friends. How had he found Skeres's Lund? Or did the cold-blooded lamprey just have an eye on every money-lending book in London, lying in wait in the dark, ready to —

"Mr. Walsingham!"

Tom turned on hearing his name called. A dozen steps away a man emerged out of the gloom in the most outlandish costume — a doublet made of diamond-shaped patches of all colours, and big slops over the brightest yellow hose, and fierce black lines painted around his eyes. What could this scarecrow want now?

"Mr. Walsingham!" The man trotted up — and it took Tom's sluggish wits a while to recognise Leicester's clown.

All he lacked now… "What do you want, Will Kempe?" he asked, thrusting Lord Burleigh's letter in his sleeve — and his voice sounded jittery to his own ears.

Jittery enough that the clown frowned for a heartbeat before his face hardened into a glower.

"I know who you are," he said. "Mr. Scory says you search and pry for Mr. Secretary. Walsingham's ferret, he calls you."

"Does he!" Truly, Scory — a fool among Leicester's satellites! Still, a fool who, a few years back, had been haunting the French Ambassador's table. "If I were you, I'd be wary of what Sylvanus Scory says."

Kempe pursed his lips — perhaps he didn't much like the slippery Scory, either — but was quick in recovering his bluster. "I don't care — but look you, Master: whatever you call yourself, it won't make a pin of difference if your friend killed Jack!"

Oh, Jove fulminate all stubborn clowns! Tom took a deep breath, and counted to ten in Latin. *Unus ... duo ... tres...*

"But why the devil are you so certain that Marley killed him? Or that he was killed at all, for that matter?"

"I..." Kempe blew out his cheeks. "Marley and Jack near come to blows, then Marley follows Jack to the stables, and then Jack is dead! What am I to think?"

"Perhaps that Marley just found the body, as he says?"

"You weren't there to hear them, Master. Jack knew how to taunt a fellow, but not when to stop. He mocked the shepherd tyrant, and what would shepherds know of swordplay and fine fighting, and did Marley want us to play battles with crooks."

"Is that how you choose your plays? According to the battles?"

"Jack was particular on it. Not that he chose the plays, for he was just a hired man, but he knew what's done with swords. Ever boasting the he'd learnt the Italian style. He'd even played prize to become a fencing master once, and never let us forget. And that lad of yours... You should have seen him when Jack said it took a gentleman to understand these things."

Oh Jove — just the jeer to send Kit Marley flying in a dudgeon.

"What of the German? Perkin near came to blows with him, too."

"Ha!" Kempe looked very pleased with himself. "I spoke with the man who fined Warner that day. Says he came in from the side of the Inner Court, soaked with snow. Can't have been him, can it?"

Did the clown *see* himself, meddling with matters of life and death in his motley and paint? And drawing wild conclusions, too. "Can't it? Is there no way to reach the Inner Court from the stables — and vice versa?"

"It doesn't mean —"

Tom took his sternest manner. "What it means is that you can't be sure. One thing is what you want to have happened; what truly did happen may well be another." This left the clown speechless — just long enough to press another point. "Besides, didn't Marley tell you about Perkin's bookseller at St. Paul's? And of the bookseller's daughter here at court?"

"'Tis true, then? I thought…" Kempe blew out his cheeks again. "But see: you won't take Warner at his word, and I won't take Marley at his."

Which was, considering, fair enough. "And what of me? I spoke to Goodwife White, learnt of her daughter…"

Some inner debate passed over the clown's face like clouds on a windy day — calculation chasing doubt as it chased opportunity in turn. In the end bluntness won the day. "I don't know that I take you at your word, either, Mr. Walsingham…"

And then another player in motley trotted up to Kempe, fretful and vexed, wanting to know if Will had left his wits abed this morning, and His Lordship waiting…

"Go and do your playing, Will Kempe," Tom ordered. "I'd stick to that, if I were you."

The clown might have protested, but that his fellow cut through him with a portentous snort.

"Play — don't we wish! Tumble, that's all we do, Your Honour. Playing, that's for the Queen's Men, these days! Come, Will."

Kempe hadn't gone half a dozen steps when he stopped and turned, mouth working in hesitation.

"Little as I trust your Marley, I knew Jack Perkin's ways when it came to women," he said in the end. "I'd talk to Janet, if I could find her. Not that I haven't tried — but it isn't easy to ask questions around here when you're a common player."

With that he let himself be dragged away, heads together with his fellow, grumbling at each other — and Tom was left with the impression that perhaps the clown did see himself after all.

Tom being no common player, nobody would raise an eyebrow if he asked a few questions…

It was the blink of an eye — and then the thought of Robert Cecil seized him again. Prison — but, he found, going to prison was the least of it. Betraying Sir Francis's trust, opening his own guard to the little hunchback. And so much for the Cecils' new friendship — meaning to use his witless self against his cousin in this time of weakness!

Well, he'd help nothing by standing rooted there, would he? Shaking himself, Tom started off towards the court and the stables at as brisk a pace as he could without drawing attention. Jump in the saddle, ride back to London, and then…

And then be quiet, Cowardice whispered in his ear. *Perhaps the Cecils are only sounding the ground. Perhaps they'll stop if you don't yield. Or, even better, they can be fed careful false words…*

And here Sense made itself heard: *The Tom Walsinghams of this world presuming to play chess with Lord Burleigh! And Sir Francis going to war for the sake of a spendthrift fool!*

Don't play, then. *Bide your time.* And whether this was Sense or Cowardice speaking, Tom didn't quite know.

He stumbled to a halt. There was this story about a tortoise — his very first Latin translation as a small boy: the tortoise retreated inside his carapace, thinking the eagle would see him no more, and go away.

And you know how well it ended for the witless beast! Sense taunted.

Cowardice's answer was swift: *Would it have ended any better, if the tortoise had stuck his head out?*

Only a fear that those passing through would take him from a bedlamite kept Tom from laughing aloud. Ruin awaited on all sides: prison, dismissal from the Service, the Cecils' schemes, Sir Francis's contempt… Sir Francis, sitting alone at Barn Elms, reading of Hannibal while he reeled under the weight of grief, and ingratitude, and betrayal. Had Hannibal had doltish kinsmen to make it all worse? And must it happen just when Stafford's…

But then, of course it must: Lord Burleigh had always been lukewarm when it came to the affairs of Mary Stuart. Why wouldn't he try to fathom what schemes might be afoot, even to interfere. Why, could it be that Perkin…?

A giggle dragged Tom out of his musings. A dozen steps ahead, two pageboys huddled together in the embrasure of a window were eyeing him as he stood frozen in place. *That's Mr. Secretary's man. He's lost his wits, for sure!*

Because, of course, this was the Royal court, full of eager ears and eyes. With all the dignity a grown man can summon while doing his best to ignore children, Tom resumed his way — but not to the stables, not yet. Whatever else he did or did not do, he could at least untangle the matter of Perkin's death, beginning with the whereabouts of Janet White.

A servant who would have looked askance at a player asking where the Coates where lodged, had no objection whatever in answering a gentleman. That Lady Coates was at the church service Tom had more than half expected. In fact, he'd counted on it, hoping it would be easier to talk with Janet in the absence of her mistress. It would have been, had Janet been there, but, it turned out, she wasn't.

Young Janet, Coates's manservant grumbled, was gone. Tom's first, slightly wild thought was that she'd died too — but…

"Ran like a chicken, the silly little thing." The man twisted a damp cloth between his hands. "Late on New Year's Day she began to whine and wail that she must leave Sir John's service. Master told her very well, as soon as we're back in London — but no, next morning she must run away. Ungrateful little fool — with her lady unwell and all!"

Run where, the man neither knew nor cared. But had they seen her go? They had, he said slowly, with her bundle and a basket … and as he spoke, doubt gathered like clouds on his face of what did this stranger want with Janet.

Tom had his lie ready. "Janet's aunt used to be my mother's servant," he said. "She's very ill, and would see her niece one last time."

After all, most people have aunts, and the manservant jumped to the easy conclusion that word must have already come to Janet.

"Why didn't she tell? Master would have understood. Silly girl…" With a glum shake of his head, he accepted a penny, and went back to his work.

This time Tom made his way to the stables in earnest — and in some haste, meaning to ride back while there was light — and, as he hurried down stairs and corridors, he tried to sift through what little he'd learnt.

So Janet White had wanted to leave court right after Perkin's death, and had gone as soon as she could, leaving behind good employment. As with Elias Werner, it sounded plausible: Janet saw Perkin at Placentia, followed him when he wouldn't speak to her — or perhaps he, out of lust, brought her up to the empty hayloft. Either way, they fought, and, pushed or not, Perkin fell from the window: wouldn't this have young Janet fleeing in blind terror? Surely her flight spoke of guilt — or did it? Couldn't it speak of grief and shock at her lover's death? An unfaithful lover, according to her mother's journeyman — but then the fellow's whispers were all there was to show that Janet and Perkin had been lovers at all. Could there be another reason for Janet's disappearance? What if she'd seen how Perkin had died? Seen who had pushed him out of the window? This would still have her run in fear, surely? And it would have the murderer go after her? Oh, there were many questions that Tom would ask of Janet White if he could find her — supposing that she was still alive, and that he didn't get thrown in gaol first.

Sunset and curfew were near by the time Tom reached Seething Lane, but nobody was in a haste to go home. The feasting of Twelfth Night and the Three Kings was dragging, with music and laughter spilling out of every tavern, and apprentices running wild in bands, heedless of the cold.

Dark and cheerless, Sir Francis's house was the exception.

As he entered the gloomy hall, Tom shivered. This had been his home for years now, ever since returning from France. If he confessed his debts to Sir Francis, if he didn't, if the mysterious Lund sent him to prison — no matter what he did, it was all lost to him. And so was Scadbury. Where would he go? Every foolhardy expense came back to needle him now — each piece of fine clothing, each long-ago card-game, each book...

Then, of a sudden, there was noise from the back of the house, and light in the kitchen passage, and Fisher saying to call Mr. Phelippes, and Mrs Jeffreys answering that Mr. Thomas was at home, had been half an hour...

Oh Jove — had they come to take him already?

After a wild moment, Fisher marched in, shielding a candle's flame.

"There's a messenger for you, Mr. Thomas. From Mr. Davison."

Bless good old steady Fisher and his stolid ways. One just could not show nervousness before the man — although what could Davison want so soon after they'd met?

"In my room, Fisher," Tom ordered. "And call Mr. Phelippes."

For all that there was no one but them in the hall, the servant stepped close to whisper in Tom's ear: "Mr. Phelippes was called away, Master. His father is much ill. With the cold." There was a colour of reprehension to the tidings, and Tom had to wonder just what was reprehensible: being much ill with the cold, or deserting one's post to a much ill father's bedside? It was a brief wondering, forgotten the moment he entered his writing room to find Davison's messenger perched on the windowsill, rubbing his hands together. The fellow rose in haste, showing a young face, and the beginning of a yellow moustache. One of Davison's usual couriers.

"Please you, Master," the lad said. "From Mr. Davison — and thank the Lord I found you! Else, I was to ride ahead to Barn Elms, or back to Placentia..." He fumbled to unearth two letters from his sleeve — half crumpling them between chilled fingers.

Tom dismissed him to the kitchen for warm ale, and sat down with the letters, and a penknife, and a good few misgivings. What could be so urgent now?

One was for Sir Francis; the other, though, was addressed to Mr. Thomas Walsingham. It was a short missive, scribbled in haste by the look of it — and, to Tom's surprise, it came from London.

What I wouldn't tell you before Douglas, Davison wrote, *is that the Frenchman d'Estrapes was caught this morning and brought back to London. This afternoon, Sir Christopher Hatton and I left Greenwich and went to Newgate, to question the man Stafford claims was willing to murder Her Highness. Michael Moody will not admit to it. We have therefore thought it convenient to have d'Estrapes brought to Ely House tomorrow very early in the morning. This haste is most necessary and, as Mr. Secretary's illness keeps him from having any part in the proceedings, it is felt that you should be present, to report to him more fully than a letter could. I trust then, Mr. Walsingham, that you will meet us tomorrow at seven at Ely Place — and, meanwhile, convey to Mr. Secretary the note I send to you.*

Fates be thanked! Tom sat back, and blew out a long breath, shoulders unknotting for the first time in days. Here was the Council, falling for Stafford's tale — not swallowing it whole yet, but taking a good bite — and glory be. Despite Stafford's witless blunder, despite Perkin's death, the game was afoot at last.

And so much to be done yet! Brisk with new resolve, Tom went to the door just long enough to shout for Chandler, then wrote a note for Davison — acknowledgement of summons, thanks for solicitude, the usual in this most unusual circumstance. By the time Phelippes's apprentice appeared, the note was ready and sanded and folded — and one for Sir Francis begun.

"Seal this for me, Toby. Address it to Mr. Davison and send the messenger on his way." He considered the glooming twilight past the window, and the wind whistling and rattling at the casement. "Is it snowing?"

The scrivener shook his head.

"Then have a horse saddled, and someone ready to ride out to Barn Elms."

The lad scurried away, and Tom sat down to write to Sir Francis. He couldn't ride out himself now, could he? Not when he had to be at the Frenchman's questioning early in the morning. After that, having much to report, he would go and see Sir Francis. It would make little sense to do otherwise, surely…

By dint of busying himself with an overlong letter, Tom had almost managed to push Robert Cecil out of his mind, when there was some fumbling at the door and, without waiting for an answer, Nick Skeres elbowed the latch open and pushed through, carrying a trencher and a waft of spices and sugar.

"Mrs Jeffreys sends a mince pie," the lad said, laying his burden on the table. "And there's a bit of Kings' cake, and the ale's spiced."

Epiphany fare, fragrant with cinnamon and clove, such as they used to have at home in Scadbury when Tom was a boy — or at Barn Elms in happier years. Tom's smile died a quick death with the thought of Barn Elms, and Frances mourning her husband and baby, and Sir Francis, and the Cecils...

The Cecils, yes.

"Dolius," Tom narrowed his eyes at the servant, still fussing with the festive supper. "You never told Faddigan who I am?"

The scowl that met this would have sent small children running. "Did the louse come to bother you again?"

"Never mind that, did you tell him?"

One would expect some contrition, some shifting of weight and eyes — but no! Never from Nick Skeres, who instead looked greatly pleased with himself.

"Changed 'is music, 'asn't 'e?" he asked.

And why he'd hoped otherwise, Tom didn't know. Leaning across the table he grabbed his servant by the arm and shook hard.

"Have you lost your wits?" he hissed. "I told you again and again: the one thing they must never know —"

"Ay, you told me— so I never told. But look you 'ere, Mr. Tom: these are nasty folks, minded to see you in gaol. Now they'll behave." A satisfied nod.

Unus ... duo... Tom made himself unclench his fists. "Don't you understand, you lackwit? I would have gone to prison a thousand times before these people tied me to Sir Francis —"

"Ay, ay, but there's no need for that, for they'd cut their own throat before going to 'im," the lad explained, all slow and patient reason. "It takes a bigger fool than this Lund to nettle Mr. Secretary 'imself.'"

"And did it never cross your mind that he could go to some enemy of Sir Francis?"

"And 'ow would that be better? D'you know what Mr. Sec'tary would do to a tattler?" And see the Minotaur triumphant, basking in his cleverness, winking, and grinning.

Grin and wink froze on the red face when Tom rose and hit both palms on the table.

"What do you think he'll do? He'll let me go to prison, he'll kick me out of the Service — and small blame to him, for Lund, whoever he is, found someone to tell already! Devil take your loose tongue, Nick Skeres — you've harmed Mr. Secretary, and you've ruined me!"

Thunderstruck — that's what the lad was. Dumb for once, round-eyed, slack-mouthed…

"Master…" he wailed.

Before he throttled his servant, Tom stormed out.

CHAPTER 7

It wasn't full light yet when, having left the disgraced Skeres in the servants' hall, Tom was admitted to the company of Davison and Hatton. Ely House, the Vice-Chamberlain's mansion, had first been built by a bishop in the old days — and it showed. The room they'd chosen for the affair was far too tall, with an overly large mullioned window — surely part of a larger room once, now walled off and severely panelled. Unless it was Tom's own black thoughts and sleepless night making him feel both small and constricted in this place, it was well chosen for the morning's affair.

By the long table at the room's centre, the two councillors stood — one tall and broad, the other stooping — two black shadows against the greying winter dawn, and the light from a branch of candles. It was the Vice-Chamberlain who turned to see Tom hesitating on the threshold.

A new Hatton it was, a far cry from the laughing, fine-feathered fellow Tom had occasionally crossed paths with at Court.

"Young Walsingham," was the man's clipped salutation. "You were at Barn Elms to hear Stafford's side of things, weren't you? Well, now you'll hear the rest in your uncle's place."

Cousin. Tom swallowed the correction. Not that it mattered, and Hatton had already turned away to mutter to his clerk.

A less curt but no less grim Davison beckoned Tom by the table. "We want to hear d'Estrapes before confronting him with Moody," he said.

But was it prudent to let the Frenchman rehearse his tale, gauge what was held against him? Before Tom could decide what to do with his misgivings, there was a knock on the door, and a burly servant led in Léonard d'Estrapes.

A fussy pup, Bonetti had called the man. A good description for the young secretary Tom had once met at Court, all fair curls and pale blue silk, with the sulking manner of one seeing offence everywhere. This man under arrest was another matter, although even his mud-stained travelling clothes could well have passed for finery, and he still clung to his French arrogance.

"I demand to know, *Messieurs…*"

But that was as far as it went. What he'd expected, or whom, Tom didn't know — but see how he fell silent at the sight of the two councillors.

When the Vice-Chamberlain motioned to the chair, and said "Sit, Mr. d'Estrapes," there was more command than courtesy in it.

The Frenchman obeyed slowly, watching with a deer-like, twitchy wariness as Hatton and Davison sat down across from him. Tom went to stand behind them, arms crossed. When the servant who had brought him in was dismissed, d'Estrapes turned to see him leave, and swallowed hard. What did the fool fear, that they'd murder him at Ely House?

But then perhaps he did, reckoning by the quaver in his voice as he asked: "When will I be allowed to see *Monsieur l'Ambassadeur?*"

"Oh, you'll see him soon enough, *Monsieur* d'Estrapes," Davison said. "Meanwhile, you'll be so good as to tell us how you know a gentleman named William Stafford."

It couldn't come as a surprise, this particular question — so it must have been fear that made d'Estrapes's Adam's apple bob up and down.

"Stafford? But why?"

"So you know him?"

A shake of the head. "But yes — a little. He asked to travel with *Monsieur* de Bellièvre who was about to leave for France. I could not grant the request myself, of course, so I promised I'd put it to His Excellency."

"And did you?"

"But yes. And there was some question of why he would ask for it. *Monsieur* Stafford is brother to your Queen's Ambassador in Paris, is he not? And yet he asked to travel with a French diplomat. So I was charged to question him — and I did."

"What reason did Mr. Stafford give?" Davison asked.

"He said that he was not in good standing with his brother, that he suffered much…" D'Estrapes made a gesture, as though searching the air for the English word. "Much unfairness because of his sympathies for the Catholic faith. That he had enemies at the court."

"And your Ambassador didn't think these good reasons to secure his passage to France."

The Frenchman's lips thinned. "These are uneasy times, *Messieurs*. Our every step must be chosen with great caution, and His Excellency was considering his decision…"

"Considering what young Stafford could do in exchange, perhaps?" Hatton leant forward, chin propped on the back of his hand.

"In exchange?"

"In exchange for safe passage. Recommending someone, perhaps. A man suited for a certain sort of enterprise?"

For a heartbeat there was only the soughing wind outside — then…

"Do you know a man named Michael Moody?" Davison inquired. "He's a prisoner atNewgate."

"Moody — but yes." D'Estrapes grasped eagerly at the name — gathering together his lie, or perhaps the truth. "You ask whether *Monsieur* de Châteauneuf did not set a price on Stafford's passage to France — but you are wrong, *Messieurs*. It was Stafford. As His Excellency bade his time, Stafford grew desperate. He told me that he had something to offer in exchange. The name of a man, he said, who was imprisoned for debt, and would do anything to be released. *Anything.* I tried to laugh it away, at first — but Stafford would not let it rest. He insisted, and insisted, whenever we met."

"Where, at Salisbury Court?" Davison tilted his head. "Did Stafford come very often to the Ambassador's house?"

"*Et bien…*" There was the shortest hesitation. "But yes, at Salisbury Court. Again and again he came there to inquire, and every time he pressed this matter of Moody with me."

Tom shifted his weight. At Salisbury Court — and yet at least some of it must have happened at the fencing hall. Why was D'Estrapes lying? Or had Stafford lied — or Bonetti? But, even if he were welcome to ask questions of his own — which he much doubted — Sir Francis's man could not, *must not* know about Blackfriars. There was nothing for it but to keep his counsel and stand still while Davison hunted on.

"With you, and you alone?"

"*Mais oui.*"

"You say Stafford came there again and again. How many times?"

" I don't know — three … two."

Having never thought Davison one for much subtlety, Tom wished he could see the councillor's face while he asked in the politest disbelief: "And he never met *Monsieur* de Châteauneuf?"

"But no!" D'Estrapes leant forward. "Never. He was to meet His Excellency only if it was decided to grant his request."

"And this decision," Hatton pushed back his chair and rose to his feet. "Was it never reached?"

A shake of the head. "Before His Excellency could decide I... I let Stafford's insistence persuade me —"

Hatton would never make a good questioner — impatient to the point of interrupting the fellow, leaning forward with both palms on the table. "And you went with him to Newgate. When was this?"

"On New Year's Day, while His Excellency was at court for the festivities."

And perhaps the Vice-Chamberlain would have pounced again — but he stopped when Davison shifted in his chair and said nothing. Had the two of them done this before, Tom wondered. Questioned prisoners together, enough to know each other's manner? Hatton rocked back on his heels, crossing his arms. Both councillors stared at the Frenchman, and so did Tom, hearing Sir Francis's voice in his mind: *Silence, Thomas, can wear on a man's stubbornness as well as the most relentless questioning.*

It didn't take long.

"This Moody," D'Estrapes cleared his throat. "He said that he would conceal a bag of gunpowder in the Queen's room — under her very bed..." Nothing but stony silence met this. "When I asked, is the Queen not guarded day and night, Moody said that there were ways. Then I marvelled at Stafford, for his own mother is a close companion to the Queen — or so he had said. Would she not be put in great peril by a scheme like this?" The French colour was thickening, the faster the spoke, until he choked to a stop. Saying enough of the truth, quite likely — and perhaps wondering of a sudden just how wise this truthfulness was?

Davison asked: "And what did Stafford have to say to this?"

The Frenchman looked from him to Hatton, pausing between the two just enough to glance at Tom.

"I believe he had not thought of this," he said, "for he was shaken. And then Moody laughed, and said that a poisoned glove would harm nobody but its wearer. That he had seen it done."

"And you believed him?"

For the first time, Tom wondered if d'Estrapes might not be an empty-headed fool after all. He had at least, it seemed, the wit to know a trap — though not enough to keep from showing it. "I…" The blue eyes darted from man to man. "I had no reason to believe him or not, *Messieurs*. I went to His Excellency, and set it all before him — all as I have told you."

"And this was the first *Monsieur* de Châteauneuf heard of the whole matter?"

"Of the murder, yes. It made him very angry. He forbade that Stafford should ever come to his house again." And, deep in trouble as he was, trying as he was to exonerate his master of all misdoing, Léonard d'Estrapes could not help sulking. "His Excellency berated me very strongly."

Oh, he must have, poor Châteauneuf — whether he believed Moody or not — and wished himself rid of them all: Moody, and Stafford, and D'Estrapes with them. *And when was it decided that you'd travel to join Bellièvre?* Again, Tom shifted, torn between asking questions of his own, and not letting D'Estrapes know him. But then, he rather thought he knew the answer.

The silence stretched as the Vice-Chamberlain rose and went to loom over the Frenchman.

"Will you be much surprised, *Monsieur*," he asked, "if I say that William Stafford tells a different tale?"

D'Estrapes feigned bewilderment — feigned it quite badly.

"He says that he was asked about..." Hatton paused, as though raking his memory. "About the means of freeing England."

D'Estrapes drew a sharp breath, but said nothing.

"He says that he was asked in exchange for passage —"

D'Estrapes at last found his voice. "But he lies!"

"In exchange for passage to France," the Vice-Chamberlain forged on. "An exchange he accepted out of his great despair. He also says that he was asked by you — and by *Monsieur* de Châteauneuf himself."

There must be something to this, because his words caused the Frenchman to stiffen. "But this is not true, *Messieurs*!" he choked out. "William Stafford is a liar. He cannot be trusted, or believed!"

"And still," Davison continued, "you trusted him enough to follow him to Newgate, didn't you? To meet a man who'd murder the Queen of England."

It was plain to see, the moment when it occurred to d'Estrapes that he couldn't deny this, and he paled.

"Yes," he said, voice quavering. "I was very foolish — but His Excellency had nothing to do with it, and Stafford lies if he says otherwise. I'll put it all into writing, if that is your pleasure."

Davison said that a written statement would be welcome. Hatton called for a clerk with ink, quill, and paper, and, under the surveillance of the man who had brought him from the Tower, the Frenchman was left to his writing.

When the two councillors left the room, Tom followed them to a smaller parlour, with a fire crackling in the hearth. Hatton strode straight to a sideboard where claret wine and custard tarts were spread.

"Lying through his teeth," he pronounced, and bit into a tart. "What would you say?"

Davison, bent before the fire to warm his hands, hummed in thought.

"At least in part, though I won't say I have much faith in young Stafford." He straightened with a grunt. "Ah, but I grow old!"

Hatton laughed as he poured the claret for the three of them. "We all do, Mr. Davison!" he said — for all that he, like Davison, was still well shy of his fiftieth year. "We all do — but for young Walsingham here. What do you say, lad?"

The jest of it was, Tom alone knew that d'Estrapes wasn't truly lying — and yet worried most because of what he did lie about. But this was not for the two councillors to know, and — to Tom's surprise — Hatton was truly waiting for an answer, eyebrow raised and goblet of wine in hand.

Well, this was the chance to ask a question instead of answering. "I wonder … was he carrying any letter when he was caught?"

"Why, no, nothing of import, I believe?" Hatton turned to Davison, who considered.

"A letter from Châteauneuf to Bellièvre — a most mundane affair."

And now to play obtuse and lead the Council down the right path. "No great reason to send a messenger, then — much less a secretary?"

"Unless Châteauneuf learnt of Stafford's arrest, and tried to send d'Estrapes off to France — but by then it was too late.

Yes, by God!" Hatton hit a fist on the sideboard, making the fine glass goblets tinkle. "More proof that d'Estrapes lies, and Châteauneuf is at the heart of it all."

Or that Châteauneuf knew nothing, and only truly worried when Stafford's arrest came to his ears. Tom looked at Davison, who stood with his head tilted, stroking his greying beard.

"What I cannot fathom is how he came to hear of Stafford." The councillor pursed his lips. "I'm sure he lacks no friends at Court, but the matter was kept under silence."

Never one to stand still for long, Hatton paced to and fro. "'Tis worrying, ay, and it must be resolved — but for now it's little help to Châteauneuf. Even if d'Estrapes were telling the truth — and I don't believe it — the fact remains that our esteemed Ambassador knew of a plot against Her Highness and kept it to himself."

True enough, and yet, as he sipped his claret, Tom couldn't rid himself of Davison's question: how had word of Stafford's arrest reached Salisbury Court so quickly?

"Ah well." The Vice-Chamberlain clapped his hands together. "Before young Walsingham rides back to his uncle, we might as well see this man Moody."

Michael Moody, brought from Newgate and wearing the stench of it, must have been a big man once. Now not only his worn, discoloured clothes, but his very skin hung on him in none-too-clean folds. Once he was marched in, he stood beside d'Estrapes's chair, his deep-set eyes blank, and his whole demeanour that of a hunted deer.

He barely raised his head on being questioned, sparing an incurious look for d'Estrapes before he answered in a dull, rusty voice.

Ay, Moody knew the French gentleman from a visit in gaol with young Master William — that was Master William Stafford, brother to Sir Edward, whom Moody had served in Paris.

No, Moody did not know who Mr. d'Estrapes was — nor his master.

("But that is not true, *Monsieur!*")

Ay, Moody knew the reason of this visit: a kind deed of Master William's, seeking to interest his French friend to Moody's plight. Moody had been very willing to serve Mr. d'Estrapes, if the gentleman looked into the matter of his debts.

No, Moody had not spoken of any particular service. ("*Messieurs*, the man lies! I told you what particular service—")

No, Moody had never mentioned the Queen — much less the means to harm her.

("*Bon sang*, but a bag of gunpowder — that's what he mentioned! Did not Stafford himself say so?")

No, Moody didn't know why the French gentleman would say so — but, please Their Honours, had Master William been arrested?

And, for the first time, there was a note of unease in Moody's rumble, and a flicker of alarm in the dull gaze.

Michael Moody, Tom thought, had missed his calling. See how he faltered, how he tugged at his ragged hair, how haltingly he admitted that ay, maybe he'd said that he would balk at no service, as long as he was freed… At no service at all — but that had been at Master William's urging, and Mr. d'Estrapes's, too, and it was all that was said…

Mr. d'Estrapes sprang to his feet in a red rage. "But you see that he lies, this scum! *Vous le voyez bien!*" he cried. "You will take his word over that of a gentleman?"

"Gentlemen have been known to lie, my master." Hatton rose in turn, towering over the Frenchman by a good head, and glared at him most quellingly before he turned his displeasure on Moody. "And so have servants."

My master... See how d'Estrapes stiffened and thinned his lips. Clearly the Vice-Chamberlain shared Bonetti's notion that the Frenchman lacked blood, and had no qualms in using it.

It was a pity that right then a knock on the door interrupted the questioning, and the Vice-Chamberlain's clerk scurried in, to murmur urgently in his master's ear. Hatton turned to glower at d'Estrapes.

"Have Moody sent back to Newgate," he ordered the clerk — and, with the slightest curl of the lips, added: "And have some wine brought to our guest here."

Then he motioned at Davison and Tom, and they followed him out into the empty corridor.

"Well, Moody begins to relent, doesn't he. Stafford was telling no fables —" Davison said as soon as the door closed behind them — only to find himself interrupted most unceremoniously when Hatton swung around to face him.

"Yes, Mr. Davison — no fables. And meanwhile someone talks to the French! Or why would a man of Châteauneuf's be here, demanding to see d'Estrapes?"

And twice could be no chance — not that Tom had ever believed it was to begin with... "Oh, devil take it!" he cursed — and winced under Davison's glare, and Hatton's amusement.

"Well, the lad's not wrong," the Vice-Chamberlain chuckled. They'd reached the open gallery by then, and he motioned for Davison and Tom to stop there, where an oaken screen, finely carved to resemble a trellis of vine, allowed two men to stand and listen unseen, while he went downstairs to meet the visitor.

There were Hatton's unhurried steps, and a French voice echoing under the tall truss-beams.

"*Monsieur* de Hatton, I am sent by His Excellency *Monsieur* Guillaume de Châteauneuf, Baron de l'Aubespine, His Majesty King Henri's Ambassador to your sovereign." A cold, stiff voice. Tom knew it before the man announced: "My name is Pierre de Cordaillot."

"The other secretary," Tom whispered to Davison, as downstairs Hatton made his greetings with the most perfect courtesy.

"Can I be of service to you, Mr. Cordaillot?" One could feel the raising of eyebrows in the Vice-Chamberlain's words. "It must be a matter of urgency, at this time of the morning?"

Not that it was very early anymore, and it was no great surprise that Cordaillot should ignore the hint.

"It has come to the ear of His Excellency, that one of his secretaries was seized on his way to Dover. As *Monsieur* d'Estrapes was travelling as a courier, and carrying diplomatic papers, His Excellency wonders what grave matters can have prompted his arrest."

"And a spoken message rather than a letter!" The smallest smile flitted across Davison's intent face. "Châteauneuf must feel the ground unsteady under his feet."

Downstairs, Hatton's manner had hardened. "In truth, I can't imagine how such tidings came to His Excellency's ear."

It was calculated to make Cordaillot bristle — and bristle he did. "But you do not deny that he is a prisoner here?"

"My house is no prison, Mr. Cordaillot."

"*Monseigneur*, I must insist." The Frenchman sharpened each careful word. "His Excellency also requests that I be allowed to speak with *Monsieur* d'Estrapes."

Tom pressed against the screen, striving to peer through the carved vines, and, finding that he couldn't, took a step back to peer around it unseen. Hatton was out of sight, but there stood Cordaillot, stiff and straight-shouldered in the severest charcoal velvet. He didn't shift a finger when Hatton spoke again.

"Ah, but if you think that your man is held prisoner, this is a request that must be addressed to Her Highness's Privy Council. And the Council sits at Placentia, as long as Her Highness resides there."

There was a huff from Davison. "Sir Christopher's name as a fine dancer is well deserved indeed."

Oh, was it not! Those who sneered that Hatton had come to Court by the galliard were half-blind. But Cordaillot knew the steps too — if he lacked the grace. His bow, his leave-taking, it was all finely judged: defeat acknowledged for the moment; a promise of more to come. And, as he turned away to follow the servant to the door, a glance over the shoulder —sweeping the hall, the stairs, and upwards…

Up in the gallery, Tom froze. Surely Cordaillot could not see the two observers there?

If he did, he never showed it — and, as soon as he was shown out, Hatton hurried back upstairs, face darkened in thunderous displeasure.

"Let Châteauneuf go cry at Placentia, if he likes," he grumbled, "I wish him joy of it. But how he heard of Stafford first, and now of d'Estrapes, I'd give an eye to know!"

And he stormed off, to give instructions for what was to be done with D'Estrapes.

Davison and Tom followed at a more sedate pace.

"How, indeed?" the councillor mused. "Douglas?"

Archibald Douglas at Placentia, chattering, listening, watching, smiling…

"He always seems to know more than he should," Tom agreed — although the pieces of glass in his mind shifted into a different shape, one he liked a good deal less than that of the devious Scot. One that he wasn't going to share with Davison, and much less with Hatton.

"This spells more trouble." Davison glumly shook his head. "I'll be glad to hear what Mr. Secretary has to say. You'll be for Barn Elms, young Thomas?"

Tom said that he was — because what he meant to do before riding out wasn't for Davison to know — and the councillor nodded.

"Good, good. He'll want to be kept advised — but I've no need to tell you, I'm sure. Ill as he is, and mourning poor Sidney, and with the Queen's present humour…" He shook his head. "'Tis a good thing that Lord Burleigh has conceived of a greater kindness towards him, these days." A questioning frown told Tom that he hadn't shown the thankfulness Davison expected. "But you must know that His Lordship has been pleading Mr. Secretary's cause with Her Highness these past weeks. Why, you know who suggested that you be called to observe these questionings? Young Sir Robert — so, you see…"

Tom's stomach clenched into a cold, hard knot. Hades and Hell — didn't he see! He saw far more than he wished: Cecil, moving him like a pawn on a chessboard, better to make use of him. It took some effort to bow, and take his leave like one preoccupied with nothing worse than the tidings he was to bear.

As he descended the stairs to the hall, full of the cold January light, Tom felt very much like that chess pawn — and a puny one indeed.

It was snowing again when Tom left Ely House. Skeres followed a few steps behind, fidgeting in the saddle, and not daring to ask — not even when, instead of going for Newgate the way they'd come, Tom turned into Shoe Lane. Considering what Davison had said of Robert Cecil, it was most wise on the Minotaur's part, for Tom had no patience to spare for his servant.

Hatton's angry question kept whirling in his mind: who was passing secrets to the French? Douglas, to Davison's mind — and it could well be — but then the councillor had no reason to suspect otherwise. To suspect another who, while not as well placed as Douglas, still knew enough — mostly thanks to Tom himself — to have set Châteauneuf a-thinking at the very least. Another d'Estrapes had lied about…

"Master!" Nick Skeres hissed.

Turning in the saddle, Tom found the servant's nag bumping into his horse, and himself grabbed by the sleeve.

"What the devil—"

"There!" Skeres pointed with such vehemence he nearly lost his stirrups. "There 'e is again!"

There stood the pinnacled belfry of St. Bride, and the Fleet Bridge they'd just cleared — ever throttling the traffic in and out of London. Under the snow, the city had awakened from its days of carousing, and the street was full enough that the crowd roiled around the two halted horsemen. Tom drew his mount to a full stop, raking the press for Faddigan. No point in being subtle anymore.

"Where?" he asked.

Skeres clicked his tongue and shrugged. "'E was there, I tell you!" Lying low on the horse's neck he peered around, nostrils flaring as though he could scent the air for his quarry. "There, by the church — cuds-me! Now I'll trounce —" He drove his heel's in the nag's flanks — of would have, had Tom not grabbed the poor beast's bridle.

"No, you don't!" he exclaimed, with a tug at the cheekpiece that had the horse fret, and Skeres near unsaddled again. "He knows all there is to know by now, and I'm not rescuing you from the Watch."

And, for once and for a wonder, Skeres didn't even grumble. Head low, he followed in silence as Tom resumed his way.

After all, if Faddigan had traced them to Ely House, there was no harm done, since Cecil himself had seen to it that Tom should be there. Blackfriars, however... Just to be safe, and with the impression that he'd done little but shake off pursuers lately, Tom entered Ludgate and turned away from Blackfriars, up Ave Maria Lane, and around St. Paul — before doubling back, down Lambeth Hill, and to Blackfriars again.

Even as he kept peeking over his shoulder, Skeres kept very quiet.

"Have you seen him again?" Tom asked, as they dismounted in the cobbled court that had once been the friars' cloister. He glared at the servant's bright coat. "He won't have had trouble keeping us in sight, with that cursed thing. You might as well light a beacon."

There was pursing of lips and a shake of the head.

"But..." The lad peeked at Tom, and, seeing no immediate rebuke brewing, gave a huff. "I'm going to throttle Cormac Faddigan this time!"

"Are you sure it was him? You saw him well?" Which was uncertain at best — and, besides, it stood to reason that Lund would have more than one man in his pay.

Skeres scrunched up his face in thought — but, before he could make up his mind, Bonetti's servant ran out to take the horses, with young Gerolamo on his heels, hatted and cloaked for the outside.

"*Signor* Walsingham!" Bonetti's nephew greeted them, teeth white in his swarthy face. "You'd like another bout? There are quite a few gentlemen today, and my uncle is busy. But if you like, I'll be back in a trice."

Another bout! As though Tom had the twenty pounds to pay for the first one — twenty pounds, Tartarus take it!

A guilty conscience, Thomas, will see offence in all things. Which, of course, Sir Francis had taught him so he'd discern the guilt of others, and make use of it — but, Lord have mercy, how fearfully well it fit his own prickliness now!

He hoped he wasn't showing it too badly, as he smiled back. "One of these days, Gerolamo. What I'd like now is to talk to the Captain."

What did the young man know of his uncle's dealings with Sir Francis? Nothing, it was to be hoped, beyond Bonetti's debt of gratitude to a generous patron; if he had been told more, Gerolamo knew to hide it, and bow the visitor inside before he left on whatever was his errand.

With many leaving the court after the Epiphany, the hall was indeed a good deal more lively than it had been a few days earlier, ringing with the song of blades, and the chattering of many watchers. Four of five pairs of pupils were scattered across the flagstoned expanse, practising under the eye of Bonetti himself, and of another instructor, a tall, sullen-faced fellow with a beard as black a soot.

"Cuds-me — and twenty pounds a man!" Skeres muttered, not soft enough by half. "'Tis a tidy living that 'e makes, this papist jackanapes…" He fell quiet abruptly, not even waiting to be quelled.

Not that Tom was in the mood to lecture his servant about keeping his notions to himself, nor was he too sure of Bonetti's religion — although, in truth, he hadn't met many Venetians who were overly concerned with it. The man *had* crossed himself on learning of Perkin's death, which could mean little enough beyond old habit or superstition — or it could mean more and worse...

Tom considered the fencing master who, a rapier under his arm, walked from pair to pair, observing and instructing: a praise, a miming gesture, a correction — and, now and then, he'd stop and demonstrate with great flair. He was in the middle of a thrust when he caught sight of Tom.

It was another maxim of Sir Francis that Suspicion often sees what it expects to see, so perhaps it was Suspicion seeing the Italian's smile stiffen at the corners. Suspicion — fed by D'Estrapes's patent lies and Cordaillot's visit at Ely House. Be that as it may, the man was swift to conclude his demonstration and wind his way among his sparring pupils towards the visitor.

"*Signor* Tommaso!" he called, though not before he was close enough that he could do it softly.

He was a man of many smiles, Rocco Bonetti: so genial in conversation, hawk-like when he was fencing, and now so bright and so wary, as he gestured to his crowded hall. "You find me very busy, *signor mio.*"

"Then I won't take up much of your time," Tom promised, with what his once-friend Watson used to name his amiable obduracy.

For the briefest moment it seemed that the Italian might dither. He stopped to applaud one young boy who made a bold assault, to the cheers of the watchers.

"*Ben fatto, Signoria!*" he called, and then turned back to Tom. "My Lord Howard's son: not yet ten, but he displays much talent." And then Bonetti sighed. "Come this way then, *signore.*"

He led the way under the gallery and through a small door into a room, or rather a narrow passage that Tom knew from half a dozen quiet talks with the Italian. The walls were so thickly hung with blades to earn a whistle from Nick Skeres. Bonetti's best weapons, and those of his most renowned pupils were displayed in panoplies in the hall proper; this place was lined up to the eaves with the workaday pieces: rapiers, swords of all sorts, daggers, misericords, veney sticks, old-fashioned Italian falchions, targets and battered bucklers — studs and edges agleam in the light from the one small window.

As he always did when he entered the place, Tom craned his neck to observe the array.

"Add a fire, and you'd have Vulcan's forge!"

"If I were a god of old, *signor mio*, eh!" Huffing in drollness, Bonetti slid his rapier sideways in the nearest rack, and propped himself against the door, arms crossed. "So, what is it that I can tell you?"

Are you telling the French Ambassador what he should never know? Have you betrayed what trust we put in you? Does Châteauneuf pay better than Sir Francis? What of the Scots…? "You never told me that Perkin was a practitioner of your noble art."

This earned a grunt. "I never told you because he was not."

"And yet, I was told that he played prize — so he must have been … what is it called? A provost?"

"A free scholar, that's the lowest rank. Then after seven years you play for provost, and then for master. I have naught to do with it — but that is the English way of things." The amused contempt made it easy to see why the London Master would resent the Italian. "Jack Perkin, though? Playing prize? I am much doubtful. Who was it that told you, *signore?*"

And if your opponent opens his guard, never you wait to enter it. A precept not of Sir Francis, but of Isaac Kennard, Tom's own fencing master — one of the London fellows Bonetti despised so much.

"Ah, who was it, now? Someone from the French Ambassador's household, I believe — d'Estrapes or Cordaillot? Whoever it was, I thought he might have heard it here…"

"Here? I do not see how he could. Perkin never was more than a servant here. Perhaps he went to the London Masters. At four shillings a lesson, there is no pig so wretched that can't afford them — begging your pardon — and perhaps they see nothing wrong with making a scholar a player and a servant. But I do not know, and if your Frenchmen heard it said, it was not here. Besides, *Signor* Cordaillot is not even one of my gentlemen. He comes to pay for the Ambassador's guests from time to time, never speaks to a soul but for me. Unless Perkin told him…" Frowning, he went to the door and called: "Gianni!"

In a trice, the black-bearded fellow ambled to the threshold, a long dagger under his arm, and asked: "*Sì, Capitano?*" in a sullen, unsmiling manner.

Was it out of courtesy, or some warning to Gianni that Bonetti stuck to English — for all that Tom had Italian enough? Ah, Suspicion…

"Cordaillot, the Frenchman," the master said. "The one who doesn't fence. Have you ever seen him talk with Jack Perkin?"

Gianni didn't answer at once. He sniffed, and rubbed at his mouth with a hand that was missing the fourth finger. "He doesn't fence," he repeated in a rough Italian accent. "He's never here enough to take notice of the servants."

Of none of us, he didn't say.

Bonetti dismissed him with a nod, and waited until he'd gone before turning back to Tom.

"I will ask Bonifacio too," he said. "And my nephew, but…" He shrugged.

Not that Tom was interested in Cordaillot… "D'Estrapes fences, though."

"So he does, but… Ah." Bonetti smiled a little when the thought dawned on him, and shook his head. "What truck I had with Salisbury Court, *Signor* Tommaso, ended back when you know. Ambassador Châteauneuf is a most mistrusting soul, not like his predecessor."

Ah well — the game was in the open now, no use dancing about it.

"And what kind of guests come to fence here on Châteauneuf's money?" Tom asked.

"Little *vicomtes*, all sorts of noblemen. Mostly young fools who believe they know how to wield a rapier."

"All of them French? No Scots?"

The Italian's brow knitted, then cleared. "Cordaillot has not paid for *Signor* Gray. Not yet, at least."

"But they have met? You never told me Gray was here."

It seemed to be half surprise and half reproach that widened Bonetti's eyes. "You never asked, *signore*. Now let me think. I believe *Signor* Gray was here the same day as d'Estrapes once. Perhaps they talked, but I have not seen it. Had you told me to watch for it…"

Which was true enough — if only Tom had known of or expected Gray's fencing excursions.

"Master!" The forgotten Skeres called, more softly than Tom had ever heard him speak. He stood at the window, nose squashed against the small glass panes. "They're making a racket out there."

He wasn't wrong: shouting, and whistling, and howls of laughter...

"*Ancora!*" Bonetti grabbed his rapier from the rack, just as the door flew open, and young Gerolamo appeared on the threshold.

"They're here again!" he cried.

His uncle shoved him aside, and charged into the hall.

It might have been the same scene from a few days earlier: three bullies in the court, well in their cups, howling and cackling, and throwing insults and handfuls of filthy snow towards Bonetti's windows. This time, though, among the three was a straw-haired giant of a man, large as a door, and thick-faced. He carried a buckler, and kept pounding on it with his fist as he bellowed.

"*Signor* Rocco! Show your face, *signor*! Or are you too fine to take on a challenge? Ah, but we know you, the Italian gentleman, eh? Show yourself!"

"*Signor* Rocco!" The giant's two fellow shrilled and whistled, in time with the pounding.

Oblivious to the confusion of his pupils on floor and gallery, Bonetti stood there, white to the lips and quivering with rage. When Tom came to stand at his side and asked who that was, the Italian didn't seem to hear.

"Austin Bagger," spat young Gerolamo. "A piece of filth — and a man of the London Masters. If only —"

"*No.*" The one Italian syllable cracked like a whip — and at that moment Tom believed that Bonetti had truly led men in the armies of Venice. "Don't move, boy. That's just what they want."

He half turned when young Howard's tutor strode close to protest that it was preposterous to subject his charge to such a spectacle, that they were leaving at once. Most of the others gathered around, noisily agreeing with the tutor.

"As you wish, *signori*," Bonetti's voice never quivered. "But if I were you, I would go by the stables door —"

Before the half-insult could sink in, a projectile sailed through the open window, a chunk of ice that splintered on the flagstones, and sent the protesters scattering to the back of the hall with much exclamation.

Outside, it seemed, the miscreants had caught sight of Bonetti standing at the window — and, more unpleasant than unexpected, a gaggle of beggars, children and shrill women were joining the mischief.

"*Signor* Rocco!" Bagger redoubled his yelling. "The only cunning man in the world with your weapon, ain't you?" Ain't it what they say?"

"*Padrone*, let us go and teach them…" The brigand-faced Gianni stepped to Gerolamo's side, together with the servant Bonifacio, all seething and armed.

Without even turning, Bonetti shook his head.

"You brag that you can thrust and hit any Englishman on a button, eh?" Bagger howled. "Come and show us!"

And see whether the Minotaur hadn't joined young Gerolamo's troops — never mind who the foreigners were, and who the Englishmen! — growling in outrage at the words.

With a great flourish on his buckler, Bagger turned to harangue his fellows, louder and louder. "But Italy wasn't big enough for him, lads — no: he must cross the sea, sent by God himself to teach the gentlemen of England! And yet, will he fight *us*? Too good for us, is he? Or maybe there's some other reason…"

Young Gerolamo tensed, and Tom grabbed him by the arm. "Look at them: mad with drink. If you go out there, blood will be spilt."

The boy didn't have the time to answer as Bagger drew his sword, and slammed the hilt against the buckler before pointing it to the window.

"The reason's that you're a cowardly fellow, *Signor* Rocco! If you're not, come out here and fight!"

It was too much. Bonetti sprang to the nearest panoply, and tore from it a two-handed sword.

Gerolamo grabbed the man's arm, and Tom followed suit on the other side.

"Bonetti, don't —"

It was like a baited bear shaking free of the dogs. Gerolamo crashed into the bench under the window, and Tom would have stumbled to the ground, if Skeres hadn't caught him.

"The man who comes in between, I kill him!" Bonetti growled, eyes burning, and then strode out.

They followed to the door, spilling into the court — Bonetti's men, Tom, Skeres, and one or two of the pupils. In the middle of the frozen grounds, Rocco Bonetti was already swinging two-handed, his big sword glinting in deadly skewed arcs.

"Slice off 'is 'ead, that's what 'e'll do!" Nick Skeres chortled, and slapped Gerolamo on the shoulder — only to earn a shake of the head. "What?"

"He's too angry." The young Italian grimaced as his uncle swung again. "And you don't fight in anger with a sword like that… He's tiring already."

He was right, as he would be, being brought up to the art. Bonetti, all his brisk elegance gone, swung wildly, a little wider with each stroke, panting hard. It was powerful enough that he might have mown down a smaller opponent, but Bagger was huge, tall and long-armed, and each swing he parried with sword and buckler both, arms crossed at the wrist, never once wavering, never once ceasing his cackles and his taunts.

"That's why you wouldn't play prize, eh, *Signor* Rocco? All your airs, and you fight like a peasant!" He poked at Bonetti's exposed forward leg, making him jump backwards, to great hoots of laughter from his drunken friends.

"Is this what you teach your lords and earls?" one called. "Skipping away?"

Gerolamo hissed between his teeth as Bonetti growled and moved in for another swing, and Bagger met him hard with his buckler.

Uglier and uglier it grew, and deadlier.

"That's enough!" Tom took a step forward. Would Mr. Secretary's authority cover this? He decided he'd worry about authority later, as long as it worked - boung Gerolamo grabbed his sleeve.

The youth's face twisted in anguish. "They'll say he hides behind his gentlemen, if you stop it," he cried. "He'll be ruined!"

"He'll be killed if I don't!"

The shout of many voices drowned Tom's protest, and then the clang of the two-handed sword on the cobbles. Bonetti had been hit in the right leg, and was hobbling backwards, hunched low, a hand on the wound, the other groping for the fallen sword. Bagger stood looming over him, chest heaving and teeth bared, and, just as the Italian's fingers closed on the hilt, kicked it away.

With a groan — half rage, half pain — Rocco lost his balance, and crumpled to the ground.

"Enough, fellow!" Tom shouted, and broke into a run with Skeres, Gianni, and Gerolamo in tow.

But it wasn't enough to the man. Heedless of Tom's command and of all rules of swordsmanship, Bagger viciously kicked his fallen foe, catching him in the side, and when Bonetti tried to roll away, stomped on his sword-hand and arm.

So ugly it was, that even Bagger's friends jumped in to stop the butchery.

Tom drew his rapier, the others doing the same — even a couple of students — all shouting in outrage, all armed and angry as they closed in. Even as Bagger's friends dragged him away, the ruffian squirmed free to stomp one last time on Bonetti's wounded leg. Then they all turned tail and ran, chased by Skeres and Gianni, and disappeared into the maze of the Blackfriars. Sheathing his blade, Tom knelt instead by the fallen Bonetti, together with Gerolamo.

The Master writhed in pain, clutching his good hand at the wound. It was a nasty gash, just above the knee, bleeding crimson all the way to the ankle.

"*Zio!*" Gerolamo leant over his uncle, questioning in Italian, and feeling for broken bones. When he touched the right arm — the sword-arm — Rocco screamed, face creased in agony.

When a man entered the court at a dead run Tom straightened, gripping his hilt — but it was Skeres, alone, puffing and sweating — with no prisoners in tow.

"Lost 'em — the whoresons!" he panted, and then looked at the wounded man, and hissed through his teeth at the gruesome sight.

"He needs a surgeon," Tom said. Bonifacio was binding the wound with a bit of cloth, with a briskness that spoke of past soldiering.

"No surgeon!" Bonetti gasped. "Do not let them cut off my hand!"

The memory rushed to Tom's mind of himself bleeding away in this same place, and Bonetti running to the rescue…

"Go find Master Lopes, Skeres" he ordered. *And a constable,* he nearly added — but didn't, for the local law would help nothing, and likely add trouble.

Above all, they had to move Bonetti inside, for he was trembling hard, where he lay on the snow. He insisted, through rattling teeth, that he could walk if they but helped him to his feet. They did, and, as soon as he was upright, the poor fellow lost what little colour he had, and swooned in their arms. By the time they'd settled him on a table in his lodgings, all the pupils had fled, and Bonetti's Gianni had returned, alone and muttering of revenge. Tom drew young Gerolamo back to the hall — so different now that it was deserted and strewn with discarded weapons, with a path of red stains marking the flagstones.

"Keep your people under a tight lash now, Gerolamo," Tom ordered. "Unless you want a bloodbath."

The youth huffed bitterly, older than his years all of a sudden. "Gianni and Bonifacio may be fools, *signore,* but I'm not. I know we're few, and foreigners to boot, and the London Masters … ah, there's a whole mob of them!" He kicked at a target abandoned on the floor — and who could blame him?

"Are you sure it was the London Masters?"

Black eyes flashing, young Gerolamo made to retort — then thought better of it, and shook his head. "The other two I didn't know, but Austin Bagger…" He ran a hand down his

162

face. "For years your Masters have tried to goad my uncle to a duel, and some of them were furious that he wouldn't take the bait. At the play the Italian *Capitano* will draw on you for a sneeze — but in truth, you never fight unless it touches your honour. My uncle taught me that."

"And Bagger called him a coward."

Gerolamo watched sombrely through the window as, across the court, Skeres trotted out of a passage, followed by Ambrose Lopes.

"You've seen the sort Bagger is: a ruffian and a bully — but *this* he wouldn't do on his own."

Which to the lad meant, as night follows day, that the Masters must have hired the rascal to do it. Then the hall's door banged open, and Skeres barged in, together with Lopes. The medicus exchanged a greeting with Tom that would have been solemn without the one quirked eyebrow.

There was no doubting what the eyebrow meant.

"Hardly a matter for a physician, I know," Tom began, only to have it waved aside as Lopes, who had a satchel slung over his shoulder, followed Gerolamo to the lodgings.

They weren't out of earshot yet when Nick Skeres snorted. "Little papist upstart! You'd think 'e'd be shy of 'aving Master Lopes mind 'is uncle."

"He's used to greater names under his roof," Tom said. Howard, Willoughby, Raleigh, North, to name but a few. It made it all the more unlikely that the London Masters should risk the displeasure of half the court to settle a grudge. With any luck, though, Gerolamo and the constables would see just that: a grudge settled, a beating to humiliate a rival. And meanwhile Tom could find Bagger for himself.

"Go pace the horses, Skeres," he ordered. "And find mine, while you're at it. We're off as soon as Master Lopes is done."

The Minotaur scurried away, and Tom spent a grim while considering how to go about finding one ruffian in London. He had formed a notion by the time Ambrose Lopes emerged from the door to the Master's lodging.

"I'm coming to think I'd like to be a surgeon." The young physician sighed. "My father will carve me up with a lancet when he hears of it. And he'll carve *you* up, it being mostly your fault."

It took some practice to recognise Ambrose Lopes's jests, glumly delivered as they were. Tom knew enough to huff before he asked about Bonetti.

"I've stopped the haemorrhage, and splinted both the radius and the ulna — the arm bones," he amended, seeing himself not understood. "The hand is a ruin, though, and I bound his ribs, but I mislike the way he wheezes. I'll be back."

It occurred to Tom that, having summoned him perhaps he should pay his fee — a fee that he would never be able to note down as Service expense. Ah well, it wouldn't matter once he was in prison, would it, except that young Ambrose would end well down the list of creditors. Still, he nearly offered — and then didn't. What the devil, at twenty pounds a lesson (and some spoke of forty or even fifty) Bonetti was a good deal wealthier than Tom, for sure! So he took leave of the young physician, and went out to find Skeres with the horses.

"'Tis home or Barn Elms?" the lad inquired.

Both one and the other, in due time — but first… "You saw the fight, Skeres. What do you think Bagger had in mind?"

Perhaps, Tom thought a little sourly, he should chastise the lad more often: not only was this new Minotaur quieter and more obedient but, instead of tossing out the first answer that came to mind, he considered, scratching at his gingery beard. "Out for murther — that's what 'e was if you ask me. 'Tis just that there was 'alf a score of us, and 'is own friends dragged 'im away — or your Captain Bonetti…" The thumb across the throat and the click of the tongue were not to be mistaken.

"And do you truly think the Masters would do that — assassination in front of half of London?"

There was some humming, some tilting of the head this way and that. "They're a bad lot, fencing masters — but murther… I don't know. Still, if it ain't them, then who? Ah!" Had Skeres been a hound, he'd have pricked his ears as the notion hit him. "Cuds-me — do you think…?"

"I'm not sure," Tom said, as he lifted himself into the saddle. "Still, Perkin first, and now Bonetti… Come now: we're for Whitefriars."

When compared to Bonetti's lavish place, Isaac Kennard's low, dark room hardly merited the name of fencing school, or perhaps the Italian was right in calling his own a college, if this one was a school. But the fees were affordable, and the place respectable enough — in spite of lying at the edge of the less than savoury maze of the Whitefriars. The cheapest of the better sort — or the best of the cheaper, Tom's once-friend Watson had liked to call it. Watson and Tom had fallen out since — but Kennard's hall was still a haunt for penniless younger sons and students from the Inns of Court, as long as they came no more than two or three at a time.

One reached it through the narrow court of the Bolt and Tun tavern, knocked at a scrupulously painted door, and found the fencing master in desolate solitude but for his one boy — usher, scholar, and servant all in one. Kennard himself, with his long nose, cold hooded gaze, and hair down to the shoulders — not to mention the earring and the habit of wearing an open jerkin over his shirt, looked more like a filibuster than anything else. Until he smiled, and came to shake Tom's hand with every mark of the greatest cheer.

"Ah, Mr. Walsingham!" he cried. "We haven't seen you in some time! Come for a bout or two, have you?"

It was in the nature of things, Tom supposed, that the fencing master should boast of having Mr. Secretary's kinsman among 'his gentlemen', not unlike Bonetti boasting of Lord Willoughby or Walter Raleigh. Not the most flattering of comparisons, when one observed the mouldy walls, and the rough wooden floor. Ah well, each to his own — and, once he was gaoled in Newgate, he'd remember this place like a lost paradise.

Shaking himself out of his melancholy, he answered Kennard much like he had Gerolamo not two hours ago.

"Some other day, Master Kennard. What I'd like now, is a word with you."

The man's eyes went cold again, and the reckoning was plain on his face: must he hope that Mr. Walsingham had come to settle his debt?

"All the words you like, Master." He gestured to the uninhabited room. "Most of my gentlemen are still sleeping off their wassail, I think."

More hopeful than subtle, he led the way to the small cabinet where he kept his books and his personal weapons, freed the one chair from a pair of fencing gauntlets for Tom, and perched against the table. His face all but fell when, instead of sitting and producing a pouch of coins, Tom asked if he'd heard of Bonetti.

There was little chance that he had, of course, for it hadn't been an hour since the uproar in Blackfriars — unless he'd either known it was going to happen, or been told by someone who saw it. But all that Kennard did was lean back against the table, and exhale with an air of tried patience.

"What's he done this time? Unless someone's sent him packing back to Venice and its armies, at last…"

A stupidly brash thing to say, if the man had been involved. Having never found Isaac Kennard to be either brash or stupid, Tom fixed him well in the eye.

"I'd say the intention was to send him a good deal farther away. 'Tis by the Lord's own mercy that he's still alive."

Tom told the tale, as the fencing master shook his head.

"Good Lord! I never was Bonetti's friend — but truly, this…" And then he stopped, and asked slowly: "Why have you come to me with this, Mr. Walsingham?"

"Because you are the one London Master I know — and it seems that the masters had been sending their men to harass Bonetti at Blackfriars."

"Ha!" Kennard laughed bitterly. "How many times have I told them?" He ran a hand down his face. "Now, Mr. Walsingham, you don't know how it is. We're not a guild proper… Well, we were, but then the Queen, bless her in her wisdom, never renewed the statute her father'd given us back in the day. So now all we can do is stick together after the old ways, but if some foreign upstart up and says 'I teach fencing here and to the devil with you all', there's naught we can do."

"Which is what Captain Bonetti did."

"Captain my foot!" was Kennard's retort, and then he sniffed. "But no, I can't even say that. Oh, we tried to give him the lie, when he arrived strutting with his cursed Italian style. Paid a glass merchant to find out in Venice — and what d'you know? He was a captain in truth — God smite him!"

"Inconsiderate fellow," Tom murmured, earning a sour glance.

"Well, so we say to him: join us. Play prize, become a Master."

"Better to have him among you than against?"

"Ay — but he's a gentleman, didn't we know? Lord forbid he should fence with us — high and mighty cocket! And when he opened his cursed college — Lord also forbid it should be called a school — all who could afford it went to him like geese to water. And there were precious few who could, mind, but still, all the best names…"

"And there was naught that you could do."

"I won't say some of us don't hoot at him in the streets now and then. Why, I once ran nose to nose with him myself. Tried to take me to court for it, though nothing came of it. When he found some trouble for himself, and we saw no more of him, all we had to say was good riddance!"

"But then he turned up again, with another cursed college. It must have irked you all a good deal."

There was a snort from Kennard. "Can you blame us? But what could we do? We tried again, but he wouldn't join us, he wouldn't play prize, he wouldn't fence one of us for all London to see — the Italian style against the English. We challenged him so often we lost count, and he never showed up."

You never fight unless it touches your honour. Clearly proving himself to the Masters of Defence was beneath Bonetti's dignity.

"So you thought you'd raise the stakes?"

In the two or three years of their acquaintance, Tom had seen Kennard brusque, and impatient, and right out of patience; now he saw him incensed.

"That we're no guild by statute, Mr. Walsingham, doesn't make us a band of ruffians! If you think we set out to cripple

168

him…" The rest he bit down, spinning away before he cursed Mr. Secretary's kinsman for a fool.

Would it have appeased the man to know that Mr. Secretary's kinsman rather agreed with him? Not much, most likely, since Mr. Secretary's kinsman was going to let the Masters be suspected all the same.

"You'd better get used to it, Kennard. This rivalry is no secret, and you can wager I won't be the only one to wonder."

With a long sigh, the fencer crammed the gauntlets in the rack.

"I won't say…" he began, stopping to listen to the wooden clack of veney sticks from the hall. "Oh, good Lord — yes: some of the younger provosts swore they'd goad him into a fight. It never worked, for he's as cold as cold iron, that one — and that, I swear to you, is all there is to it."

"I don't know that it didn't work. Bonetti was goaded well enough when Austin Bagger called him a coward —"

"Austin Bagger!" Kennard turned sharply, lips twisting as though with a foul taste.

"One of your numbers, I hear?"

"Oh no — not at all. I don't remember now who had the misfortune to call that dirty-fighting lurdane his student, but when it came to throwing him out, we were all in agreement. Played prize for free scholar and failed, which doesn't happen often, I'll tell you. And if you think we sent him, you're much mistaken. Why, he's so bitter toward us, that he'd run through one of us as soon as Bonetti."

Which wasn't the same as saying that none of them would try to hire him — or that Bagger would let a grudge come between him and a purse of money.

A sudden crash from the hall had them both leaping through the door — and see the sight that met them! Skeres stood red-faced and sweaty on one side, still brandishing a veney stick over his head; Kennard's boy — of which it would take three to make a Minotaur — sprawled against the rack.

"What's this?" roared Kennard, as he yanked his own miscreant to his feet.

The boy rubbed at his shoulder. "We were having a bout, Master — just for sport. But..." He glared Skeres's way. "He's a Bedlamite, this one!"

Skeres lowered his stick, ducking his head between his shoulders.

Unus ... duo ... tres...

"I can't let you out of my sight, can I?" Tom hissed, tearing the veney from the lackwit's hand and thrusting it to Kennard. "Write my servant's lesson under my name, Master Kennard. And any damage he has done."

And then he strode outside into the empty yard, with Skeres scurrying on his heels.

Quattuor ... quinquies ... sex...

"Master —"

"What have you done with the horses?"

The horses, it turned out, were warm and cosy in the Bolt's narrow stables.

"I've payed for it, Master," Skeres hurried to assure, all round-eyed earnestness. "And I'm paying for Kennard's lad, too."

As though the few shillings would make a difference! And yes, doling out his own money was as great a sign of a guilty conscience as the Minotaur had ever made — but still, didn't the fool see what he'd done? Or perhaps he did — only it baffled him that he couldn't set it aright with his fists or a few coins. Shaking his head, Tom climbed into the saddle, and

170

frowned down at the dunce. "God only knows what am I going to do with you, Nick Skeres — for I certainly don't."

He nudged his horse into a brisk pace, without bothering to wait. It was snowing again, and getting dark already. Bank upon bank of glowering clouds rolled in from the east — the sea, France, the Low Countries — eating away what daylight remained, as the first windows glowed yellow. Where had the whole cursed day gone? Surely now it was too late to ride to Barn Elms under the snow. Davison's words echoed in Tom's mind from the candle-lit gallery at Placentia: *You'll break your neck, and then what use will you be to Mr. Secretary?*

It wasn't until Tom was in Fleet Street, slowing down so he wouldn't trample on the scant few standing in line for water at the conduit, that Skeres caught up with him, still peering around, with all the stealth of a trained band with drums. Seeking Faddigan, for sure.

Tom ignored the lad, just as he ignored the protests of the few muffled-up servants with their buckets. Davison again spoke in his mind — only, this time, it was from the morning at Ely House: *You know who suggested that you be called to observe these questionings? Young Sir Robert — so, you see…*

Oh, didn't he see! Not quite what Cecil wanted, having him followed from Ely House — but the little hunchback was bound to have a reason, if only that of reminding Tom that he was under scrutiny.

He nudged the horse ahead, and never mind the curses of the fellow who barely scampered out of harm's way. There was nothing for it but to confess all to Sir Francis — and then go to prison.

Resolution and resolve were not one and the same.

Tom mused on this long enough to try — and fail — to turn it into a Latin hexameter. Long enough that the ink continuously dried on the point of his quill, as he torturously wrote his letter to Sir Francis.

There should be no letter, by right. There should be Tom himself, riding out in the morning to talk to his cousin — report his tidings, and confess his faults. But resolution and resolve were not one and the same, so he sat alone at his writing table, and scratched a half sentence at a time, ink drying between each and the next.

Oh, it was no question of what he should write: Ely House, d'Estrapes, Moody... Why, there should even be a small measure of triumph in that the Council seemed to be biting at last into Stafford's plot. Even with the grimmer news of Bonetti, he should be eager to write this particular note. Eager to ride out to Barn Elms and tell Sir Francis himself.

And whenever his thoughts danced that full circle again, he'd make to crumple the note, and stop, and hunch in his chair, and go back to his pointless Latin. *Consilium suscipere et animus...*

Oh Lord! It was so cold in winter, his writing room — so dismal in the one candle's light. Not that it was his at all. It never had been, and would be even less afterward. Just like the room upstairs, that he shared with Skeres (who soon wouldn't be his servant anymore) and sometimes Phelippes...

Phelippes! All day Tom hadn't thought to inquire after the cypherer or his ill father. For sure, someone would have told him if the old man had died — but shouldn't he find his way to the cubicle in the scrivener's room, and ask? *'Tis good of you to ask, Mr. Thomas* — and later Phelippes would only have quiet disapproval once he knew of the debts, the disgrace...

Tom sat back and blew on his cold fingers. The cypherer's disapproval was nothing. Sir Francis's disappointment was what bore no thinking. Hannibal carrying the weight of Carthage on his shoulders, plagued by thoughtless dolts putting his designs in jeopardy. And there was Lady Ursula. And there was Frances... That last thought Tom tried to push away. Frances had so much weighing on her poor heart, that there would be no room left for his disgrace, surely? He couldn't tell which cut deeper: Frances not caring, or Frances disappointed.

Would Tom's father have been disappointed? His mother? His brother Guildford? All of them dead, and past caring — unless in Heaven they still could be disappointed in the living? It was an irony that Edmund, who was alive and well, wouldn't give a straw...

Edmund. Tom sat up straighter.

Let Ned still be in town, and there was something that he could do, perhaps. One last thing, before he threw one more burden on Sir Francis. He picked up his quill — dry again — and resumed his note. One last thing before he went to Barn Elms, so the letter was needed, after all.

CHAPTER 8

It had seemed good counsel last night. Now Tom didn't know, and misdoubted more with every moment that passed.

In fact, as he stood and fidgeted at the back of St. Andrew's church in Holborn, craning his neck to keep an eye on the high-crowned hat that belonged to his brother, his misgivings kept ebbing and tiding.

It was very much like one of those old plays, with an angel whispering on each side of a befuddled man.

Better that he should go, one angel said. Run before the function ended, and pretend he'd never come to ask — no, to beg for Ned's help.

But, said the other, if Ned could only be persuaded, if he relinquished even only Tom's last annuity... Four and twenty pounds would go a fair way into repaying Lund, untoothing Robert Cecil's threats before telling Sir Francis...

Did angels sneer? This one did — and sourly. And just what would persuade Ned, short of a Court ruling?

A concern for his own name, perhaps? Especially if he had hopes of marrying Sir Ralph Shelton's daughter?

And squandering money on a brother's debts would be more to old Shelton's liking, surely!

This angelical debate was still raging when the last hymn came to an end, and the flock of St. Andrew loosened its ranks to disperse to Sunday cheer — and what must Sir Edmund Walsingham do, but turn around and catch sight of his brother?

Well, it was a known fact that circumstance will at times negate argument. And before either argument could best the other Ned himself decided the matter, sailing through the crowd, and glancing not once, but twice over his shoulder to a quietly conversing knot of people by the pulpit. The knot, it was worth noting, comprised the rector, an old gentleman and two ladies, one of them wearing a green, fur-trimmed hood.

Oh, better and better! Ned wasn't alone, and Tom could have laid a wager as to who his church-fellows were.

Their company surely hadn't disposed Sir Edmund to brotherliness.

"What do you want this time, Thomas?" was his salutation.

Which was most unfair, considering that Tom had never sought to cross paths at Placentia. Before he could say so, though, Ned caught him by the arm and, with a last peek at his companions, led him through a side door and out to the graveyard.

It was a smallish walled square ground, blanketed with snow — ankle deep after the night's fall where the paths lay, a good deal deeper over the graves themselves. The walls were overhung with ivy, heavy and near black against the snow. Not the most cheerful of places.

"So?" Ned asked, crossing his arms in impatience under his fine cloak. "But mind: if it's about money, brother…"

Good counsel, indeed! "'Tis my annuity —"

And there went the mirthless chuckle, as Ned looked up to the heavens — witness, O Lord, the lead-skulled brother you burdened me with! "Father always called you the brightest of us, Thomas, but what this makes *me* I don't know, for you've the wits of a snail! What will it take for you to understand?"

"Twenty-four pounds a year from Croydon Vicarage, that's what I understand — plain and simple in Father's will. It's been two years, now, and I have yet to see a farthing!"

Which wasn't quite true, but close enough that Ned didn't bother to deny it.

"Ay — and Croydon's encumbered, and so's Scadbury, and Footscray, and Burwell, and every inch of land I own, for Father left debts like an Earl's, and a will full of squandering provisions like your twenty-four pounds. There's no money, plain and simple! Or must I put it in Latin verse for you?"

"Not that you'd know how," Tom muttered — and he must truly have a snail's wits, taunting the brother he'd come to beg from.

Whatever else he was, Ned wasn't deaf. If he grew any redder in the face, he'd glow purple, no matter how he tried to sneer down at Tom. "Ay, well, some of us were learning to run an estate, while you played at poetry."

"And, having learnt, see how well they run them…" Tom bit down the rest. Why was it that they always had to rub each other the wrong way? "Ned, I'm not saying… Oh Lord, but you must see: I'm your brother, your heir, I bear your name. How am I to live if you keep the annuity from me?"

As soon as he'd uttered them, Tom wished he could take back the words. Oh, this was a mistake! See how Ned tilted his head, eyes narrowing, as the outburst's gist penetrated his thick head.

"Doesn't Sir Francis pay you wages?" he asked slowly.

"He does! 'Tis just —"

"'Tis just that you're too deep in debt, are you? Oh, Father's bright lad — but then, you're just like him!"

And under the triumphant sneer, down went the dam of Tom's short-lived meekness, and all the bitterness flooded out in a torrent. "Ay, devil take it, deep in debt! And I'll go to gaol if you don't help me. Why, 'tis not even for help that I'm asking: just the annuity Father left, that's due to me. I'm not asking you to pay my debts —"

"'Tis a good thing that you aren't, Tomkin — for that I wouldn't do if I had the money." Sir Edmund Walsingham drew himself tall. He could have sounded righteous, but for the malice in his gaze. "Gambling, and pride, and vainness," he reached to flick at the enamelled clasp of Tom's cloak. "All of them ugly sins: it would be unchristian to buy you out of your right punishment." And with this pious speech, he turned on his heel — only to turn back and lean close to hiss in Tom's face: "'Tis a good thing that you'll never have Scadbury. After the damage Father did, you'd sink the place into the moat!" Then he stalked away, head thrown high, and cloak fluttering, like some Roman Scipio in an etching.

Oh Lord — why couldn't the heartless dolt step on some patch of ice, and slip, and drench his fine clothes in mud, since pride was such an ugly sin? With a curse that would have given their mother the vapours, Tom kicked at a clump of snow — and, as he did, caught sight of someone at the graveyard's other end.

A woman — no, a lady, wearing a green hood trimmed with fur. And the fur framed a small face with a pointed chin and measuring grey eyes. Oh, wasn't this all he lacked! Who must have been there to observe the brothers' spat — who else but Etheldreda Shelton!

The little eavesdropping mouse! Not that she blushed under Tom's glare, or gave any other sign of maidenly shyness.

"Mistress Shelton," he saluted curtly — just this side of discourtesy — and looked her up and down, from the fur trim atop the hood to the dampened hem of her cloak. "Were you seeking something — or someone?"

She motioned at the wall behind her — out of which, framed by the black tendrils of ivy, stuck an iron staff wrought in the shape of a pointing hand.

"I like sundials," Etheldreda said. She had a deep voice for so slight and so young a woman, for she couldn't be older that Frances.

"Do you?" Tom groused, past grace or manners. "Well, you'll find one in the gardens at Scadbury. Old and plain — but perhaps my brother will have a new one made for you."

And if he'd thought that she'd blush or simper, Tom had been much mistaken. She pursed her lips instead, and tilted her head in cold consideration. "You and your brother share this notion that I'll consent to be Lady Walsingham."

"And you won't?" It surely flew in the face of reason that Tom should feel compelled to defend his miser of a brother to this woman? "Ned isn't such a bad catch. We go back to the Lords of Little Walsingham, you know. Over in Norfolk." And why she should give a straw for Norfolk, he didn't know.

Of course she didn't — judging by the way she pursed her lips again. "It's that I've little liking for niggardliness. Not that I have more for drowning in debt." A little toss of the head under the hood. "Oh, most gentlemen have debts. It's the drowning that I find ungentlemanly. But a lack of generosity repels me."

Well now! Were these Ned's hopes impaled on the sundial's gnomon? And what sort of simpleton was Tom, that he must feel a pang of guilt over it? A very great one, for Ned had been crowing for all of London to hear. Besides, if his brother's prospects were dashed, it was a blessing, not a matter for regret! And still Tom was gaping, speechless before the sharp grey eyes and one fine arched eyebrow. Lord, but she must think him a dunce!

Before he could conjure up a word to say, the church door swung open, and a woman leant out to call. "Come, Mistress Audrey — your father waits!"

With a click of the tongue — more impatience than contriteness — the disconcerting young lady gathered her skirts to go.

Audrey... the soft French name didn't seem to fit this sharp young person. "Audrey?" Tom blurted out, for no reason at all.

One pattened foot on the doorstep already, she turned to glance at him over her shoulder. "You never think I'd call myself Etheldreda?"

"I wouldn't, if I were you," Tom said — to thin air, for she had already disappeared inside the church. At least he wouldn't have this one for a sister-in-law!

But it was scant consolation, when one thought of it — and Tom did think of it very much, as he slowly followed inside the church. It was empty now, but for a sexton busy sweeping the floor, so Tom found a pew in the back and sat there to brood on his troubles.

With or without Etheldreda Shelton, or any other wife in fact, Ned would not change his mind — and why he'd thought he would, Tom didn't know. If — no, when he went to gaol, Ned would like it only too well. Jealous still, even now that their father was dead, and petty, and short-minded... But, no matter how many names he called his brother, no matter how many of them were deserved, the ugly fact remained: Thomas Walsingham would soon drown in debt and join the ranks of gentlemen in Newgate or the Marshalsea.

The rustle of the sexton's broom sounded just like Davison's rumbling: *And what use will you be to Mr. Secretary then?*

But then, what use was he being now? Oh, no matter: he'd be thrown out of the Service soon enough — and even if he wasn't… Sir Francis appeared in Tom's mind: haggard with illness and grief, stern, hard-eyed, disappointed. With a groan, he leant forward — elbows on his knees, head in his hands. Of course he'd be thrown out. And small punishment it would be for the idiot who'd managed to expose himself to the wiles of the Cecils, wrecking the whole matter of Stafford — all of it just at a moment when Mr. Secretary was most vulnerable to ruin and disgrace.

The sudden silence pushed its way through the cobwebs in Tom's mind. The sexton had stopped his sweeping and stood in the middle of the nave, leaning on his broom, and eyeing the madman in the pew with the blank curiosity of a bird. What did he think he was seeing? A bereft husband? A ruined merchant? A betrayed lover? A conscience-ridden malfeasant?

Well, that last he was, one could say — although perhaps the bird-sexton thought him more a murderer than a spendthrift. Tom had the sense to swallow an urge to explain that he was no such thing. Instead, he turned away and in a moment, for a small mercy, the broom's progress resumed.

Not a murderer, no — but one who failed to find murderers. He'd have to tell Phelippes all he knew of Perkin and of Bonetti, so that the cypherer could at least know what was afoot. Not that Tom himself knew too well. What *did* he know, in fact?

With a sigh, he leant back in the pew, frowning at the whitewashed vaults above as he marshalled his scant certainties and many questions.

Item: Jack Perkin was to have discovered Stafford's plot to Lord Leicester on New Year's Day — but…

Item: Before he could, Perkin had fallen from a window in the Royal stables and died of a broken neck.

Item: According to Ambrose Lopes, it could have been an accident as well as a murder — but...

Quaestio: Wasn't it all too likely that someone had killed the man to stop him from revealing what he knew?

Item: There were others who held a grudge against the dead man — namely two jilted women, and a German player Perkin had wantonly disgraced. However...

Item: It seemed unlikely that Sarah White had been at Placentia on New Year's Day.

Item: Elias Werner was there, but would have had little chance to do the deed.

Item: Sarah White's daughter Janet was also at Court, and had disappeared since, so perhaps made a more likely suspect, but all described her as a small woman.

And then...

Item: Rocco Bonetti, who had helped set up Perkin to reveal the plot, had been assaulted with a violence that only by chance hadn't resulted in his death.

Item: The assault seemed a result of the rivalry between Bonetti and the English fencing masters — but...

Item: The London Masters, at least in the person of Kennard, denied that the assaulter was one of their own, and denied the charge of having hired that assaulter.

Item: While either Perkin's death and Bonetti's misadventure could have been accident or unrelated mischief, they had both happened within a few days of each other, and of the uncovering of Stafford's supposed plot.

Quaestio: Was it reasonable to believe the three unrelated?

A most rhetorical question, whose answer, like many of its kind, only bred more questions.

"But if Perkin was killed to shut his mouth, why try to kill Bonetti when Stafford had let the cat out of the bag already?" Tom asked of the ceiling. And suddenly it was as though someone had reached in to rattle the glass pieces inside his mind, tossing them so that they fell into a new pattern.

He sat up straight. "Because Bonetti knew who had been there to overhear Perkin and Stafford!" he answered his own question, loud enough that the sexton, a dozen steps away, stopped his work again, and peered at the Bedlamite who talked to thin air.

"Master?" The old fellow asked in head-ducking wariness — and see how tightly he gripped his broom.

It must be no great reassurance when Tom grinned at him, and asked: "And why wait a full week before acting?" He held up a forefinger. "Because that's when it became a threat!"

Even as he jumped to his feet, Tom dug in his purse for a penny. "I have wits as slow as molasses, my good man! Sulking about my woes." He flicked the coin to the disapproving sexton, who caught it awkwardly, dropping his broom with a great clatter.

Perhaps, at least, before being thrown in prison, there would be time and means at least to straighten the joints and flexures of this matter for Sir Francis.

By the time he dismounted in the deserted courtyard at Blackfriars, Tom's new eagerness had dimmed. It hadn't taken him long to think that trouble was not be sought only among Rocco's students — and so much for glib thoughts about never knowing about the Italian's religion. Perhaps he should have concerned himself much earlier — or perhaps...

You will find, Thomas, that loyalty, money and faith are three separate paths that seldom cross in most men's lives.

And Sir Francis was right, of course: never mind faith or loyalty, and no matter what he said of Châteauneuf, Bonetti knew of Stafford's game, though not the game's nature, and of Perkin's unwitting part in it. Whatever he made of the plot, he knew enough to sell that knowledge first, and later to be a danger to whoever had bought or heard. And the same could be true of the nephew and the servants.

It was in a grim disposition that Tom knocked at the fencing hall's door. Such a large door, with its fine carved lintel, and a knocker in the shape of a winged lion's head. The lion of Venice, Bonetti had once explained.

It took more knocking — the echo hollow beyond the barred door — before the bolts were drawn, and a grim-faced Gerolamo appeared.

"*Signor* Walsingham," he greeted, stepping back to let in the visitor. "Have you come to see my uncle? He isn't well."

The hall didn't look well either. How it had changed in just a few days — empty, and silent, and dusty, the flagstones stained with mud, the panoplies dull, the gallery dark ... no matter how softly Gerolamo spoke — as though he were in the sick-room already — it carried in the hollow silence.

"Master Lopes was here again late yesterday. He said to watch for a fever, and now the fever has come..." The youth shook his head. "*Per tutti i Santi* — but the Masters will pay for this!"

Oh yes: all they lacked now was a civil war of fencers in London! And a baseless one, most likely — although Tom wasn't going to point this out. "You know how dangerous it is to think like this, don't you?"

"So I must trust to the constable, who doesn't care a whit," the lad snarled, and then stopped short, brow creasing.

"Weren't you chasing a murderer, *signore*, when you first met my uncle?"

Half hopeful, half fierce. How old could Gerolamo be? Youthful as he might seem, that didn't make him unaware of his uncle's less public dealings, nor incapable of treason or greed. Still, he wasn't the one with the certain knowledge, and many acquaintances in many places, not least Salisbury Court.

"Let me talk to the Captain," Tom said, and the youth obeyed, shoulders slumping.

Once in the narrow, darkened sick-room, it became clear that Bonetti was at his weakest. Lying abed, propped against a mound of pillows, his splinted arm lying across his chest, the Italian had the ashen face and flushed cheeks of the very ill — and, as Lopes had said, he wheezed badly. He opened too-bright eyes to squint against the open door's glare. "Gerolamo…?" he rasped.

"'Tis Thomas Walsingham." Tom dithered on the threshold, loath to step in the close air, where not even the odour of sweat and vinegar could mask the sickly sweetness of a festering wound. "How are you faring?"

"*Signor* Walsingham!" A quiver of a smile. "I know I have you to thank that I am alive, and being physicked very finely. A couple of days, and I will be on my feet again…" Bonetti sank deeper in the pillows, winded for the dozen words.

Not that Ambrose Lopes would ever make such promises. Ignoring the half-boast and waving aside the thanks, Tom pushed the door ajar and went to stand at the bed's foot.

"I'm trying to find out what happened," he said.

The weak smile again. "I knew you would."

"For one thing, are you sure the Masters of Defence sent Bagger? They say they've long thrown him out."

"Did they? Good for them, *signor mio* — but I don't know… You heard what he said."

"There's not a soul in London who ignores your rivalry. Anyone could have hired Bagger, telling him what to say. And…" Tom lowered his voice. "I have to wonder: could someone other than the fencers want you dead?"

Bonetti held Tom's gaze for a few ragged breaths, then rolled his head aside. "I have told no one, *Signor* Tommaso. I swear to you by God and by Our Lady, I have not…" the splinted fingers twitched, and the Italian choked on a gasp of pain.

"Then someone saw or heard something here."

"Perhaps Perkin told the wrong person. I knew him for a braggart, but…"

"A braggart, and a greedy ruffian, I'm told," groused Tom. "A fine fellow, you've chosen for me!"

"I reckoned that he would want to earn the Earl's good will for himself."

It was hard to stay vexed as poor Rocco fisted and unfisted his good hand in the sheet.

"Lay still, Captain." Tom leant closer. "Lay still and think. Could Perkin have known what you were doing?"

"No." Weak as it was, there was no hesitation in the rasp.

"Then someone must have seen him eavesdrop on Stafford and d'Estrapes — or observed as you arranged for it. Who's been around when Stafford was here?"

Between one shallow gasp and the next, Bonetti groaned. "Jesu — half of London was around! We were busy — that is why I reckoned no one would notice… All who were not at Court — but who would want to uncover your work?" Agitation made the Italian loud, and Tom stepped close to shush him.

"Peace, Captain! Do you want..." He stopped short as it sank in. Who would want to uncover his work? He'd thought so, but... "Why, whoever killed Perkin, never meant to uncover my work!"

Bonetti blinked and shook his head, eyes bright and empty as glass. There was no point in explaining that, if the murderer had meant to expose Mr. Secretary, they'd have known it by now. No — whoever killed Perkin believed Stafford's plot genuine, and had tried to keep it going, to buy time, perhaps even to save Mary Stuart's neck. And then, when Stafford had confessed, the murderer had found himself in danger of being singled out by Rocco.

"Bonetti, heed me. Think: who was here around the year's end?"

But the poor fellow was forspent: he weakly tossed his head this way and that, sweating and muttering half in English, half in Italian.

"All sorts of people, *signore*. All come and go these days. All come and go. *Signori e medici e buffoni...*"

"Gentlemen, physicians, and... I hope you don't mean me by *clowns*," Tom said, not expecting an answer, and startling when there was one — from behind his back.

"He means that player, *signore*."

Unnoticed, Gerolamo had come to stand in the doorway, craning his neck to see his uncle beyond Tom's shoulder. How long had he been there, listening?

"What player?"

"Leicester's clown. He came here this morning. I was away, and Bonifacio, like the dunce he is, let him in to plague my uncle with his questions."

Which was as broad a hint as the lad would dare, but Tom was past caring. Lord smite all meddlesome players!

"Will Kempe!" He growled, and strode out of the room without waiting for an answer. He was halfway through the hall, with Gerolamo on his heels, when Reason elbowed her way past Fury. Because, truly, what was he going to do? Descend on Kempe in wrath, warn him off the Blackfriars — and show himself to be in Bonetti's confidence? Demand to know how much Lord Leicester knew, and reveal his game even more plainly? How was he to know how the clown had found Blackfriars, and steer him away to safer paths? But wait — there was a way.

He stopped so brusquely that Gerolamo all but walked into him. "I need to write a note," he said.

The lad turned to the alcove under the gallery, where a green carpeted table sat. It was one of the college's luxuries, carrying fine paper, quills, ink and sand for the gentlemen's use... Only, the ink had been left to dry in the commotion of the last day. With a clicking of his tongue and a glower that promised retribution on the dunce Bonifacio, Gerolamo showed the way into a small room with a writing table on which a thick book sat open. He hurried to scoop the book away, but not before Tom saw what it was: a ledger.

"You keep records of who comes here and when, don't you?" Of course they did, or how would they ever manage to be payed?

Gerolamo nodded, wary of a sudden. "Yes."

"Then I would see those for the days ... oh, between Christmas and New Year."

There was a beginning of protest in the lad's mien — the thinning mouth, the creased forehead — but in the end he put the ledger back on the table, and opened it to a thickly written page ruled in columns.

"Here," he pointed halfway down. "This is right before Christmas. They're never very busy days."

That Rocco had said differently, Tom didn't point out as he ran a hasty forefinger down the columns — perhaps uncle and nephew had a different notion of a busy day, for there were several names, and notes, and fees. It would take too long to study them right then, and the ledger was large and thick. Suppressing a wince at mistreating a book, Tom tore away the Christmas page.

"*Signore!* What are you doing?" With the nimbleness of his calling, Gerolamo leapt to catch the page, and only stopped from snatching it back because Tom held fast.

"Don't you want to find out who sent Bagger to harm your uncle?" Which was a lie, for whatever Tom found out would never be meant for the ears of Bonetti's nephew.

That in the end the lad relinquished the page didn't prove him unknowing — just possessed of wits enough to see that anything else would seem suspicious. But the dark eyes were troubled when he asked: "What's it in truth, *Signor* Walsingham? You don't think it was the Masters, do you? What trouble has the Captain found for himself?"

Unwitting words — or else a culprit's lure to sound a foe… In truth there was never knowing, was there? Tom folded the page in four and slipped it in his sleeve. "I'll return it," he said. "I misdoubt you'll be giving much instructions these days. Now for some ink and paper."

Gerolamo hovered in the room as Tom jotted his instructions to Skeres, just far enough that he couldn't read.

"My man can carry it for you, *signore,*" he offered, eyeing the way Tom didn't bother sanding the few lines.

But there was never knowing, was there?

"I'll have your page returned," Tom said, and, taking his leave, found a street boy to run to Seething Lane and made his way to Cripplegate, to wait for Skeres and Marley.

All one had to do, after all, was to let Marley loose: poets in their affronted rage were a good match for stubborn players. For a while, more to Skeres's amusement than Tom's, the two shouted at each other in the yard of Kempe's landlord — Marley clamouring that Kempe was out to ruin him for no good reason, too lazy in his suspicion to seek any other path.

"I've sought other paths!" roared the clown, stabbing a forefinger Tom-wards. "Ask your master: that bookseller woman wasn't at court, the German was, but elsewhere, and the bookseller's daughter ... between her and you, I know who makes a likelier murderer!"

"Do you!" Marley bristled. "You pig-headed, ignorant lurdane —" He broke off when Tom shoved him aside.

At the same time Tom glared at the clown. "Your prejudice is hardly proof, Kempe. Have you found the daughter? Have you talked to her?"

He had, the clown announced, arms crossed and chin jutting. "And I say that a murderess would have found a better place to hide than her mother's shop!"

Which was true enough, and still didn't explain Kempe's visit to Bonetti.

"If all murderers were clever, hangmen would work a good deal less," Tom groused. "I'm going to question Janet White myself."

So they all trooped to Foster Lane, where Sarah White lived — Kempe disgruntled, Marley with head thrown high, and nostrils a-quiver.

"*I'm* questioning her, Kit," Tom warned.

And when the lad's only answer was the stiffest, most soldierly nod, Tom didn't find it in his heart to chide Skeres for his snort.

It wasn't until they were inside the city again that the servant drew close enough to mutter in Tom's ear.

"And why you don't throw Corpus Christi here to Kempe, I don't know. You want 'im to chase the wrong 'are, don't you? Then give 'im the wrong peacock — and good riddance!"

That Marley's Cambridge airs and gentlemanly pretensions had found disfavour with the Minotaur came as no great surprise. "Because being a nuisance is no reason to be thrown to the wolves, because a cornered peacock might blurt out just whose peacock he is — and also because, but for him, I might have ended up on a Papist rack, back in Rheims."

The old Nick Skeres would have had a huff for that. This new disgraced Skeres, though, just kept his counsel, face knotted in displeasure.

The Widow White, it turned out, owned a narrow, half-timbered house in Foster Lane, part warehouse, and part lodging. For being less than glad of having four strange men invade her neat little hall, angry at each other and demanding to see her daughter, Tom found he could hardly blame her.

"If I let you speak to her, will we be done with Jack Perkin?" she groused. "I don't give a straw how he died — and neither does that little minx!"

But the little minx did — oh, she gave all the straw in England! With a little more flesh on her bones, Janet White would have been much like her mother, and perhaps even pretty. Hollow-cheeked and red-eyed, though, she looked worn, even in what had to be her church best, made finer through the art of a lady's maid and what had to be her mistress's cast-offs. Worn and sullen: see how she glowered at Kempe.

"I told him already —" she began, only for the clown to interrupt her.

"Ay, and now you tell them, for fine folks don't bother to believe a common player. Servants, though…" He darted a venomous side-glance at Marley.

Which had Marley stiffen, ready for some tirade on how he was no servant. Skeres elbowed him quiet.

Oh Jove! Tom glared at the three men, and turned from them to Janet. "Please, tell me of Perkin."

She took a great gulp of air, and latched her hands against her stomacher.

"My mother calls Jack a scoundrel, and me a minx. She isn't wrong, but she should call me a dolt as well, and herself, while she's at it. Jack made no secret that he was after her — and you'd have to be blind not to see he'd like my father's shop for his own." A sniff. "Well, I'm not blind, so I must be stupid, for when he began turning sweet on me… Old and ugly as he was, he had this fine voice, like velvet, and he made me laugh… A player, ay — and he played me like a lute. Then Mother found out, and the thought came to Jack that my husband might inherit the shop someday, but Mother's husband would have it at once — and that was the last I saw of him."

"Until you met him again at Placentia, on New Year's Day."

She tried to snort, and turned away when it broke into a half sob. "Met him! I was going to the kitchen, to fetch some warm wine for my mistress who wasn't well, and there he was, on a dark staircase, groping a servant-girl. When I told her to be wary of the likes of him, she near scratched my eyes out — and all the time Jack laughed. He called me *child*, he tried to kiss me — the gall of him! I kicked his shin, and he laughed again, and bowed. Ay, all laughter — until I told him…" She flattened both hands on her belly. "And then he didn't laugh. Oh, no — then he ran like a hare. I followed him into the kitchen passage, where it's always full of people, and he made up he'd seen a friend of his. From his fencing days, he said, and off he went. So what was I to do?" She looked away again, pressing her belly, as though she might squeeze it out of existence.

Poor Janet White — no matter what her mother said, it would be a long time before they'd be done with Jack Perkin. And it was unchristian, surely, that, of all the poor woman's woes, Tom should latch onto one thing alone — the one thing that he couldn't pursue in front of Kempe. Jove rain on all clowns, and on the dunces who let clowns go along!

Kit Marley, of course, had no such compunctions: "A friend from his fencing days?" he asked.

With an air of expecting nothing better from a man, Janet clicked her tongue. "He'd have made it seem he'd seen the Pope, just to get rid of me!"

Which was beginning to sound likelier with every word Tom heard about Jack Perkin — but it didn't mean the fencing friend was an invention. Reckoning the jaunt at Blackfriars, Kempe must have thought the same, and now must be steered clear of Bonetti and his pupils.

"So you saw neither the Pope nor the friend," Tom said. "You didn't follow Perkin? Or sought him again?"

No, she hadn't, Janet said — why would she? It wasn't as though she could make him marry her. She'd gone back to Lady Coates, and been scolded for not bringing the wine, and the next morning she'd run. To her God-sister in Aldgate first, and then…

"Four days it was, before I found the heart to come home. And found that Jack is dead."

Yes, poor Janet — turning away again, her head bent, her shoulders shaking.

They filed out a little awkwardly after that, but as soon as the widow's door slammed on their backs, Kempe stabbed a finger towards it.

"Now tell me that poor girl threw a grown man out of a window!"

And perhaps the playhouse was the right place for Kit Marley ... see how he threw back his head to laugh. "And you tell me that poor girl had no reason to be angry at Perkin!"

"Ay, but she couldn't wed a dead man, could she?"

"And couldn't she get angry? A push, a shove —" And Marley demonstrated.

"That bit of a girl?" Kempe shoved back and, being half as big again as Marley, sent the outraged poet careening back into Tom.

It was a good thing that the lane was empty at that time, but already windows were clattering open.

"Enough!" Tom held fast onto Marley's arm before he could jump at the clown. "A brawl will prove nobody's innocence, or guilt."

For good measure, Skeres shouldered in between and, over his shoulder, the two glared at each other — a seething Pyramus to a furious Thisbe, with Skeres as the wall.

Some amusement could have been found in how the clown turned away first, and covered it by addressing Tom. "Come now, Master: she didn't even know Jack was dead until her mother told her! Do you truly believe that poor little thing killed him?"

Not for a moment, in fair truth. "Women lie just as well as men — and she *had* reason. Aren't you a tad eager to discount her?"

It wasn't to be expected that Marley should keep quiet.

"Anyone but me, he'll discount!" he groused. "The German isn't the sort, the maid is too small and sweet. What of the fencing friend?" He stood on tiptoe to better sneer in the clown's face. "Did you even hear that, you churl?"

And so much for keeping *that* out of the way.

"Ay, I heard it fair!" Kempe broke out of his posturing to pace in a tight round, rubbing at his neck in vexation. "So well I heard it that I went to that Italian who keeps school in Blackfriars. He's ill, and his boy kicked me out. Plaguing the Captain, I was…" A snort. "But I'm going there again, and I'm having my answers, by God! If there *is* a fencing friend, I'll find him, and we'll *see!*"

This last was half-shouted at Marley, with much reddening of face and bulging of veins.

Oh, but there was no blaming Skeres when he advanced a step on the clown, who was too incensed to stand back.

"Do I trounce 'im, Master?"

Yes! Yes, before he goes back to Bonetti, before he learns that Perkin…
"No, you don't." It came out rather brusque, and the Minotaur stiffened in place as Tom stepped around him to face Kempe.

"The Italian in Blackfriars — Rocco Bonetti?" he scoffed. "The one who charges twenty pounds for teaching?"

The low whistle from Marley, they all ignored, and Kempe humphed.

"Jack knew the Italian manner — he taught us! And he played prize, so at some point he was taught…"

But he never played prize. Tom bit down the objection. "To the tune of twenty pounds an hour?"

"God's teeth!" Kempe yanked the soft cap from his head, and twisted it, and for a heartbeat or two he stood there, jaws working, raking his brain for an answer he didn't have.

And wasn't it a fine moment for Marley to remember his Aristotle!

"Which doesn't mean there was no fencing friend, though!" he announced in logical triumph. "He must have fenced somewhere else, or perhaps —"

"Or perhaps," Tom stepped in, "Janet made up the fencing friend to divert suspicion from herself. If I were you, Kempe, I'd consider her more closely. And also Elias Werner, for that matter."

"Or him." The clown jerked his chin at Marley — and that was when Tom had enough.

"Devil pinch you, William Kempe!" he snapped. "The widow, her daughter, the German, Perkin — must you take everybody's word over Marley's? It's been a week now: what have you found against him, other than your own suspicions?"

That this, at last, should silence the fellow was an irony — for the White women and Werner were most certainly just as innocent as Kit Marley. Ah well, let only Kempe keep baying up the wrong tree long enough for Stafford's plot to reach the Queen's ear!

And what if an innocent was charged? But no, for Perkin's death had been ruled an accident, and it would take more than Kempe could uncover to reverse that. Let him just not uncover enough to make Lord Leicester suspicious.

For the moment, the clown was flustered enough to cram the cap back on his head askew, and grouse at Tom: "But mind you, Master, I'm not done with this!" And, turning on his heel, he stalked away towards Maiden Lane in the leaden afternoon.

Fates keep him flustered long enough — but, just as precaution…

"Follow him a little," Tom ordered Skeres. "See where he goes."

Off the Minotaur trotted, and Kit Marley waited until he was out of sight before he spoke.

"If you'd told me Kempe must be kept away from this matter of the fencing…" And, for once and for a wonder, the lad sounded rueful.

Rueful — and not all that wrong, either.

Tom's sigh curdled to vapour in the chill air. "No, he must not. And yes, I should have warned you. With any luck, he'll tire of running around in circles, but I'd stay out of his way, if I were you. Go back to Cambridge…" He stopped short when Marley winced. "You're never still after Leicester's Men, are you?"

"Those chuffs!" To see him scoff, you'd never think he'd been courting them so doggedly not a week before. "There are better companies in London. The Queen's Men, the Admiral's…"

"I thought it would be term time, now. Don't you have attendance?"

A thoughtful hum. "Ay, there's that — and I've to tread carefully. Already old Norgate's making a noise about denying me my mastership as a papist. Rheims and all, you know."

"Who's Norgate?"

"Ass-head at Corpus." He stopped, frowning. "But he can't do that, can he? Considering…"

Couldn't he? Would the Service step in — considering? Tom tried to look not too dubious.

"I've no idea," he said. "But missing attendance will hardly help your case."

"Ah well." A shrug. "A couple more days will make no difference. You'll come to see my *Tamburlaine* when they play it? It's a tragedy like no other. No rhyme, that's true, for I made up my own kind of verse — like no other. Listen: *Nature*, *that fram'd us of four elements, warring for regiment within our breasts, doth teach us all to have aspiring minds!"*

It took Tom by surprise — the beauty of it. *To have aspiring minds…* The vertiginous flurry of images, the notion itself, the burning pulse to the rhymeless verse.

"Yours?" he marvelled. "Why, Kit Marley — you *are* a poet, after all!"

And, of all things, the lad blushed crimson, and smiled very, very brightly.

Tom was about to ask for a few more lines of *Tamburlaine the Great* when Skeres reappeared, and jogged up to join them.

"Turned into Wood Street, to Cripplegate," he called, when he was still a dozen steps away, loud enough for the whole lane to hear. "Goin' 'ome, if you ask me."

Had there been any point in chiding him, Tom would have; instead, he nodded. "At least he isn't for Blackfriars again," he said — and then turned to the still grinning Marley. "But, if I were you, I'd wait to be a Master of the Arts before pursuing glory and fame."

"Why wait?" The brightness dimmed down to cheerful calculation. "Besides, they pay four of five pounds for a play, you know. Nothing compared to the twenty your Italian takes to fence — but still…" He drew a sharp breath. "I'm thinking that I could go to the school, pretend I want to study there, find out whether Perkin —"

Oh yes — and get yourself killed too! "And I'm thinking you could scurry back to Cambridge at once," Tom scoffed. "Why, if you don't, I'll feed you to Kempe!"

Which seemed to amuse the young fool greatly.

"Well, unless you do, I'm much in your debt, Mr. Walsingham," he said. "How I'll repay you I don't know, but

I'll find a way." And where the cobbler's son had learnt his fine bows, Tom didn't know.

He shook his head as he watched the lad disappear into Cheapside. Could it be hoped that at least this thread of the tangle was unravelled and done with? Skeres was unconvinced.

"Plaguey jack-sauce!" he grumbled. "Repay you, 'e says — like 'e is a gentleman!"

"Why, but he is. A Cambridge gentleman. Has he been giving you grief over it, Dolius?"

There was a sudden silence, and there Nick Skeres stood, hunch-shouldered and hopeful.

Oh yes — *Dolius*. The by-name had slipped out for the first time in days, just out of habit.

"No, you're not forgiven," Tom groused. "But I think I believe Janet White. Now let's find where Perkin had his fencing friends."

Named by Kennard as the one who kept the Master's records, William Joyner wasn't very happy to be sought out on a Sunday afternoon. He'd been about to sit down to an early supper, he pointedly said — but his demeanour changed the moment he heard his visitor's name.

There were certain advantages to being a Walsingham rather than a Guildford, Tom mused, as Joyner bent over his table, drawing the candle nearer to thumb through a stack of carefully sewn fascicles.

"Parsons, you said, Master?"

"Perkin. John or Jack Perkin. A player with Leicester's Men. If he ever played prize, it must have been some years ago."

"A player, now…" Joyner straightened, fingering his small grey beard as he frowned in thought. "Some of us have a few of those as students, but they never play prize. Well, they say that the Queen's clown, Dick Tarlton, wants to play for mastership — Lord knows why he bothers — but other than him... Are you sure, Master?"

"Not in the least," Tom admitted. "I know he..." *used to boast...* "He boasts about it, though."

"Ah, that!" The fencing master slapped the fascicle closed, with enough force to make the candle's flame quiver. "London's a-swarm with those who boast. Does he have the gall to teach?"

"Not that I know. Not past drilling his fellows for stage battles."

There was a huff. "Ah well, he's welcome to that. After all, people don't go to the play for fine swordsmanship, do they? There are prizes and bouts for that."

"It's not as though Perkin had set up school to teach, is it?"

It took a few heartbeats before the thought struck Joyner — and then he stiffened, wary of a sudden.

"You are thinking of Bonetti, Master," he said. "Poor devil, for all that he's a plague. You never think... Now, Mr. Walsingham: we're an ill-regarded lot, little better than bully-rooks to most people's thinking. What would we gain by living up to it?"

Which was true enough, and very sensible, and yet Kennard had told a different tale. "Are all your fellows so moderate?"

"I won't say we don't have a few break-necks, but even those who aren't moderate still know that Bonetti has powerful friends."

"Even the likes of Austin Bagger? I know he's not one of yours — but he used to be. Master Kennard told me he failed his prize."

"Ah." Joyner had reached for the fascicles again, but he stopped and shook his head. "We don't keep records of failures. Austin Bagger… I've heard the name before. He's the one who mauled Bonetti?"

"With a few cronies he went to the college, and goaded…" Tom stopped when Joyner took in a sharp breath.

"The college, yes," the fencing master slowly said. "I do remember a Perkin, from years ago. Didn't he call himself Bonetti's man?"

"And you didn't believe him."

Joyner shrugged. "I remember him now. He bragged that he knew the Italian style, that he could sell all sorts of Italian secrets." A snort. "Secrets, truly! What secrets are there? One only has to see the way Bonetti's students fight."

It didn't sound as though Perkin had made many fencing friends. "So you sent him back where he'd come from."

Joyner fingered his beard. "I'll say that some thought him Bonetti's spy, but I don't know… He never came to pester me. You should ask the man who took him up for a student." He tapped a finger on his fascicles. "Ah, now — who was it? Not Calvert, no… Mucklowe? Old Mucklowe, I think — but if it was him, he hasn't taught for years. I'm not even sure he isn't dead." His gaze wandered to the door, thoughts of supper on his mind, no doubt. "There are some I can ask, Master. I'll let you know."

So Tom let Joyner go back to his supper, recovered Skeres, who was gorging himself on bread crusts and vinegar sauce in the kitchen, and, it being too late for anything else, made his way back home.

Having no stomach for his own cold writing room, Tom took possession of the kitchen parlour, with its snug benches by the fireplace. On one of these he settled with a trencher of warm ale and bread and cheese, and the page he'd torn from

Bonetti's ledger. It would have been comfortable, after the long day of tramping all across London — but that the warmth soon thawed all the worries he'd shoved aside since the morning.

Now Ned's gloating refusal, and the looming disaster, and the unavoidable necessity of riding to Barn Elms came back to haunt Tom, no matter how he tried to keep his thoughts on the fencing master's records.

He must seem glum indeed, if even Phelippes seemed loath to interrupt, and hummed and hawed a little before voicing his misgivings about Moody's reluctance in confessing.

"Young Stafford has bragged before," he mused. "What if Moody is more Sir Edward's man than William's?"

Moody, yes. Had it only been yesterday that they'd questioned Michael Moody at Ely House? Tom looked up from his page. "Pray he's not having second thoughts," he said, and went back to his study.

Next Phelippes murmured that no letter had come from Barn Elms all day, not even in answer to Tom's own — an unusual circumstance, and perhaps a worrying one?

And just what do you suggest? That we chide Mr. Secretary on his tardiness? Tom swallowed the retort, but not the impatient glare.

The cypherer sighed. "'Tis no matter, since you'll ride in the morning. I'm for Leadenhall, then, if you've no need of me."

Leadenhall. Home... Oh. Tom winced in repentance. "Why, Fisher told me of your father. How is he, Philippus?"

Not that Phelippes seemed overly upset, either by his father's plight or by Tom's lack of consideration. "'Tis good of you to ask, Mr. Thomas," he said, all pious and even. "My father will mend, Lord willing."

Meaning that the old man was on the mend, or that he'd die or live as the Lord saw fit? Sometimes it was hard to tell with

Phelippes. The moment the man was gone, Tom shook his head, and went back to his study, supper forgotten as he peered at the list:

Lord Berkeley

Mr. Clinton

Lord Edward Seymour

All of them a little hard to imagine in the role of Catholic plotters.

Lord F. Stanley and his brother

These two, now, might be another matter. Then the next day…

Mr. Clinton again — a most keen student — and an Earl's son…

M. d'Estrapes

And this was on the last day of December, when Stafford had been there — ostensibly trailing after Clinton, but in fact talking to the Frenchman. Stafford's name wouldn't be on the list, having gone there only to watch. But then, wasn't this true of who knew how many more?

Young Sir W. Howard

Mr. Talbot

Sir John North

Nobody had fenced on New Year's Day, and then, on the second of January… What was this? Damn the Italian's flowery hand!

The Master of Gray.

Tom sat up straighter. Was this the Scots envoy's first visit at the college? Who had brought him? Not two days in London, and already he'd found himself some Italian fencing hall, Douglas had made a point to say — but did it truly matter? For this was after Stafford had made his appearance at Barn Elms, and was secured in the Tower…

Hades and Tartarus, this was leading nowhere! Would Bonetti or his nephew remember? Would they even know the names of every satellite of their students?

There was a glassy whisper in the fireplace, as cinders fell and, for a heartbeat, a swarm of sparks threw a coppery glow on the page. Tom bent to stir the fire back to life. He itched to throw Bonetti's list into the golden and scarlet flames, for all the good it did.

Well, it was done, now. He would go to Barn Elms tomorrow, with nothing for his cousin but ill tidings. He sighed as he sat back — and startled badly.

The door to the kitchen stood open, and on the threshold, the stocky shadow of Nick Skeres shifted his weight from foot to foot.

"What the devil...?" Tom snapped.

Head ducked and shoulders hunched, the servant shuffled into the fire's ruddy halo. The meaty face was knotted, the jaws working: the Minotaur miserable.

"Mr. Tom," he rumbled, softer than Tom had ever heard him. "I'd chop off my own tongue, if it 'elped. Me dad, 'e used to say I should 'ave been born dumb..." A huff, a shake of the head. "'E wasn't wrong, eh?"

Oh Jupiter. Tom rubbed a hand down his face, too weary to hold on to his anger. "It's not your fault, Dolius." He waved before the lad could protest. "Yes, yes, it *is* your fault, and you're a bragging, loose-tongued half-wit. But Lund was set on finding out, and Faddigan was going to, with or without you. And besides, before you're to blame, I am — for a scatter-good and a fool."

It was as though someone had poured water on a withered gillyflower: the Minotaur seemed to swell and expand with his relief.

"You're not turning me out?"

"It's you who'd better find another master. Once I'm in prison —"

"Never say that, Mr. Tom!" Skeres shook his head furiously. "And the whiles, I want no wages — not a 'a'penny. I'll tell 'Is Honour it's all my fault. I'll… I'll…"

Nick Skeres renouncing money and taking the blame — these were portents, and signs, surely. Tom didn't bother to swallow a huff of laughter — though it was most cheerless — as he climbed to his feet.

"You'll do nothing, except have two horses ready at first light, Dolius." He clapped the lad's shoulder. "We ride to Barn Elms, and perhaps Sir Francis will have mercy and take you back into his service when I go to the Marshalsea."

CHAPTER 9

They didn't ride to Barn Elms in the end — not at first light. Davison's note caught Tom with his foot already in the stirrup: faced with the rack, the note said, Michael Moody had broken down, and wanted to confess. It was with something shamefully akin to relief that Tom bade Phelippes send word to Sir Francis by a none too happy Skeres, and hastened to Ely House.

There had been an unsettled air to the place, the last time Tom had walked the echoing corridors. An air of waiting, of speculation. Today it was different. Tom felt it the moment he was ushered into the panelled room, where Davison and Hatton waited, together with the Queen's Attorney General, Sir John Popham. Today there was a sense of certainty, as though much — if not all — had been decided.

Perhaps there was still doubt in Popham's fleshy, clean-shaven face that gleamed the colour of butter, but none in Davison's — though his Puritan soul wouldn't let him exult over a murderous plot and the ruin of a defeated foe. For his part, the Vice-Chamberlain had a wolfish smile, and a spring in his step. He even clapped Tom's shoulder in a most comradely fashion.

"This morning's ado you'll tell your grandchildren, young Walsingham!" he said — and there was nothing genial in his mien.

Then Moody was brought in, with a guard and a clerk — and he was different too.

Gone was the sullen, blank-eyed fellow of only three days ago, leaving in his place an uneasy rabbit of a man, all twitches and jerks. Tom would have inwardly applauded yet another playing feat, but for the bruises that marked Moody's jaw and cheekbone, and the awkward shuffle as he was walked before the table and left standing.

Tom raised a brow at Davison. "He was put to the question, then?"

Davison shook his head, but it was Hatton who answered.

"Not that I know. He claims he was assaulted."

Assaulted! Tom hardly listened as the Vice-Chamberlain dismissed Moody's woes as common gaol fare. And yes, prisoners were known to be an unruly lot if they could get away with it, and sometimes even if they couldn't — but then Hatton didn't know of Perkin and Bonetti.

Was the murderer still at work? Did he have access to Newgate? Did he have reason to fear Moody's confession? Had he failed twice with both Moody and the fencing master — or was he trying to silence both with fear? And just what did Moody know? Not who was behind Stafford, surely...

Davison, bidding the prisoner to speak at last the truth, dragged Tom away from the questions whirling in his mind. At the table's far end the clerk sat, ready with paper, quill and ink. When the two councillors and the attorney each took a chair, Tom again went to stand behind them. All the time he observed the prisoner, gaunt frame all skewed to favour his right side, itching up the sleeve that hung torn off his arm, watching his questioners with gleaming, half-wild eyes.

Let him not lose his wits now.

And perhaps Michael Moody was thinking the same thing as he drew a ragged breath, and began.

"What I said of Master William visiting me together with the Frenchman — d'Estrapes he called himself... All that is true, I swear to God —"

"You will not swear," Davison cut in. "And you will repeat the whole for Mr. Attorney, so it can be taken down. From the beginning. When did you receive these visitors, and who were they?"

Moody started again, steadying as he talked. He repeated his rusty-voiced tale, word by word, almost — for it was well rehearsed — up until the conversation with the Frenchman.

There the tale changed.

"He asked if I knew how the Queen's life could be taken, which I took to be in jest at first. But he wasn't jesting, nor was Master William. Master William said there was hope while the Scottish Queen was still living, and that she should not die. He said he'd go to France, and find allies, and money. As long as I knew the means to destroy the Queen."

"By that you mean Her Majesty, Queen Elizabeth?" Popham asked — his voice as buttery as his cheeks, with a colour of disbelief to it.

"That's what they wanted." Moody started to shrug, and stopped with a wince. "And the best way's gunpowder: hide a bag of it under her bed, and make a trail all the way to a hidden place where it could be touched with fire. Master William misliked it on account of his mother being so close to the Queen."

Again the attorney raised a plump hand, pushing his paunch against the table's edge to lean across. "Let me understand, then: William Stafford forbade this?"

There was a jerky nod, and Moody fingered his bruised jaw. "The matter of the powder, ay. Then I said that I'd heard of poisoning a person's stirrup, or a shoe, or a glove. I'd heard it in France, and you'd think that a Frenchman should know of these things! But Mr. d'Estrapes wanted to hear it of me. To hear if I'd know how to do it — and when I swore it wasn't hard for a man that had his wits about him and wasn't in gaol, he said that his master was taking much interest in my troubles…"

"Did he say who his master was?" Davison asked — something Moody had denied before.

There was a spell of hesitation, then a sigh, and: "The French Ambassador, he said."

No, Fates be thanked: Moody had not lost his wits. The more he spoke, most of it tallying with Stafford's claims, the more he recovered his sullenness. Did he reckon he'd be safe once his confession was made? Something of a misjudgement — for Perkin's murderer must be still more concerned with covering his own guilt now. Or did Moody hope for protection from whoever stood behind William Stafford? Another ill-placed expectation, as Sir Francis would do no more than have the man's talk of regicide forgotten, and his debts quietly settled — in good time…

It was more than an hour before Michael Moody came to the end of his recitation, and was suffered to sit on a stool, with his head lowered, under the stares of Hatton and Davison — one fiercely triumphant, the other full of stern disgust. Sir John Popham's mouth twisted as though he'd taken a purgative.

"May the good Lord forgive you as He sees fit, Moody," Davison said. "A man willing to murder his sovereign — for the sake of a bag of money!"

All he knows is that, in the end, we're killing no Queen — not truly, Stafford had said of his old servant. Yet another misapprehension, when one thought of Mary Stuart. Unlike his Master William, the man was no fool: had he thought that far ahead? Did he care if he had? He seemed stung enough by Davison's accusation to look up, with something stirring in his deep-set eyes that hadn't been there before.

Tom swallowed hard, the room chill of a sudden. Oh Jove, was Moody discovering the perils of having confessed what he had? Was he going to give them all away? Had it all been for naught, for the ruin of them all?

For a heartbeat Michael Moody gazed dully at Davison, then, "Ah, Your Honour," he muttered. "'Tis a miserable thing to live in prison."

Had he not feared to give himself away, Tom would have reached for the back of Hatton's chair to steady himself. He stiffened his knees instead, and schooled his face. Lord — but this. *This!*

Once the confession was read through and signed, Hatton ordered that the prisoner be brought back to Newgate, and off Michael Moody shuffled with his guard, dull-eyed and awkward, and bruised — back to the ruffians who had beaten him.

The moment the door closed behind the clerk, the Vice-Chamberlain smiled in thin-lipped triumph.

"I trust Mr. Attorney doesn't still sit on the hedge," he said.

Popham heaved a gusty sigh as he shuffled the sheets of Moody's confession. "I have to say, this is a very grave matter." He glanced up at Davison. "He wasn't put to the question, you say?"

Again, Hatton explained the claimed assault and discounted it in the same breath, and Tom wondered even more.

Not for Michael Moody's sake — although it did seem callous to abandon the man to his fate now — but what if the murderer had the freedom of Newgate, or at least friends in there? The murderer who thought Stafford in earnest, and had killed Perkin to protect the plot, and now was so afraid of discovery...

Popham and Davison had gone on to discuss the nature of punishment, and Hatton, listening to them with only half an ear, raised an eyebrow at Tom.

"What are you musing, young Walsingham?" he asked. "Aren't you running to your uncle with this?"

Cousin. "I wonder, Sir. What if Moody was truly assaulted?"

Some might think it beneath a Vice-Chamberlain's dignity to scoff; they didn't know Sir Christopher Hatton.

"Who cares what happens to…" But then he stopped. "No, what you wonder is who'd harm the man who reveals this plot. Stafford's safe enough at the Tower, but Newgate…" The little grin grew wider. "Yes, lad — yes: I'll say that it bears watching."

And with another clap on the shoulder, Tom was dismissed.

It wasn't much, and whoever watched would seek to apprehend the murderer, not to keep Moody safe… But then Hatton was right, wasn't he? Who cared about a traitorous prisoner's fate?

It could be argued that, with Moody's confession secured, and Hatton's trap set for the murderer, there was nothing more to keep Tom away from Barn Elms. In truth, even going back to Seething Lane was a delay. Whether it was unneeded, Tom's mind and heart were fiercely debating as he left Ely House.

Go, and spit it out, and be done with it! One side blustered.

And perhaps neglect some new tidings, or some instruction from Sir Francis himself that could have arrived since you left? Scoffed the other. *Heedless to go with all the rest?*

And such is the nature of Man, that Tom had trouble telling which was Reason, and which Cowardice.

In the end, though, it was a good thing that the side arguing for Seething Lane won the day: for just as Tom reached the gate of his cousin's yard, two men half-ran up the doorstep, and one began plying the knocker with tight insistence. Dismounting in the street, and throwing the reins to the groom who appeared at the wicket, Tom hastened to meet this urgent visitor. The man himself was muffled in a hooded cloak against the cold, too intent on being admitted for distraction, but at his back the well-armed servant kept watch, and wasn't long in noticing the newcomer. When he turned around, Tom found himself facing the narrow-eyed stare of Archibald Douglas's deaf servant. What threw him, though, wasn't the lad's tenseness; it was Douglas himself, hunched and stiff before the door, knocking and knocking... Tom's stomach clenched. It must be four or five years since he'd first crossed paths with the Scot — and never in all that time, not even as they ran together from a pack of armed bullies, had he seen the man so disquieted. What could have happened that was dire enough to upset Archibald Douglas so?

"Mr. Douglas!" Tom called, just as the servant reached to touch his master's sleeve, and as Sir Francis's door opened, showing a flustered Fisher inside, Douglas whirled around — and Tom saw that he'd been mistaken. The Scot was not upset at all: he was furiously angry.

"Och, lad!" he exclaimed, eyes blazing in a face as white as paper. "But Mr. Secretary's folk slack their hands, when he's not here!"

Sure of being included in the reproof, and not in the mood to argue, Tom ignored it. "Is it with me that you would talk, Mr. Douglas?" he asked instead, steering the Scot through the door and past Fisher. "Or do you require another visit at Barn Elms?"

It was a thing of wonder to see the old man gathering the folds of his anger and laying it aside like a cloak, as he decided,

211

most likely, that Tom wouldn't be quailed. At length he nodded.

"I'll be telling ye, young Thomas," he said, like one making a great concession. "I'm reckoning ye'll be for Barn Elms?"

I was on my way there already... Oh yes – go and confide in Douglas, now! What was with him today? "We always keep Mr. Secretary advised of any tidings that warrant it," Tom said, and it was plain that Douglas had no doubt his tidings would.

Ordering Fisher to show the deaf servant to the kitchen, Tom led the way up the stairs, to the cold parlour. Fisher would know to summon Phelippes to the cupboard and, to give him time, Tom fussed a little with the unlit fire, and offered wine that was refused with a curt gesture. Instead Douglas went to stand behind the chair he'd so comfortably occupied a few days earlier, gripping the carved back.

Oh, but he was bursting with his news!

"Melville and Gray are at Salisbury Court," he announced in a quivering rasp. "Visiting with Ambassador Châteauneuf."

And you are not. Was this it, then? Being left out? Tom did no more than raise an eyebrow. "A matter of time, I reckon, once they'd made their bow to Her Highness. And." *And we all know the days are gone when you were welcome under a different French Ambassador's roof.*

Douglas said: "Iphm!"

Was there a Scot on this earth who didn't use this sound — part grunt, part hum, and part sheer Scottishness — to convey any one in the widest array of meanings? Douglas's Iphm, at this time, Tom took to mean *Baggage, lad — and don't play pert!*

Still, if this explained Douglas's vexation, none of it made it Sir Francis's business, yet. Now to say so without giving offence. "I'm sure you'll soon know what they've discussed,

Mr. Douglas. Unless you think they'll disobey their king's orders that you be kept advised."

Under the greying red beard, Douglas's mouth worked. "I know what they're discussing! Should ye ask them, young Thomas, they'll all say they're sifting through each conversation Bellièvre had with Her Highness. And shaking their heads that ye're holding Châteauneuf's man and his letters."

"We're not —"

A brusque wave of the liver-spotted hand. "Ay, ay — not Mr. Secretary. The Council, then! It is nae matter, for that's nae what they'll be discussing." He turned to stare into the black hearth. "There was word brought early this morning. Word that the axe has found Queen Mary's neck already…"

There was the icy soughing of the wind down the chimney, and a scrape of dragged furniture somewhere in the house. Could it be true, and he not know? And what of Davison, and Hatton — for it was not an hour since he'd spoken to the two councillors… They wouldn't conceal it from him, surely? Wouldn't keep questioning Moody? It troubled Tom that he even had to wonder — but, if he lingered any longer in answering, it would seem like assent.

"No," he made himself say, soft but far firmer than he felt. "Be assured, Mr. Douglas: the day it happens, it won't be kept hidden."

He held the Scot's gaze — returning the scrutiny, wondering if the heart of this prince of turncoats still knew how to stir over the fate of the woman who had once been his Queen.

At length, Douglas propped both elbows on the chair's back, and steepled his fingers.

"I'll tell ye then, lad," he murmured. "If that's a rumour, it didnae travel alone. Together with it, Melville was told that the northern counties are astir."

Oh Lord! Was this what the murderer was doing, then? Protecting the plot, protecting his own work, buying time while the North marched on Fotheringay to free Mary Stuart, and now the kings of France and Scotland —

No.

Rule your mind, Thomas, or it will rule you. Sir Francis had liked to quote Horace, when Tom was younger and given to flights of fancy. Because that was all it was: a flight of the wildest fancy — and not even his own. *Our doing,* Phelippes had said — meaning himself and Burleigh's men.

"The northern counties! Is this from the same quarter where Melville learnt of the Duke of Guise, Mr. Douglas?"

Puzzlement flew across Douglas's face, followed by disbelief. "Ye're never meaning that they lie to me! These two gowks calling themselves envoys? Why, the King himself…" And he stopped short, eyes sliding aside as he moved in his mind, surely, the import of what Melville had said: King James ordering that Douglas should be kept advised…

For surely, surely, he could not be bemoaning the Scots' mistrust of him to Mr. Secretary's man — never in earnest! It was all Tom could do to swallow a disbelieving laugh. What did the Parson think he was doing, when he brought his tidings to Seething Lane? Feeding scraps to all parts, and to all lying. If now Tom laughed, if he said that Melville might have orders to be open, but surely not to be honest, would Douglas be at the envoys' lodgings by night, to curse Mr. Secretary's kinsman for a malicious pup? And to observe how very unmoved the English were by these alarming rumours?

Better to cross one's arms, and appear thoughtful — if not troubled.

"Whether they lie or not, Mr. Douglas, we'll look into this matter of the northern counties. Rumour or truth, it's nothing that has been spread in innocence. Now shall I have some wine fetched?"

It was most unusual to see the Scot — ever one to appreciate the contents of Sir Francis's cellars — shake his head in refusal, gather his gloves, and ask, would Tom report to his cousin soon?

"I'm for Barn Elms within the hour," Tom assured him, not sure how well he liked the relief that passed over the old man's face.

There was no need to seek out Phelippes. The cypherer was hastening downstairs the moment the street door closed behind Douglas's back. For his displeased grimace, Tom had no liking at all.

"I assume," he said without preamble, as he met Phelippes halfway up, "that the northern counties are just as ours as the Duke of Guise?"

The cypherer's pale brows shot up before he caught himself and nodded eagerly. "Why yes — yes, our doing." A huff. "Whether Melville hears his rumours from the French, or the other way around, though…"

Through the years Tom had learnt that Phelippes's fits of peevishness were best ignored. "I've been meaning to ask you: did you ever find out whether they knew of the Guise at Burleigh House?"

The cypherer blinked, as though caught by surprise — as out of sorts, in his own way, as Parson Douglas.

"Lord Burleigh's men, Philippus! Had they heard of it before we did from Douglas?" At once Tom regretted his brusqueness. What with his father being sick, some heedlessness was to be expected. But Phelippes distracted, Sir Francis ill, Skeres less trustworthy than he'd been, a murderer at large, the ploy still teetering between success and disaster, prison looming… Tom shook his head. "I'm sorry —"

"Burleigh House, ay." Was the shake of Phelippes's head dismissing the reproof, the apology, or both? "No, they'd heard naught about it yet." He paused. "Or, if they had, they didn't tell."

There had been a time when it would have been easy to tell whether the cypherer was nursing doubts of his own, or just deferring to Tom's. Now Phelippes had grown more inscrutable — and Tom less observant, as likely as not.

Ah well. "Skeres isn't back yet?"

"No. Are you riding there? You may well meet halfway."

"I'm riding, yes — but before…" Before, if the murderer wasn't done, if Châteauneuf and the Scots were conspiring among themselves, if Douglas was playing games again, there was something else that must be made certain. "I want to see Joyner again. I want to know if he found Perkin's fencing haunt. And if Skeres arrives, I want him to mouse out Austin Bagger."

Which earned more perplexity from the cypherer, who was only half-advised of Tom's inquiries. But it would be too long to explain, and it was beginning to seem that time was in short supply — and, all considered, Phelippes could remain curious a while longer.

William Joyner had done his work: Perkin had fenced with a William Mucklowe, a skinner as well as a fencing master. Now too old for either trade and alone in this world, this Mucklowe lived in the Skinners' almshouses in Little Wood Street. All of it said with a measure of bland contempt: the old man, it seemed, had never been much regarded among the Masters.

Tom had little trouble believing it as he made his way along a row of squat timbered houses that bordered the narrow alley off Little Wood Street. He'd left his horse with an urchin, and asked an old woman. Both had shaken their heads when Tom described the old fellow as a fencer; then the woman had shrugged, and pointed a knobby finger at the last of the doors.

"I know naught of fencers, Master. But if it is Wilkin Mucklowe that ye seek, then down there's where 'e lives."

Even among the poor, Mucklowe had little in the way of standing.

Also, perhaps, in the way of hearing. It took a good deal of knocking before the door — the most scuffed and untidy in the whole row — opened by a crack, and an old face peered out.

A thin, sallow face, it was, knotted in distrust, fringed with wisps of white beard and whiter hair, and the fingers that held the door were gnarled as a mandrake root. No wonder the fellow couldn't fence anymore.

"Master Mucklowe?" Tom asked.

He'd been expecting a reedy kind of voice, but the old swordsman rumbled instead: "It's been a long time since anyone called me a Master." He squinted some more. "Did Mr. Corley send you?"

"Why, no…" Whoever Mr. Corley was. "I'm here to ask you about a fellow called Jack Perkin."

The old man snorted. "If it's for the door again, Master…" He let go of the door, holding up both hands. Not only were they contorted, but shaking a good deal. "How can I scrape the

217

cursed door and paint it, eh? I don't know who told you, but…" He leant out of the door, peering this way and that.

Tom held firm. "I care naught about the door, Master Mucklowe. A word about your old student, and then I'll be gone."

"Student?" Mucklowe's face furrowed as though he'd been asked about the Antipodes of India. "It's been a while," he repeated, but he opened the door at last, stepping back to let Tom through.

The Skinners' almshouse was a goodly room, modestly flagged and wainscoted, with a glazed window, a bed on one side, and a fireplace on the other. It showed some effort at tidiness, but there was dust on the mantle-shelf, and ash on the hearth, and the reek of soot and smoke hung in the air. Then again, it was unlikely that the old man could do much in the way of housekeeping, with those palsied hands and, perhaps, an addled mind. It was with some dismay that Tom accepted one of the chairs by the half-stifled fire, and held the watery gaze that studied him head to toe.

"One of them, were you, Master?" Mucklowe asked, as he sat in turn with the wariness of old aches. "My students?"

Oh, better and better! Addle-minded, short-sighted, and what else? Tom bit down his impatience. "No, not I. Jack Perkin. Do you remember him?"

"Oh, I thought… But then I never had fine gentlemen among my lads. Never one to make money, I was — not like some others." Mucklowe jerked his chin at the room. "'Tis a good thing that I stuck to skinning."

Less and less likely as it seemed that anything useful could be learnt from the old man, Tom forged ahead. "Jack Perkin was a player, with —"

The laugh rumbled up from the depths of Mucklowe, a bark that shook his whole frame, and ended in a great, hawking cough. "Players, ay! Those I had by the cartful. God knows I charged cheap enough for beggars!"

"Did you have many from Leicester's Men? Jack Perkin was one of them."

"Never asked nor cared whose men they were, Master. As long as they paid. One or two, I had to kick out, mind you — threadbare chuffs!"

A crumb at last! "Was Jack Perkin one of those?"

Mucklowe frowned and muttered, "Perkin…" As though he'd never heard the name before.

Oh, Jove! Tom leant forward to catch the old fellow's eye and spoke louder. "Jack Perkin, the player." Ah, but of course, if Mucklowe remembered anything… "Bonetti's spy."

And there it was, the flash of recognition, and that harsh laugh again. "Ay — that one! Lord spare us. The Italian, we called him. *Signor* Perkino! But, Master … a spy?"

It was disconcerting to see the old face light up, all vacancy lost, wiped away by a cheer full of malice.

"Many of the Masters thought him one…"

"Many of the Masters have their wits addled!" Again, Mucklowe started to laugh, and ended coughing. "Spy! What need had Bonetti to spy on us — much less on the likes of me? Teaching players, I was, and a few more that… I'll wager you, Master: some of my lads were church-robbers and bullies — not that I ever asked. *Signor Capitano* was welcome to spy all he liked."

"So you took Perkin as a student?" Tom cut in, before the old man wandered into bitterness again.

"If I could learn something of the Italian style from him, why not?"

"Didn't he want to be paid for it?"

A snort. "Ay, so he did, high-and-mighty beggar! Halve his fee if he taught me something worth the pain, now that was another matter — and did he jump at it! Only…" Mucklowe bent low to tap Tom's knee. "I'll tell you this, Master: he'd precious little to teach, that one! That low stance, those silly guards, that way of lunging… Italy's great art of the sword — ha!"

So Perkin had been a greedy charlatan, unlikely to have many friends. "What of your other pupils? Were they as disappointed as you were?"

"Disappointed, them!" The old man's lips pursed. "The swaggering fools drank it all up like it was the Gospel! Not that they liked him, nobody did, but still… Even young Horne, who should have known better. Played prize for free scholar, young Horne did. I told him I'd make him my provost in time – but no, mad for Perkino's Italian ways, just like the other churls!" Mucklowe broke coughing again, and it became a fit.

There was a tin beaker on the hearth: the old man grabbed it and gulped down the contents between coughs, fit to drown himself. In the end the coughing subsided and Mucklowe sat back, wheezing and hiccupping, and wiped a sleeve across his streaming eyes.

"Going to be my provost, he was," he whined. "And then, just like that, off he goes for a soldier! Young fool — gone to the Low Countries…" And likely never come back, reckoning by the tears that kept falling well past the coughing fit.

"What of the other students, Mucklowe?" Tom pushed. "Who were they, those who fenced with Perkin?"

"Students? It's been a while…" He choked on another cough.

Oh Lord — back to the beginning! And there was no time to begin again, for right then the door flew open, and the old woman appeared, leading Nick Skeres. Skeres — back from Barn Elms already.

"Is this your man, Master?" the woman asked. "'E's making a racket —" Then she caught sight of the wheezing Mucklowe and, for all her spitefulness earlier, she hurried at the old fellow's side, to pat his back, and pick up the beaker, all the time glaring at Tom.

Ah well. It was doubtful that there was much more to learn from the old fencer — and, on the threshold, Skeres danced with impatience, making faces, and beckoning: the Minotaur fancying himself subtle.

With a sigh, Tom took his leave — unheeded — and joined his servant in the street.

The wind had picked up while Tom learnt precious little from old Mucklowe, unfurling a grey lid over London, and starting a fall of iced snow that stung like needles. Tom wrapped his cloak tighter around him, and drew his soft cap lower on his brow.

"You've been fast," he told Skeres. Urgent orders, surely — at last...

The lad blew out his cheeks. "I didn't see 'Is 'Onour. Ill in bed, sleeping, for Master Ambrose's dad says 'e must rest."

A shiver clawed its way up Tom's spine. What must it be, that Dr. Lopes had been summoned... "Did they say...?"

A fierce shake of the head. "'Er Ladyship says you don't worry, Master, and she'll show 'im your packet soon as 'e's awake. And that you ain't to worry your 'ead."

Lord bless Lady Ursula, knowing just enough — or shrewd enough without knowing — to keep the matter even from her husband's secretaries — for none but Sir Francis, Tom himself and Phelippes wholly knew the nature of Stafford's plot. Bless Lady Ursula, yes — and if Sir Francis was so unwell, perhaps it was no use to ride out before the morrow? News of Moody's confession was at Barn Elms already, and of Perkin's murder there was little enough to tell, and if there was no way to discuss either — or anything else...

"Oy — but I'm a lackwit, Master!"

The lad slapped his own forehead, and rummaged in his sleeve until he extracted a crumpled letter.

"'Ere! Mr. Phelippes says it came after you'd gone."

He handed Tom a thin note addressed to Tho. Walsingham Esquire and bearing an unfamiliar seal.

"And who sent it?"

Chastened and in disgrace Skeres might be, but not too chastened to shrug in that manner that said '*Ow would I know? Read it and find out for yourself*, before he scurried off to fetch the horses.

And, with a shake of his head, Tom turned his back to the snow-laden draught, and slipped off a glove to break the seal.

The missive consisted of only four lines in an almost too careful secretary hand.

Mr. Walsingham, it read. *On being advised of Michael Moody's intention to confess his wrongdoings, I trust you'll be prompt in advising Mr. Secretary of the man's words. I confide the tidings will not discompose Mr. Secretary too badly in his ill-health. I would regard your reassurance on the matter as a sign of friendship — since I hope to be, in this matter and others, your helpful friend, Robert Cecil.*

The wind, the needle-like snow, the peddlers' cries ... it all whirled madly around. Tartarus take Robert Cecil — the helpful friend! What had Moody said? *'Tis a miserable thing to live in prison...* And Tom had wondered just how miserable.

Miserable enough to pretend regicide? Miserable enough, to Cecil's thinking, to betray Sir Francis's trust?

"Oy, Master!"

Tom stiffened in surprise as Skeres shook him by the shoulder, wide-eyed with worry.

"Are you ill, Mr. Tom?"

When the lad glanced at the letter, Tom's impulse was to crumple the cursed thing and throw it in the snow. Instead he drew in a gulp of air, letting the cold burn in his lungs steady his thoughts.

Never let yourself be swept into a course of action, Thomas, until you've considered all its necessities.

And here was a necessity indeed: that Sir Francis, no matter what happened, must see the treachery of the Cecils! Gritting his teeth, Tom thrust the letter under his cloak, and into the breast of his doublet, before snatching the reins of his horse from Skeres.

"I'm for Barn Elms," he said, leaping into the saddle. "You go back and tell Mr. Phelippes."

And he would have spurred the horse, but that Skeres grasped the reins, digging his heels into the iced mud as the beast danced.

"Lord love you, Master!" the servant cried. "What's the 'urry? 'Is 'Onour's ill — they won't let you see 'im! At least let's go back 'ome before —"

Tom tore free, and leant low to glare at his servant. "Do as you're told for once, Nick Skeres! Go and tell Mr. Phelippes."

"Tell 'im what?" The lad threw up both arms. "That you've gone 'orn-mad?"

Which the Minotaur was likely to do in earnest — and Phelippes would think disaster had occurred in some form, and take measures perhaps . *Never let yourself be swept into a course of action…*

"Tell him that I must go, but it has naught to do with the affair at hand!" Or perhaps it had. "Tell him to keep his counsel when it comes to Burleigh House. And you, find me Austin Bagger — as quietly as you can."

As he turned his horse, spurring it into a canter that was more than half reckless in a city street, the last image Tom had of his servant was of drooping shoulders, cheeks scrubbed red by the cold, and an unhappy scowl.

When, by mid-afternoon, Tom thundered out of the gathering gloom and into the stable yard at Barn Elms, covered in snow and chilled to the bone, the household took it that he must be carrying momentous tidings.

By the time he was thawing by the fire in the dining parlour, with a goblet of warm wine between his hands, and old Gawton and Lady Ursula hovering, he was thoroughly ashamed of his wild arrival. No better than Stafford a week earlier, and with much less reason, when all was said and done.

Oh Lord! Cringing inside, he thrust the goblet at Gawton, and made to rise, seeking Lady Ursula's worried eyes. "I beg your pardon, Madam — it was thoughtless of me. In truth —"

She pushed him back into the chair. "Is it something that my husband needs to hear at once, Thomas?"

He opened his mouth, and then closed it. The Cecils. Moody. The murderer at Newgate. The Cecils… And in truth there was nothing for it but to shake his head and admit: "Nothing that can't wait until tomorrow."

And bless the good lady, who dismissed the servant, and quietly sat by her husband's half-witted kinsman, and waited while Tom gazed at the flames, and wished he could unburden himself to her.

"I'm sorry, Madam," he said at length. "I've lost my head…"

Lady Ursula tutted most motherly. "How long have I known you, Tom? Since you were a small boy — and even then, you were quieter and steadier than most children. Never, not once in all this time have I seen you lose your head. If you truly have this time, I won't think it was for nothing." She clicked her tongue when he would have protested. "Even if it's naught that will sink England in the waters tonight."

It was the wan amusement in her voice that made him look up, start to speak — and stop when she shook her head.

"You don't have to tell me, dear. Why, you must not, most likely." She reached to pat his arm, frowning a little as she studied his face. "You'll have some rest, tonight. What would your poor mother have said, to see you like this?"

Nothing much, as likely as not. Or at least, nothing much that was kind — for Lady Dorothie Walsingham had always been practical, and a little brusque when it came to her children. The effect of losing so many of them as infants, perhaps… He pushed aside the unbidden memory of his mother to find Lady Ursula watching him, thoughtful to the point of calculation.

"And since you're here, Tom, would you do something for me?"

As though she could believe there was anything in this world he wouldn't do for her or hers!

He should have known.

Oh, he should have, for Lady Ursula wasn't blind, much less when it came to her daughter and, fond as she was of Tom, the good lady wasn't above making use of him. And there was no blaming her — although a part of Tom wanted to — as soon

225

as he saw Frances, lying sunk in a mound of pillows and blankets by a blazing fire in her mother's parlour. So thin she was, her triangular face the colour of parchment in the firelight, her braided hair coiling dull and limp over her shoulder … there seemed to be nothing left of her. Nothing but the eyes, huger and darker than they'd ever been, and lustreless as she stared unseeingly at the window, where the flames reflected on the leaded panes.

There was a maid kneeling by the fire, poking at it for all that it roared tall, and she startled when Tom entered the room.

"Her Ladyship asks that you attend her in her room," Tom told her.

The woman hesitated, glancing at her young mistress and then at the visitor she knew for a kinsman. Frances didn't stir as her maid rose slowly to her feet — and what she thought he'd do, Tom didn't know. She curtsied, in the end, and left, not without pausing on the threshold to glance once more at Frances, and leaving the door ajar.

Tom went to stand by Frances's couch, leaning low to seek her gaze. "Poppet," he murmured, and his heart ached when she cringed, as though the childhood name pained her. When slowly, slowly, she turned her head, her eyes were like the glazed window she'd been staring at: the surface gleaming in the firelight, and only darkness beneath.

Lost for words, Tom went down on one knee, half wishing he could take her hands, half thankful they lay hidden under the covers — afraid she'd shy away from his touch. *She won't see you*, Lady Ursula had said on his previous visit, *but I trust that she will*. Which now only went to show what the mother knew, not what the daughter wanted. Time stretched, alive with the crackling of the fire, while Tom's heart pounded in his chest, when all he wanted was to hold her.

"God is punishing me, Tom."

The whisper startled him. Had she not been in front of him, he wouldn't have known the strained voice.

"Lord, Poppet — no! He's not —"

"He punishes me for loving you." She pushed herself a little straighter against the pillows, breath catching with the small effort. "I had a fine husband, a daughter, another child coming. Do you know it was another girl?"

Your mother told me. Tom nodded, unseen as she squeezed her eyes shut. Daughters, no matter how he might love them, were not what a man like Sidney needed. Or a man like Sir Francis, for that matter.

"I told myself that, if I loved you in silence, if I just held it in my heart that you loved me from across the sea… I told myself it was a very little sin, surely?"

It tore at Tom's heart how weakly she freed her hands from the blankets. He clasped them in his, kissed the cold thin fingers.

"And now Philip is dead." She little more than mouthed it. "And my baby was never born, and it was a girl…"

Ay, Philip, who all the time had loved another woman, and anything but quietly — so if anyone should be punished… It was hard to swallow his anger at the man. His anger at himself, he would not.

"Dear love, if anyone's to blame for this, then God should punish me." And wasn't He doing just that? Ruin, the loss of Scadbury forever, of his cousin's trust, of Frances's love…

But perhaps not that: with the softest sob, she reached up to touch his face.

"Not you, dear, dear Tom. Never you."

When the log crumpled on the hearth, the swarm of sparks shone in Frances's tear-filled eyes. *She never weeps.* And still she didn't, blinking away the tears, setting her mouth to shoulder it all, so much braver than he'd ever been.

It felt too late now, too feeble-hearted this urge to claim the sin for his own. "I'd little care for your marriage, I betrayed your father's trust —" Tom's words deserted him when she touched her fingers to his lips.

"And that was my doing too!" she gasped. "I put myself between you and Father. God has taken my husband, and my baby. And because I don't learn and love you still, now my father…"

I love you still. Lord — it cut so painfully, this burst of joy! Tom bent to kiss her hands again, not knowing what showed in his face, forcing the murmur past a tight throat.

"Your father will mend, Poppet. And so will you. You trust Dr. Lopes, don't you?"

The weak shake of the head had nothing to do with the physician. "Father is ruined, Tom. He's lost the Queen's trust, he's lost my husband, and he's ruined. Philip's debts will finish him, it's thousands of pounds, and Lord Leicester…" For a heartbeat the flare of anger made her much like her father, even as her breath grew short and shallow. "His Lordship played at kindness very well, but won't pay a penny! He's just another enemy now. Father has so many of them, all baying, snapping at his heels — and it's all my fault! You must not desert him too, Tom, you must not —" She broke into sobs, her thin chest heaving.

He gathered her to him then — and let God punish him for it! He held her close, stroking her hair, kissing her temple as she wept against his chest.

"I won't desert him, Poppet," he shakily promised. "I won't desert you." And how he'd keep that promise from his prison cell…

He looked up when the door opened. Over Frances's dark head he saw Lady Ursula peeking from the threshold. He couldn't read her expression in the half darkness, while she must be able to see him quite well in the coppery light — weeping as he cradled her distraught daughter. But Lady Ursula had known, hadn't she? She bowed her head, and retreated, closing the door.

For a long time Frances sobbed, and Tom held her, and kept holding her well after she grew quiet and limp in his arms, while the fire died away unattended, and the wind rattled the casements, and hissed down the chimney like a thing wild and sorrowing.

CHAPTER 10

Sir Francis stirred very little, in either movement or expression, as he listened to Tom's confession. His mouth grew taut a few times, especially at the mention of the Cecils, and now and then he tapped his fingers on the spine of the book he held in his lap — still Polybius, Tom thought. All signs of a building anger.

It was a short confession, in the end — how long does it take to say *I'm up to my ears in debt, and your enemies know, and try to make use of it?* Even shaken as he was after his conversation with Frances, Tom knew better than to ramble.

Once he was done, there was a long silence — and the tapping of fingertips on the parchment, and the creaking of the armchair, as Sir Francis sought a less painful position, perhaps. Some tiny red thing lay tangled in the matted rushes on the floor, of a most vivid crimson. A winter berry, dragged there under some visitor's shoe, half crushed and of no consequence at all, but that it was easier to stare at it than face Sir Francis's quiet wrath.

It was its own kind of relief when the crisp question came at last.

"How much is it?"

"Ninety-two pounds, Sir." And this was without counting the twenty he now owed to Rocco Bonetti — but mentioning that would sound like asking the Service, asking Sir Francis to fund the stupid fencing lesson.

Whatever debate Honesty and Shame waged against each other inside Tom's mind was cut short by Sir Francis's vexed sigh.

"Why is it that young men...?" A click of the tongue. Thinking of Sidney, no doubt. "Why didn't you come to me earlier with this?"

There must be a good answer to that, one that was reasonable, but Tom didn't have it.

"I hoped... I tried..." He looked up at last, meeting his cousin's glare. "I'd go to prison a thousand times before making trouble for you, Sir. Before having you think I'd ask..."

"Books, I imagine, and fine clothes, and fine swords — and what else? Gambling?"

Tom bowed his head. "Back in France —"

"Which is not just a sin, but a most stupid sin!"

But I haven't played cards in a while now — little or naught since Paris... At the very last moment Tom stopped himself — and might as well not have, for Sir Francis's glower darkened just as though the witless excuse had been uttered.

"My brother..." he tried instead, earning an impatient wave, and it came as the mildest of surprises that, among his myriad preoccupations, Mr. Secretary should know Sir Edmund's disposition better than Sir Edmund's own brother. "But, Sir, it wouldn't have mattered, I'd have gone to prison — I *will* go to prison without a word, but that the Cecils think to use my stupidity against you. I wouldn't burden you with my petty troubles..." Petty indeed, in the face of Sir Francis's own ruin, of Sidney's thousands. "But this I thought that you should know." *All the more so now that your guard is so open, as I have from your daughter. Now that Lord Burleigh pretends friendship.*

Hard as it had been to drag his eyes up from the red berry, now Tom found that he couldn't look away, couldn't hide from Sir Francis's narrowed gaze, and the tapping of the finger. Counting in Latin, perhaps, to rein in a burst of the famed, if rarely seen, Walsingham temper — or building up to it, perhaps. *Unus … duo … tres…*

It was a sign of Sir Francis's weakened state that what explosion there was came with no more than a palm hitting the chair's armrest. "And in all London, you managed to borrow from a man under the Cecil wing!"

Oh Lord!

Tom's heart sank, and his mouth went dry, and before he knew it, he'd taken a step forward, words tumbling out with little rhyme or reason. "But never for a moment, Sir — I never… No matter what the Cecils do, nothing would ever make me betray you, or…" *Or your trust.* But that he'd done already, hadn't he?

How long the silence stretched, before Sir Francis nodded, just once.

"No, nothing would, would it? I believe I've known that since the day I took you into my house. The Cecils have reckoned wrong."

Fitted with a betrayer's clothes, and most firmly absolved in the same breath. Light-headed with it and speechless, Tom bowed low — if a trifle unsteadily. *Lord God, but one would go through fire for him.*

And then Sir Francis sighed — a long, weary sigh, and his shoulders sagged. "You speak of *the Cecils*, Thomas. Are you certain that my Lord Burleigh is a player in this game of yours?"

This game where I'm a pawn, rather. As for being certain… Tom stopped to think. Was he truly? He went back to the small, warm cabinet at court, with the bright-hued tapestries, to all that had been said, to young Cecil's smile. *You could find a good friend and a support in my father…* And then nothing in yesterday's note.

"In truth, I only have Sir Robert's hint for it — and that in terms that were vague enough."

"I see." Sir Francis said. "Not that I'd put making use of my cousin beneath the Lord Treasurer's dignity — but neither would I put it beyond young Cecil to offer you to his father as a New Year's gift. Sometimes young men can cling to animosity, long after their elders have grown weary of it, can't they?"

True of the hunchback, and even truer of Tom himself. Did he even want to think Lord Burleigh innocent of his son's little machination? He felt the blood rush to his face.

"'Tis that Sir Robert…" *is a cold, slimy, sly lamprey.*

The hum from Sir Francis was something of a surprise. "I wonder if anyone truly likes Sir Robert, but for his father. Still, he's a very intelligent man. Have you given him any grand refusals yet, Thomas?"

Oh ,he should have, he wished he had – but the hunchback had not given him the chance at Placentia, and then there had only been Davison's assurance at Ely House, and the note. Tom shook his head, most wretchedly. "No, Sir. Not yet, but I'll —"

"You'll throw his dishonourable offer back in his face, I'm sure. Or else, you could accept it." Was that a gleam of amusement in the sunken grey eyes? "Never look this shaken, child. Young Cecil thinks that he can play you like a fiddle. Wouldn't you like to play *him* instead?"

And see how Sir Francis leant forward in his chair, some animation returning to his mien. Could it be that the trust wasn't lost, after all? Trust, and some faith too — for a plan like this had crossed Tom's mind, and he'd judged it beyond his ability, but now his great cousin thought him good enough for it.

The eagerness was more than Tom could help. "Accept out of desperation, and grudgingly tell…"

"Tell — and yes, most grudgingly — that Mr. Secretary is ill and despondent, and he sees threats in every corner, and grows fretful when he thinks whose brother Stafford is. Yes — I think this will do for now. It will keep young Cecil thinking, and you out of prison."

Stafford's brother — the hostile Ambassador in Paris… Oh, this was perfect! It would depict Sir Francis as unaware, and protect the ploy! It was hard work to resist the light-headed urge to smile — hard and ineffectual, reckoning by the reappearance of Sir Francis's frown.

"And don't think for a moment, Thomas, that you are not a fool." A forefinger rose in admonition. "Though one possessed of greater loyalty than Robert Cecil is able to conceive."

This time, when Tom's smile broke through his contriteness, and he bowed low to hide it, Sir Francis said nothing. Instead, he sat straighter, and asked of Perkin's murderer.

Oh Lord: Perkin. Tom would have given much for some firm answer to that question, just to show that he had some other quality beyond being loyal. Instead, as he tried to array all his findings and his conjectures like troops for a general's inspection, the ranks seemed mostly comprised of possibilities excluded.

"So I believe —" was all the conclusion he had to offer — "that the same person killed Perkin to protect Stafford's conspiracy, and then later, once Stafford confessed, hired Bagger to kill Bonetti, who might now have dangerous knowledge. I can only think of either Châteauneuf or the Scots — with or without Douglas's help."

"Most likely, yes. Still, if you are right and the murderer believed Stafford, we have no lack of Catholics, rabid Marians, and plain discontents. And how many of them fence with Captain Bonetti?"

"I'm trying to find out. And I'm seeking Bagger: I misdoubt he'll be loyal to the man who hired him — or expect much loyalty from him. I also misdoubt he knows what truly was at stake in silencing Bonetti — but, in his place, I'd be hiding too."

One thin hand gripping the armrest, the other the book on his knee, Sir Francis sought Tom's eye. "So, in weaving Stafford's plot, we've flushed somebody else who's ready to do murder so that Her Highness will die. For Mary Stuart's sake."

I'll ask you to bend your conscience, Sir Francis had once told Tom, back in the Royal park at Richmond. And then there had been Father Ballard's burning eyes on the scaffold, so certain, while he was being cut to pieces, that more would come after him. And he'd been right in his blood-soaked faith, hadn't he?

Tom held his cousin's gaze. "Michael Moody said so yesterday," he said. "And he was right: they'll have hope as long as the Scottish Queen's alive."

What Sir Francis saw or heard now that had been lacking before, Tom didn't know – but something there must have been, for Mr. Secretary nodded most gravely. And then, "Before you go, Thomas," he said, "there's a case on my writing table."

It was a handsome affair, square and flat, and finely inlaid with the Tudor rose on the lid.

"Open it."

Inside, on a bed of blue velvet, gleamed a chain of gold, arranged in many layers of different lengths. The clasp bore again the Tudor rose.

"My Lord Burleigh, in his renewed friendship towards me, has been reminding Her Highness of how my long and difficult service had depleted both my health and my finances. A service that, His Lordship was good enough to say, has more than once preserved Her Highness's life." An edge of bitterness crept into the quiet words. "Her Highness said that she stood rebuked, and would act accordingly. And how she acted, you see there. A chain, Thomas. Bearing Her Highness's device."

A collar. Tom's jaw clenched as he turned to his cousin, who sat weary and pained, worn in all ways by his long service, still struggling for the good of England, for all English souls, and for a thankless mistress... Hannibal after Zama — or not quite, because Sir Francis carried the weight of no defeat on his shoulders. But still, fighting to save his country from its own folly, and receiving no thanks for it.

"I want you to bear this in mind, Thomas, since you are decided to stand by my side. We do the Lord's own work, and the Queen's, but in ways that may well earn us the Lord's damnation. As for recompense in this world..."

As for it, the Queen's chain sat between them, as a caution and a taunt. Another thought for the long nights in gaol...

Most likely it was a good thing that, before Tom could voice that sour thought, there was a knock on the door, and Davies entered, as stolid and blank-faced as ever.

"Mr. Thomas's man has just ridden in again," he announced, and carried a sealed letter to his master.

From Phelippes, surely? Oh Lord, what now? And it would have been proper to turn away, to retreat to the window, even to follow Davies outside, perhaps... Ah well, propriety was more than Tom could manage at the moment. Why, he openly watched as his cousin broke the seal, and read, eyebrows rising higher and higher with each line… What the devil now?

It seemed a long time before Sir Francis looked up, the faintest curl to his lip, and held the paper to Tom.

Her Highness instructed Mr. Davison, the cypherer wrote, *that I should see the letters from Mr. Châteauneuf's packets, that were detained on my Lord Burleigh's order. Upon much insistence from the French Ambassador, these packets are to be returned tonight or the morrow. Her Highness commands that, before night, I should bring what letters of the Ambassador's that we may have, and assist my Lord Burleigh in making the papers ready to be delivered. Therefore, please Your Honour, I cannot much delay in leaving for Greenwich.*

Oh Jove! A laugh wanted to make its way up Tom's throat. The Queen was convinced, at last. What use would Lord Burleigh have for a cypherer of Phelippes's ability, unless it was to find what Châteauneuf was hiding in his correspondence?

"It may well be, Thomas, that you won't need to play young Cecil for long, after all." Sir Francis frowned over his steepled hands. "Ride at once, tell Phelippes that on no account must he find anything other than what Châteauneuf put in there. I trust there will be, at the very least, a confirmation that he believed the plot true, and never thought to denounce it. And, Thomas…" The forefinger rose again. "Whether the confirmation is there or not, find your murderer. If he truly believes in Stafford's intentions, it will surely serve to make firm Her Highness's mind."

As she had one week earlier, Lady Ursula met Tom in the gallery. He stopped short, wanting to ask about Frances, to see her again, perhaps…

And Lady Ursula knew — was there anything she didn't know? — because, before he could find his words, she said: "You're riding back, I'm sure? Have a safe journey, Tom."

Her husband's wife, dealing out as kind and as firm a dismissal as could be.

What did you think — that she'd bless you to court her daughter? Feeling every inch the fool Sir Francis had called him, Tom gaped as the formidable lady advanced on him.

"Frances is sleeping, has slept all night — better than she has in a long time." She took his hand. "I believe that talking to the dear friend of her childhood was a medicine to her." And the smile that went with this was thankful, and very sad, and unyielding.

A dear friend — and never let yourself think you can ever be more than that.

It was like the passing of a sentence. If Frances's mother had guessed before, now she knew, and for her knowing, if Frances had been out of Tom's reach before, she was utterly lost to him now. A most useless, most unreasonable thought, for what had he ever had to offer to the daughter of Sir Francis Walsingham? *His heart*, a rebellious voice raged deep inside — which was laughable, really. Tom bowed deep.

"I'm glad, Madam," he said around the knot in his throat. "Please give her my love when she wakes."

It didn't matter now, did it? Not with Lady Ursula. She nodded, and Tom believed her. He believed that she truly would tell her daughter, and be sad about it, and them both. Only, it changed nothing — nor must it.

It was in the saddest humour that Tom half-ran downstairs, boots echoing upon staircase and empty hall, and recovered Skeres from the kitchen. In the stables, as they waited for their horses, Skeres kept glancing askance at his master, face creasing and knotting this way and that with questions that once he would have blurted thoughtlessly — and, for a mercy, now he wouldn't dare.

Once in Seething Lane, having half-expected to find Phelippes raring to go, it was unreasonably annoying that the cypherer should be at work in his cupboard — though dressed and booted to ride. He had no misconceptions on his task, and listened intently to Sir Francis's instructions. It was as he related them that Tom remembered something from the cypherer's letter.

"Why should you *bring back* Châteauneuf's letters?" he asked. "Do we have any?"

Phelippes shrugged. "Only the three I've had from my Lord Burleigh's man." He patted the satchel that waited ready on his desk. "I'm bringing them back."

From Burleigh's man... "Does Sir Francis know of this?"

The cypherer blinked at the sharpness, mouth thinning. "I sent word to His Honour yesterday with Skeres, when I received the papers. His Lordship's fellow wanted another pair of eyes on a French dispatch or two. I'm sure I must have told you, Mr. Thomas."

"You have not." But then, yesterday had been the devil of a day, and Sir Francis had been ill, and not seen the packet from London until much later, and then this morning Tom himself had arrived with his confession... "And was there anything?"

"Not that I saw." A pursing of the lips. "Either they're a slack lot at Burleigh House, or they kept the best to themselves, no matter what their master says. Well, there's a Royal order now, isn't there?"

"So there is." There was indeed, and now a cypherer who had been working for two masters could no longer keep it hidden, and would try to make it appear innocent, wouldn't he? *I thought I told you of the letters… I thought you knew of the false rumours…* Tom stared at Phelippes, briskly shaking sand off the paper he'd been writing, brow puckered.

Oh Jupiter. Was he going to misdoubt his old friend, Sir Francis's trusted head-cypherer? Had the Cecils sunk their talons there too? Had they revealed Tom's predicament? Given reason to distrust him? Or was the man quietly, secretly playing some game of his own?

"Here are the letters copied." Phelippes held out the papers. "The others, I'll try to copy, if I can — or to make notes at least." He hitched the satchel on his shoulder. "I'd better be going now, Mr. Thomas. I'll take a man with me, so I can send him back. Will you be here?"

At Blackfriars, and who knows where else, chasing Perkin's murderer, and that Bagger if I can… Tom fingered the copies. The letters Burleigh's people had sent. "Mostly, yes," he said. *There is less danger, Thomas, in trusting too little than in trusting too much.* And the uncertainty must have shown, for Phelippes hesitated at the cupboard's door, waiting for something more — or something else.

"Your father?" Tom asked.

A tilt of the head. "So and so. He's grateful that you asked."

And the cypherer was gone.

"I never find you other than in a kitchen, stuffing yourself!" Tom said, and it was a measure of either the Minotaur's recovery or of his worry that, instead of squirming, he grinned around a mouthful and held out the plate of gingerbread bits.

Ah well. Tom took a piece and bit into it, nearly cracking a tooth, it was so hard. Making sure that Mrs Jeffreys wasn't around to see, he threw it on the fire, much to Skeres's chagrin.

Why, the lad downright pouted when Tom took away the plate and asked of the search for Austin Bagger.

There hadn't been much time, Skeres said. He'd nosed about in the Blackfriars, asked beggars and the like. Some knew Bagger in passing, none knew where he might be.

"But let me catch 'im, Mr. Tom!" The lad scowled portentously. "Murtherous lurdane — kickin' a wounded man!"

"Yes, but I don't think he thought it up by himself. No matter how he disliked Bonetti, I'll wager that he was hired to kill him."

"And botched it!"

"Of that you may give thanks. But now whoever hired him will want *him* dead too."

"Good," Skeres grunted, reaching for the gingerbread again.

"So I want you to find him, and tell him we'll protect him — "

"With a cudgel to 'is lousy 'ead, I'll protect him!"

"And tell him we'll protect him if he gives us the man who wanted Bonetti dead."

Unconvinced but obedient, Skeres grumbled. "'Ave to find 'im first, though. If nobody talks…"

"Go back to Kennard," Tom ordered. "He said Bagger was one of the few to botch his prize."

A snort. "Some are just good at naught, ain't they?"

"With any luck, he won't be very good at hiding, either." Provided he was still alive. "But if he tried to play prize at all, he must have been someone's pupil. Ask Kennard who it was — or at least when. Pester him for anything he can remember."

With a great suspiration, Skeres braced himself upright. One would be forgiven for thinking him Hercules at his labours. "And where do I find you?"

"Where is the one place in all of London where the murderer could see Perkin, *and* Stafford, *and* Bonetti, *and* hear of Moody?"

Behold Skeres scrunch his face in deep thought, and then all of a sudden light up, and slap his thigh, and holler: "Bonetti's!"

Tom nodded and fingered the right breast of his doublet, where Rocco's ledger page waited. "Hoping that someone will remember just who was there watching the fencers."

The list was meant more as a pretext than anything else, but it didn't matter much, in the end.

Young Gerolamo met Tom in the hall, that lay as dusty and disordered as though a sennight, and not three days, had passed since its master's mishap.

The youth shook his head when Tom asked about his uncle.

"He was out of his senses all day yesterday, and we couldn't raise him. Master Lopes came at two, and had him carried to the hospital, the one at St. Bartholomew. He never stirred as we moved him."

"The hospital!" Tom wished he'd sounded less startled, but weren't hospitals for the poor who lacked friends to tend to them, and the money for a physician? He kept from looking around at the neglected hall, as a thought of the twenty pounds stirred in his mind. How much of Rocco Bonetti's wealth lay in no more than his students' reputations? And how many of them — like Tom himself — had left unpaid fees?

Gerolamo only shook his head. "Master Lopes is at work there. He says he can keep an eye on the wound..." His voice broke, poor boy, and the young face twisted in some fierce manner that could have been pain or anger. "Are you still trying to find who hired Bagger, *Signor* Walsingham?"

"Yes," Tom said, wary of what the youth could ask.

Instead, Gerolamo had something to say.

"The first night, when he was still in his right mind, I was cursing the English Masters for a pack of murderers and my uncle said: *Forse che sì, forse che no.*"

Perhaps, or perhaps not.

Not for the first time, as he withstood a long level scrutiny, Tom had to wonder just how much Gerolamo knew. Enough, it seemed, to lower his speech to a murmur: "I know whose man you are, *signore* — and that's all I know, for Rocco never told me. Now he can tell no more – to me or to you, and you'll have questions. Ask what you will. If I can, I'll answer."

They stood in the centre of the hall, facing each other like a pair of swordsmen. The last time, it had been as instructor and student, under Rocco Bonetti's watchful eye — and Cordaillot's. Now it was as one inquiring and one who might have answers, the shadow of the hapless Rocco presiding, half a ghost already, as the poor man lay dying over at St. Bartholomew.

Unless, of course, Gerolamo himself had betrayed them all in the first place — if only to the extent of selling Perkin... Ah well, there was only one way to know. Trying to shake the feeling that both he and the Italian were taking up their guard, Tom drew a deep breath and began.

"Jack Perkin worked here around the end of December, didn't he?"

"That good for nothing!" Gerolamo clicked his tongue. "I'll never know why my uncle keeps taking pity on the fellow, after he'd gone to the London Masters! But yes, he was here. Down at the heel, crying because the players were going to Court without him. But why? You never think —"

"When was that?" Tom cut in, before the youth forgot he was to answer and not to ask.

"Right before Christmas, but he began to work after St. Stephen's Day. And then, on New Year's Eve, up he comes and says that Leicester's Men are taking him back after all, and so he's leaving. I told my uncle that, if it was up to me, I wouldn't have Perkin ever again. And he only laughed."

On New Year's Eve — before the Master of Gray ever heard of Bonetti's college. But then, someone had brought the Scot here. Someone who might well have caught Perkin eavesdropping…

Gerolamo was still venting his disgust at the feckless servant. "Like a hare, he ran. Bragging that he wasn't on God's earth to scrub floors."

Smelling his way to some of Lord Leicester's money, surely. "Do you know what made him so boastful?"

If Gerolamo knew aught of his uncle's affairs with Mr. Secretary, he also knew how to hide it very well. See how he blew out his cheeks, raked a hand through his black curls.

"That one was born boasting, *signore*. There's no other way with him: either he whines, or he brags. In truth, if I never see the man again, then good riddance."

Tom eyed the youth closely. It seemed that Rocco truly had never confided in his nephew — not even about the death of a wayward servant. Well, revealing as a reaction to these tidings might be, Gerolamo needn't know yet that his wish was granted, and he'd never see Perkin again. Instead, Tom took the folded ledger page from his doublet.

"I'm giving this back to you, — but first, you must tell me two things." He unfolded the paper, and pointed at the dates.

"These are the students who took their instruction between Christmas and New Year — but who was here watching them? Also," he turned the page to find the second day of January, and tapped a forefinger to one line. "Who brought the Master of Gray here? And who paid for his instruction?"

The lad took the page and skimmed through the list. "I'm no good at this, *Signor* Walsingham. My uncle knows them all, students and watchers — and Gianni does too, the snake! You remember him? The moment the Captain was laid low, he ran. Ran to the London Masters, I'll wager you, stealing two fine rapiers, and money, and I'm praying he won't steal half the students too." He crumpled the ledger page and flung it to the floor.

"This is no help, Gerolamo," Tom cut in sternly. "Unless you think this man could have something to do with the assault on your uncle?" Gianni had chased after Bagger together with Skeres — and come back empty-handed… Could he have betrayed his master for money?

Perhaps not, reckoning by Gerolamo's confused astonishment. "But he was well paid, treated as one of the family. Why, my uncle hired him when he was a drunkard no one wanted…" He stopped, shaking his head at Tom's raised eyebrow. "But say all that counts for naught, *signore*. Say there's no gratefulness in this world. Still, there's no soul, in London or in Venice, that'd pay him better than Rocco Bonetti."

No other fencing master, perhaps — but what of an ambassador, or the friends of a dethroned Queen?

"Two fine rapiers and money, you say. Have you gone after him for them?"

"*Certo!*" The lad stamped a foot. "The day he was gone. And he said he never touched a penny or a blade — the gall of him! He says he's afraid to work here after what happened!"

"I take it he didn't hide?"

"Hide? And why?" The lad gave a mirthless laugh. "I didn't see him steal the rapiers, and he says he doesn't have them. So what can I do?"

Tom nodded at the crumpled page on the floor. "You can answer my questions, and help me find who hired Bagger — and if Gianni had anything to do with it."

The reckoning was plain behind the black eyes. *And how will it help my uncle if you find out? He was harmed in your service. It's your enemies that you're after...* Still, Gerolamo bent to pick up the paper, smoothed it and went to sit on a bench under the window, where he could hold the writing to the cold grey light. For a while he considered, running a forefinger down the list. Now and then he stopped.

"I think there were two masked ladies with Sir Henry Danvers. Very beautiful." He pointed at a name listed for the twenty-eighth, and therefore too early. "And the Stanley brothers never move without a flock of fawning popinjays. Gaudy wastrels, but they mostly behave, for Captain Bonetti was strict." He frowned. "Was this when one of them almost came to blows with Master Clinton? That's the Earl of Lincoln's son. But no, that was earlier, because towards the end of the year he started bringing a friend with him."

And that had to be Stafford, but he'd never been fool enough to fight, had he? "Did they quarrel again?"

"Oh no, I tell you: the Captain was..." He stopped with a small gasp, catching himself as he spoke of his uncle as of a dead man.

"And what of the Frenchmen?"

Gerolamo shook himself to attention again, and tapped a finger to the name. "D'Estrapes. The French Ambassador must pay well, for this one is some sort of secretary, and still fences here often enough for a Lord. Mincing fellow... Good footwork, though. And then there's the other, Cordaillot, who never fences. He must be the Ambassador's purser. Now I haven't seen him since the day Rocco was wounded — but I'm thinking..." He tapped another name down the list. "Perhaps it was him who brought that Scot of yours, *signore*. Perhaps even... Now wait." He leapt to his feet and called: "Bonifacio!"

When nobody answered, Gerolamo strode to throw open the lodgings door, and called louder. "Bonifacio!"

This time there was an answer of "*Ohi, Padron Gerolamo!*" But it didn't sound from the master's rooms. The door to the courtyard opened instead, and the servant Bonifacio entered, brushing snow from his sleeves. He stopped short on the threshold when Gerolamo asked him in uncomplimentary Italian where the devil had he been.

"But in the stables, *Padrone*," Bonifacio answered in the same language. "There was the gentleman's horse, it's all a coming and going of people asking about the Captain, what with a man from Sir John, and the French gentleman, and then these two arrived..." He pushed the door wider and, together with a gust of snow-laden wind, who must enter but Nick Skeres in his lion-coloured glory, dragging another man by the arm.

"Oy, Master!" Skeres bellowed, as he pushed forward his prisoner. "See what I found!" The Minotaur triumphant.

So very triumphant he was, and so huge the other man, that for a moment Tom thought it was Austin Bagger.

It wasn't, of course.

Not tall enough, for one thing, though he was built like a clothes-press, and far too placid for a caught murderer. See how he gaped around at the huge hall, the fine gallery, the panoplies on the walls.

Still he must be a ghost — for here was Skeres, bursting with pride as he announced: "This 'ere's Roger 'Orne, Master. The fencer. Old Mucklowe's boy!"

Well now.

There was a scowl from Gerolamo, and from Bonifacio curses in Italian, for it must be a great indignity to have a man of the Masters treading Bonetti's flagstones.

Ignoring them both, Tom observed the man's stocky frame, the would-be fine cloak, the scuffed tall boots, and the ragged plume on his hat. "I thought you'd gone for a soldier, and never come back."

Horne sighed. "Master Mucklowe told you, didn't he, Master? Lord bless his old pate. Not that I didn't go — but the Low Countries weren't to my liking, so I came home years back, and found work as a butcher, like I was 'prenticed as a boy. Master Mucklowe never liked it."

It was a jest of the Fates, surely, that a man so ox-like should be a butcher? But a murderer?

"So you knew Jack Perkin, I take it."

The man smiled, gap-toothed. "Oh, *Signor* Perkino…" He held up a hand to forestall the suddenly incensed Gerolamo. "No offence, Master. That's just what we called him in jest, for he always bragged … ay, well."

Ay well, indeed. If looks could kill, Roger Horne would have been as dead as a roasted pigeon. But Tom had one interest only in the fellow.

"And have you met Perkin again, of late?" he asked. "On New Year's Day, perhaps?"

Horne pursed his lips, rubbing at his beard as he pondered — and how this one had ever been swift enough of foot and wits for swordplay, Heaven only knew.

"Why, no," he said at length. "Haven't seen Jack in years. But he's never still fencing, is he?"

"Not quite." Tom ignored Skeres's snort. "Why would you say so?"

"That's where I was on New Year's Day, Master: doing bouts on the ice at the Horsepool."

Some Italian mutterings met that: clearly these bouts were a most inferior form of fencing.

"Ay well," Horne shrugged good-naturedly enough, as he sized up Tom. "You're too young, Master, to mind when the river froze all over."

And indeed Tom had heard tales of the Thames freezing so thickly that one could walk all the way to Southwark, and fairs were held on the ice, with music, and dancing, and a market... He'd never seen the charm of it.

Horne did, if his gap-toothed smile meant anything. "There ain't ice enough on the river these days. The old Horsepool, though, out in Smithfield — that's frozen thick and solid, and they do a bit of a winter fair there. It will break up, now — not cold enough these past nights — but never you mind: 'twas there on New Year's Day. Stalls as sell sweetmeats, and some dancing and singing, and mummers, and a few of us doing bouts. 'Tis tricky on the ice, mind you, and the Masters scoff at it..." He grinned at Gerolamo. "Just like these Italian gentlemen — but folks like it well enough, and pay to see, so..." Another of those placid shrugs.

"And you were there all day?"

"Ay, Master. 'Twas striking ten just as we began, and we were at it 'till dusk, on and off. Ask who you like at the Pool."

"I will," Tom said, wondering how long it would have taken Horne to ride from Smithfield to Placentia and back, never mind to seek out Perkin and kill him.

But there was something else that perhaps this butcher-fencer could tell. "You wouldn't know a fellow called Austin Bagger, would you, Horne?"

The man's gaze had wandered to the nearest panoply, lovingly running over the fine weapons. At Tom's question it snapped back. "Bagger? It's strange that you should ask, Master."

"Why strange?"

"Well, Bagger, he's one of us as play bouts at Smithfield Pond —"

"What?" Tom exclaimed, just as Skeres elbowed Horne in the ribs, and barked, most unreasonably: "And ye kept it for pudding?"

An elbow from the Minotaur had been known to bruise ribs. Horne didn't even flinch. "You never asked," he protested, all mildness. "Besides, he ain't there anymore."

The glass tiles inside Tom's head tinkled as they fell into a new pattern. "Since New Year's Day, perhaps?"

"Ay, Master." Horne nodded in slow surprise. "Right on New Year's Day, it was. He never showed up — that day, or ever since."

No, of course he hadn't — for he was at Placentia. "And he knew Jack Perkin, I'll wager?"

"Why, yes." Now Horne gaped, round-eyed, as though Tom were a fortune-teller at the fair. "We were all with Master Mucklowe for a time. Me, the Perkino, Bagger, boy that he was, and a runagate already..." He chuckled. "A fine beggary lot, come to think of it!"

"Cuds-me!" Skeres slapped his thigh.

"So is this one in it, too?" Gerolamo asked. Bonifacio just glared up at the butcher who was half as tall again.

Tom grabbed Horne by the sleeve. "You say that Bagger disappeared?"

"Not that I sought him out, Master. Not after…" Horne let it trail, wary of a sudden.

"But you'd know where, if you wanted to?"

Horne, all stolidity gone, tried to back up a step, smacked into Skeres, and stopped there, eyes darting, and fixing on Tom at last.

"He has a woman."

"What woman?" Tom asked.

"A laundress as washes linen for the Hospital at St. Bartholomew."

"How do I find her?"

"Gillot, he calls her. I think she lives in Cock Lane or thereabouts —"

A clatter startled him into silence. It startled them all, coming as it did from under the gallery. It was a heartbeat, then all sprang into motion, as another noise came, and a clang of irons. It was the door to the armoury. Bonifacio reached it first, and cursed in Italian.

"Open!" he called.

They all barged in, Gerolamo first, only to stumble, and he would have crashed into the mess of fallen blades, had Skeres not caught him. The room was a shambles — the window crashed open, the nearest rack half empty, its collection of daggers and rapiers strewn on the floor, and a scrap of black cloth snagged in a falchion's quilloned cross-guard.

"*Buon Gesù!*" Bonifacio tore the black cloth free. "The Frenchman." He ducked his head under the combined glares of his master, Tom and Skeres. "He was here, he'd come again to ask about the Captain, right before the *signore* arrived." He glanced sideways at Tom. "I thought he'd gone."

The Frenchman. Not since the day Rocco was wounded. Oh Lord! The glass tiles shifted again — settling at last into clarity.

"And instead he was here, listening to what we all had to say of Perkin and of Bagger." Tom clapped his servant's shoulder. "Quick, Skeres. The horses."

"*Signore!*"

There was no mistaking Gerolamo's intent, earnest and fierce, and already arming himself from the racks — sword, and dagger, and a wicked *misericordia*. Bonifacio, dunce as he might be, was doing the same, all brisk and soldierly. The armies of Venice... Tom considered the use of two more resolute swordsmen, and discarded the notion, for these two knew naught, and so it must remain — and, if he was right, there would be words spoken in Smithfield that they must not hear.

"Stay here, Gerolamo," he ordered sternly, and leant closer to catch the lad's eye: "You know whose man I am, you said: well then, don't even think of disobeying."

And, pushing past a round-eyed Horne who lingered on the threshold, he ran.

CHAPTER 11

Why he had thought it would be easy to find a laundress named Gillot in Cock Lane, Tom didn't know.

"At least she ain't a Moll or a Bess," Skeres grumbled. "We'd be a-swarm with those!"

Which was as might be, but no great help, since every other soul in Cock Lane seemed to know some Gillot, or Gillet, or Gill — though none of those lived there or washed linens for a living. And that was supposing that Horne hadn't lied or misremembered.

Tom would have prayed for patience — but it was time that he lacked more. So he did what he should have done to begin with: he left Skeres to work his way up the lane, and went to the hospital.

St. Bartholomew's court started narrow, and then became a vast quadrangle hemmed by columns — a cloister in the old days. Under the portico where the monks had walked, Tom paused to contemplate if he should ask for Ambrose Lopes. But then, what would a physician know of those who washed the linen? So he stopped the first Sister he came across, and asked for a laundress named Gillot... And at once saw the extent of his mistake.

They had no Gillot there, the Sister informed him, with a withering glare, nor did she see what business of His Honour it was, since they were not permitted to have anything to do with men. An assurance that it was a matter of the strictest and most urgent necessity, earned a sniff; a farthing obtained a slow admission that, now, if it was Gill Gurney that His Honour meant, she was a Sister, too.

And Tom lacking even the time to count in Latin, drew tall instead. "Yes, Sister — Gill Gurney. On Queen's business."

Oh, she looked up from the coin she was studying in her palm, then, but only to glower in disbelief. Jove fulminate all greedy and suspicious women!

Glaring back, Tom hissed: "Unless you think it wise to hinder a Queen's man." And then ruined it all by thrusting another farthing in her work-rough palm.

Such a comfort to the poor sick she must be, with that sour mien! But, be it the coin or the implied threat, she said he'd find Gill Gurney in the laundry-house, and explained the way.

One could only hope that a foreigner would have found it even harder to reach the squat building past the hospital proper, and the low-ceilinged room, ill-lit and damp with the steam from two rows of vats. Two women, in grey aprons and grey coifs, moved among the vats, stirring with wooden sticks, raising clouds of unpleasant vapours — witches at their cauldrons.

They turned into hospital servants again when Tom called for Sister Gurney. One barely turned, the other startled. There was no doubting which one was his quarry.

Gillot Gurney couldn't be much younger than thirty, with a bleak, long face that was now flushed with the heat of the laundry-house. She was also wary to find a harried gentleman asking for her.

"Is Your Honour wanting something with me?" she asked, pushing a limp lock back from her sweaty brow.

"Not you, Sister. Austin Bagger."

A bitter lack of surprise, more wariness, calculation, flashed across the narrow face, making it most unconvincing when she shook her head, and said: "I've never heard of him —"

"Oh yes, you have. You know where he is, what's more. And if you don't tell me, he'll be dead very soon."

It was alarm, this time, the fingers kneading the apron at her waist.

Her eyes slid towards a door that stood ajar in the shadowy back of the room, but she dragged them away again. "I've never heard of him."

Why was it that bad liars always thought an unblinking stare would seem innocent?

"He's there, isn't he? And you've told someone already."

When Tom made to step past her, Gillot Gurney gripped his arm with hard fingers. "He said…" She peeked over her shoulder at her fellow among the vats, and lowered her voice. "He said he'd brought Austin's money. Nothing good, I'm sure — for you don't hide for a week for your good deeds — but he said after today Austin needn't worry anymore."

"Dead men need worry of naught, Sister." That he, too, meant to see Bagger on the scaffold, she didn't have to know. "A Frenchman, was he?"

She nodded, and glanced at the door again — not that there had been much to doubt.

Tom shook free of her and strode for the door, drawing his rapier. There were uneven steps behind him — Gillot Gurney following — and shrill demands to know what did he think he was doing.

The door led to a storeroom of sort, cold and smelling of piss, and stale sweat, and vomit. Large, two-handled baskets filled with soiled linens were piled everywhere, and some lay overturned. What a place to hide — and what a place to fight for one's life.

And then Gillot careened into Tom from behind, and sent him stumbling, hanging on to him, and kicking at his shins, as she shouted.

"Austin, run!"

"You fool!" Tom shoved her away — hard enough that she tumbled into a heap of foul-smelling bedding — and rushed across the storeroom, where a window gaped open. Followed by the woman's curses, he vaulted over the sill, and found himself in a snow-blanketed walled garden. The place was quite long — and there scurried one solitary figure.

"Austin Bagger, stop!" Tom shouted — not that he expected the man to obey — and gave chase. Unless it wasn't Bagger at all, unless Bagger was lying dead back in the laundry-house, and it was the Frenchman, fleeing in great leaps. But no — too big…

Catching his foot in a snow-covered hole, Tom stumbled and caught himself against a winter-bare bush. Sir Francis would scowl to hear his kinsman curse in English, Latin, French and Italian as he recovered his footing and ran on. Ah well, Sir Francis wasn't here — and, for a blessing, the fugitive had lost his wits, rushing headlong not for the tangle of alleys of Little Britain, not back to the crowds of Newgate and the city, but towards a row of small houses at the garden's end, and, past that, the open stretch of Smithfield.

Yes, mercilessly open it seemed, as Tom reached it through a passage narrow enough to graze his elbows — and yet…

He stumbled at a breathless halt at the edge of the market ground, and cursed some more at the inexplicable unfairness of it. It was no horse-market day, was it? The much-trampled ground, the fences, the few clumps of bare trees, it all should have been deserted, and white, and windswept — but for one fleeing man. What were so many people doing, taking the air in

Smithfield on a Tuesday? Not a thick crowd, but enough that Tom's quarry could be any one figure among the idle bunches of men, women and children strolling across the ground, mostly, towards a huddle of stalls with brightly coloured awnings, and shrieks of laughter, and peddlers' calls that carried on the wind.

The thrice cursed fair!

Horne's winter fair at Smithfield Pond — Lord smite all fair-goers, and peddlers, and idlers!

And, as no smiting seemed to be forthcoming, there was nothing for it: Tom tightened his cloak around him, and grimly descended into the market-ground to join the cheerful numbers, very much wishing he'd taken the time to go back for his horse.

Smithfield was like a shallow bowl, with half a dozen streets and lanes running into it, like rivers into a lake — but several of those were on Tom's side of the ground, and his man couldn't reach them without crossing his path and going against the straggling current. Of the others, across the field, one he could glimpse between heads and shoulders, and he thought there must be one more past the pond, hidden beyond the fair. Surely that was where the man was aiming to go?

"I would, in his place," Tom muttered to himself, as he pushed past a knot of apprentices who should have been at work earning their bread, instead of clogging up an unsanctioned fair-ground! Because, the closer Tom drew, the plainer it became that this was no well-ruled fair. The pleasure-seekers were too ragged, the peddlers — and their wares — too beggarly, the stall-holders too sharp-eyed. Tom would have wagered that most of it lay just outside the boundary of Farringdon Ward, where London law ended. He walked gripping his hilt, sparing a hope that nobody would chose just this time to pick his pockets, and glad it was the giant-like Bagger that he was seeking — easier to spot, if nothing else.

And yes — there he was! A dozen yards ahead, past a clutch of laughing women, a big head with a flat cap bobbed over the crowd, like a cork in the water, as its owner walked in jerky steps, stooping and ducking, trying — not very well — to hide among the flock.

To keep his quarry in sight, Tom picked up his step, elbowing his way between those gaping at a player of cups and balls on one side, and a pair of half-naked wrestlers on the other.

For the first time it occurred to Tom to wonder: what was he going to do, alone against this mountain of a fellow, violent in nature and made reckless by fear — in this lawless place, where Bagger knew his way and likely had friends? Surely he hadn't fled this way by chance. Memories of hunting with his father and brothers as a boy came to Tom's mind, and of his father's harsh scolding that only lackwits follow a cornered boar to its lair...

And then he felt a touch to his arm. He lashed out unthinkingly, catching backhanded not the pickpocket he expected, but a painted woman, who yelped and let loose a stream of shrill abuse, all the time clutching at his cloak.

"Your pardon," Tom said, as though it would help. And, as he wriggled to extricate himself, he managed a peek over his shoulder, catching Bagger as the man turned towards the commotion. Their eyes met, the bully's going wide.

Oh Tartarus! There Bagger went, whipping around, and slipping between two stalls, while Tom struggled amidst a gaggle of angry prostitutes, and cackling onlookers, and whistling children. Discarding ill-guided thoughts of throwing a farthing to the woman, of drawing his sword, of invoking

Queen's business, Tom shoved at the termagant, tore free and dove after Bagger at a stumble — followed by a storm of hoots and insults.

It all faded behind, together with the peddlers' calls, and the tuneless music, as Tom turned around a ramshackle wooden shed, and found himself at the edge of the ice — where he stumbled to a graceless halt.

Ice.

Cursing under his breath he tried to move quietly along the pond's edge. It was easier said than done. At some point Farringdon Ward or the horse-market people must have ordered Smithfield Pond to be enclosed, but whatever was done, hadn't lasted. The crumbled remnants of brickwork, eaten by frost and neglect, stuck out like broken teeth and shifted underfoot with each step. There were half a dozen rough stalls on the ice, on this side of the pond, all of them empty, and in part dismounted. It looked as though the fair had stretched away from this place, like a drunken sleeper turning, and thrown a gaudy, raucous arm along the pond's other side. From there, the sounds of boisterous business floated across the ice, together with the smoke from a brazier that someone had lit right on the edge.

But look! Perhaps Bagger hadn't considered his flight too well after all, for only on the market side the brick enclosing had fallen into disrepair: elsewhere, climbing over it would be an awkward, slow affair, not to be achieved in such a short time. Nor, if he was minded to lose himself among the crowd on the other side, could the ruffian have already crossed to safety. He must be hiding among the abandoned stalls out on the frozen pond — on the ice. Curse whoever had first dreamt up a winter fair! Tom ventured a step, and then another, and another. He wasn't going to think of the moat at Scadbury and

the hound Silver and the dark, burning water. He wasn't...
Shivering, he halted on the ice, near-black where last night's
snow didn't cover it in patches like a leper's scabs.

Oh yes — now let Bagger rush him while he cowered in fear!
Cursing, Tom shook himself, and kept going, eyes darting
between the undone stalls and the sparse bare bushes that
stuck out of the ice along the pond's edge.

Hand on hilt, skin crawling with more than the cold, he
reached the nearest shed, hid behind it and wondered: what
now? He rather wished for Skeres's company, at the moment.
If it came to a fight on the ice... He shuddered hard as he
undid the fastenings of his cloak. *Tricky* — that was what
Horne had called fighting on the ice. And Bagger had been
doing it for a paying audience, and was a desperate fugitive,
with blood on his hands already — twice, if he'd killed the
Frenchman back at the hospital, and that wasn't counting the
assaults on Rocco Bonetti and on Moody at Newgate. And if
he'd ever counted on the protection of the ones who'd hired
him, he'd had a rough awakening among the soiled linens at St.
Bartholomew. No, Austin Bagger would make no bones about
killing again — and why should he? Tom, on the other hand,
needed Bagger alive...

Ah well. *All hesitation will ever accomplish, Thomas, is to waste time
and chance.* He wasn't going to take Bagger at all by dilly-dallying
there, with the chill from the frozen pond creeping up through
his boots' soles to his flesh and bones... Oh, the cursed,
plaguey ice!

As quietly as he could, he discarded his cloak and drew his
rapier, straining his ears for a sign of his quarry. And signs
there were to burn — but sign of what? Snatches of drunken
song, and the wail of a flute floated eerily with each gust of
wind. It was a soft wind, that made the loose boards in the

stalls creak, and now and then some frost-bitten branch would break under its own weight, or bend and drop its burden of snow, startling some crow into outraged flight. In truth, half a trained band could have been hiding, and Tom none the wiser.

Or perhaps not.

Perhaps not, because Bagger wasn't being very cautious. Who else could it be, that movement Tom caught out of the corner of his eye, between two stalls on his left, that leant together like two sack-sopped men?

"Bagger!" Tom called. "There's no running anymore. We know what you —"

The rest was lost as the man erupted growling from the shadow — a mountain of a fellow, swinging the heaviest, longest sword in England as though it were a straw.

No French secretary, for certain, a part of Tom's mind idly observed, as he padded backwards, raising his own blade in a clumsy guard, right in time to parry a rough cut, and then another. And so much for the law forbidding swords to all but gentlemen — but then, when one had already done murder...

Kennard's instruction about the superiority of defence over offence flashed through Tom's mind. *All you need is to trick your foe onto your blade* — a jest, truly, against such a big adversary, wielding such a longer blade.

Add to that the cursed slippery ground...

Look how low Bagger crouched, padding flat-footed in place, keeping well away... Well, the man had done it before, hadn't he? Tom copied the stance, and found himself a little steadier.

So much that he tried a thrust — and slipped, and nearly lost his footing. All Bagger had to do was step back, and wait, sword at the ready, left arm held stiffly up at shoulder height, tossing his head this way and that to shake the yellow mane off his face. Gone was the taunting bully who had laughed as he goaded Bonetti into a fight. Here, in the flaring nostrils and the bared teeth, was a fear too wild for reason.

But then, this was different from the games of the fencing hall. Here a mistake meant death — even if one discounted the drowning death waiting a few inches below — and Tom had trouble doing that. He had trouble doing anything but standing low, rocking on his haunches, as they circled each other, and warily touched blades now and then. Testing, sounding, gauging...

Then Bagger stomped ahead for a cut — the charge of that cornered boar Tom's father had warned against. Well, it was too late for caution now. Tom crouched lower and skidded aside just in the nick of time, as the furious blade cleft the air where his head had been, and went to bury its point in the ice with a sharp crack.

Now it was a matter of closing in, as fast as Tom could, his point swirling menacingly as his foe stood as good as disarmed.

"Now step away, fellow, and —"

And that was as far as he went, before Bagger, with a wordless roar, lurched backwards and sideways, wrenching his blade free in an angry swing.

The ice underfoot made it clumsy enough that Tom only had to circle away, noticing, as he did, what that loud crack had been: Bagger's blade was missing its point, and a few good inches of its length — left in the ice, and Fates be thanked for odds evened.

This must have enraged Bagger as much as it lifted Tom's heart: the giant swung his broken blade this way and that, grunting with each blow, padding forward with neither rhyme nor reason...

There was another crack, harder this time, and closer — like a glass of pane breaking...

Oh Lord.

A cold sweat seized Tom. *The fair'll break up, now*, Roger Horne had said with all the placidity in this world. *Not cold enough these past nights.* Breath hitching, he glanced down. Under his feet a fissure glared white against the dark ice, running and branching like a bolt of lightning.

But never — not even for a mortal threat — must one lose sight of an armed foe.

Faster than such a big man had any right to be, Bagger advanced, broken blade pointing at Tom's face. So fast, so unexpected it was, that Tom barely scampered out of harm's way — never mind parrying — to catch himself hard against a ruined stall.

And underfoot the fissures hissed and snapped...

"Bagger!" Tom shouted, dry of mouth and short of wind. "Have a care — the ice —"

Oh, but see how he advanced again, herding Tom away from the edge, towards the centre of the pond... Austin Bagger knew only too well that the ice was breaking.

Tom grabbed the stall's corner and, pivoting around it, adjusted his grip to raise the hilt just before Bagger rounded the corner giving chase.

A dirty trick, Kennard's voice chided in Tom's head, as he slammed the pommel into Bagger's teeth. But then Kennard hadn't seen this ruffian beat Bonetti within an inch of his life. Head snapping back, Bagger bellowed, and still, as he stumbled away, managed to slice through Tom's sleeve... Tartarus take the lurdane, he didn't even fall. Bent low, spitting blood and broken teeth, tears streaming down his face, he still kept his bloodshot eyes rabidly fixed on Tom and his guard high.

"Now, Bagger," Tom called, never lowering his own blade, as he reached for his parrying dagger. "We'll both drown if you keep at this. Mind the ice…"

A man with a grain of wit might have hesitated; Bagger lowed like a bull, and strode ahead again, leaving Tom hardly time to draw his dagger, and stop the vicious swing on his cross-guards. They stayed locked — and, by blood-lust or by design, Bagger turned them around, flailing to catch both of Tom's arms in his own.

By the time he swerved free, Tom found himself with his back to the centre, to the thinner ice… And here came Bagger again.

Again they locked hilts, and again the giant strove to trap Tom, to kick his feet from under him, with all the strength of his big frame, of rage, of fear, and there was no purchase on the slippery surface, and Tom's muscles burnt, and all around the ice cracked and snapped, like the jaws of a pack of wolves…

The chill water, rushing into throat and lungs, the cold, stifling darkness, fingers finding no grip…

And Frances.

One should repent one's sins as death approaches, or so they said. Tom was about to die, with his last task undone, his mentor disappointed in him, his debts unpaid, his sins countless, his only brother estranged, his soul crushed with fear of the black water that was going to swallow him — and all he could think of was Frances.

Growling low in his throat, he shoved back — not that it served.

Frances, wan, and full of sorrow, and so light as she fell asleep in his arms. *I don't learn and love you still.* Now she'd have him to mourn, too…

And then Bagger stopped.

So sudden it was, Tom fell flat on his stomach in a patch of snow, losing his grip on the dagger. Gasping, he rolled away before the giant could skewer him where he was, pin him to the ice with a broken blade…

But no.

Bagger wasn't even looking at him anymore.

Glassy-eyed, panting hard, shoulders hunched and chin stained with blood, the ruffian raised his guard again, swaying from foot to foot, with the air of one wondering whether to run or fight as he stared past Tom.

Propping himself on both elbows, Tom followed Bagger's frightened stare to the edge, and found a man in black garb. A slender, dark figure among the ruined stalls, holding a sword in a careless guard.

"*Mais bon sang!*" he exclaimed, sparing a furious glare for Tom where he lay on the ice.

So Bagger hadn't killed his Frenchman, after all.

"*Monsieur* de Cordaillot," Tom greeted — as evenly as he could while he clambered to his feet on the uncertain ice and recovered the dagger he'd lost in his fall. He sheathed neither blade — not even when the Frenchman slammed his own weapon into its sheathe. "Wishing you'd found yourself a murderer with sharper wits, I'm sure."

Brow darkening, Cordaillot moved closer — close enough to show the rip in the hem of his cloak — the scrap missing, left back in Blackfriars.

"Is this a jesting matter to you, *Monsieur?*"

"Not at all." Tom moved so he could keep one eye on Bagger, and the other on the Frenchman. "Not since a man died, and a friend of mine lies on his deathbed."

It was worth noting, Cordaillot let Bagger out of his sight, as he slowed his progress. He'd walked sure-footed — perhaps not considering the ice in his grim determination. The moment he did, he faltered and stopped, widening his arms for balance.

He quickly recovered, though. "Bonetti?" He asked, tilting his chin at the giant. "They say your English fencing masters did it to teach him a lesson."

Was the cursed ice shifting underfoot? It took some work, Tom found, to ignore it. "So they do — but they're wrong, aren't they, Bagger?"

Cornered beast that he was, Bagger blew his nostrils, the broken point of his sword moving from man to man — one wanting him dead there and then, the other offering the rack and the scaffold, both cutting his way to safety.

It might be that Cordaillot's cold composure was fraying at the edges. "You would not take this pautonnier's word?" he asked. And, when Tom only raised one shoulder in answer, flung out an angry hand. "But come now! All London knows your fencing masters hate Bonetti!"

"True, but none of the Masters was in hiding at the college today, to finish this fumbling churl's work, I'll wager — if poor Bonetti had been there." Tom flicked the point of his sword at the tear on the Frenchman's cloak. "No waste of time, though, for you hid to eavesdrop, and learnt where Bagger was to be found and killed…"

It must be awkward to keep an ambassador's secrets when having a face like that of Pierre de Cordaillot, that showed all his thoughts, changeable and transparent like water on a rock. So transparent, in fact, that even Bagger saw the calculating rage, and hitched half a step towards Tom.

"He hired me!" The giant pointed his sword at the Frenchman. "He said to follow Jack Perkin at Court. No sword there, he said. Make it an accident, he said. And then the Italian—"

"*Silence!*" Even as he reverted to French, Cordaillot's meaning was plain, as he drew and advanced on Bagger.

Tom moved to interfere. "It's a little late for that, *Monsieur.*"

The narrow face twisted, as Cordaillot dropped his cloak to the ice. "It would not be too late for *la Reine Marie*, if that weakling Stafford had not lost his head! And if this useless idiot..." the Frenchman's mouth snapped shut, and he raised his sword in an awkward guard.

And then Bagger lost his head. He howled, and charged, broken sword held high to rush them both, to force his way to safety. The ice groaned under the giant's heavy strides — two, three of them — and then cracked, and a jagged hole broke open, black as Hades, swallowing Austin Bagger but for his head and a flailing arm.

God have mercy!

A flash of movement made Tom spin around, and he raised his arm just in time to take Cordaillot's downward swing on the *forte* of his dagger.

Lord smite all murderous Frenchmen — and pinch all English dunces who let themselves be caught by surprise... So much by surprise, and with such force, that Tom had to take a step back, before he could feint and thrust back. Hardly his most elegant work, though it wrong-footed Cordaillot, who stumbled aside, flailing his free arm for balance — as uneasy fencing on the ice as Tom felt, even more so perhaps.

He never fences, Gerolamo had said. Never with Bonetti — which meant little enough.

When a ragged cry for help sounded from Bagger, Tom knew better than to turn again — much as he wanted to.

"Can you swim, Bagger?" he called, eyes fast on Cordaillot, who was moving, wary and grim, to circle him. Another wanting to herd him towards the broken ice…

"What is it to you if he can, *Monsieur*?" the Frenchman asked. "He would kill you, if he could."

But to drown in the icy jaws of Smithfield Pond… Tom stiffened against a shudder. "You're right — and besides I've no need of him. You heard: he already told me what he had to tell, and…"

And then they'd closed together, and Cordaillot thrust, aiming for the heart. Tom padded aside, one knee on the ice as he pushed his blade under the other's guard, but, instead of touching Cordaillot's arm — the arm, for this one, too, had to be caught alive — the rapier's point entangled in the man's sleeve. Steadying himself with a hand on the ice, Tom pushed upright, using the momentum to skip away from Cordaillot's side cut — to a chorus of crackles and hisses, and Bagger's cry for help.

The hair on Tom's head stood on end, the cold sweat gathering on his brow as he scampered back towards the edge.

Did Cordaillot see his fear? Perhaps, but, for a mercy, he half slipped as he tried to move between Tom and the safe ground. He stayed away, though, far enough to barely touch points. One did: no *gioco stretto* — no close play, when life and death hung in the balance.

"It won't help you, Walsingham," he called in French, a little breathless. "And when you're dead, there will nobody to know!"

Out of the corner of his eye, Tom caught a glimpse of the hole in the ice. It yawned black and empty, having swallowed Austin Bagger…

A burst of shrieking laughter rose from the fair on a gust of wind.

"Oh, but there will be!" Tom made himself lower his stance again, rapier and dagger ready. "My servant, the Italians at the college, the fellow who told me of Bagger's woman, the woman herself... Will you kill them all?"

The Frenchman shook his head. "You never told them!" he said, with the manner of one convincing himself. "You don't discuss *la Reine Marie* with servants and fencers!"

"But the servants and fencers still know you for a murderer."

Then it all happened together. There was a loud, wet gasp from the hole, and a hand appeared grasping at the edge, and Cordaillot stepped ahead and thrust, and from among the stalls came a bellow of "Master!", and Nick Skeres burst out running, sword at the ready, orange coat flying around him.

Tom parried with his dagger, thrusting in turn.

"Master!" Skeres shouted again.

Cordaillot feinted, graceless but forceful.

"Bagger's in the water, Skeres!" called Tom, as he blocked the blow.

"Austin!" a woman screamed, and Gillot Gurney darted across the ice, with Skeres in pursuit.

Oh God spare and deliver!

"A plank, Skeres! But have a care — the ice —"

Tom thought he saw the Minotaur grab the woman around the waist and hurl her back, but after that he had neither breath nor time to spare for anything but Cordaillot.

To the music of Gillot's keening, and Skeres's cursing, and the ice's deadly song, the Frenchman went at Tom in furious earnest. Oh, fury did hinder a man's wits, as all fencing masters said; what they forgot to add was that it made him strong, too.

And besides, why was it that the men Tom wanted to catch alive never had such compunctions when it came to him?

A foolish question, of course.

They fought — no longer the awkward pavane they'd danced before, but a whirl of clumsy violence. At least, Tom vaguely thought, they were close to the pond's edge, and to the bushes…

"Oy!" Skeres's yelp came from behind, distracting Tom as Cordaillot rushed in close, teeth bared in triumph and sword held high.

Oh, Tartarus take it! Tom locked hilts, and turned to catch the Frenchman's dagger arm with his own, and kicked. On any other ground, Cordaillot would have fallen; on the ice, they went down together in a tangle of limbs and blades.

Cordaillot, though, hit his head on the ruined brickwork, hard enough that he lay there dazed — and serve him right!

Dragging himself to his knees, breathless and trembling, Tom sheathed his rapier, and slid his dagger in the back of his belt. He picked Cordaillot's sword from the unresisting fingers, and braced himself upright with it. He hurled it as far as he could, and then cautiously went for the hole.

Oh Lord! Skeres was half in the freezing water, holding for dear life onto the plank that Gillot Gurney clutched half-heartedly, still screaming for Austin.

The ice crackled under each step, and the wind fingered through Tom's clothes, chilling the heat from the fight — and all the time Skeres flailed, impeded by his sodden coat, slipping back, making the plank swing as a seesaw as he grasped for it.

"Nick, be still!" Tom called, going down on his knees, and grabbed the plank just as another jolt tore it from Gillot's hold. Not that she was to blame, for the thing jumped and jarred like a thing alive.

"Don't! Just hold fast!" Tom shouted, heart in his mouth as the ice moved under the plank... And mustn't the cursed cloak get snagged on the ice's edge.

The shifting weight just failed to tear the plank from Tom's gloved hands. "Help me, Sister!" he cried.

The woman hunched on her knees, wide-eyed, her scratched palms pressed to her cheeks.

"Help me!"

She moved, for a mercy, sliding on her knees, made clumsy by her sodden skirts. She clutched Tom's arm first, and then the plank, and together they heaved, and, with a wet, tearing sound, the Minotaur was fished out of the waters.

Half his mind busy offering frantic thanks, Tom clawed a fistful of wet velvet on one side, and the woman's wrist on the other, and dragged them both away from the gaping maw. When they reached the pond's edge, Gillot Gurney dropped in a heap, sobbing and rocking to and fro. And Skeres, even as he shuddered like a rattle, and blue of lips and fingers, was forlornly contemplating the soggy rag that had been his twelve-shillings-eight-pence, lion-hued coat.

Good riddance, Tom didn't say. "Are you much hurt, Dolius?"

The lad looked up, head ducked between his shoulders.

"F-f-forgiven me, 'ave you?"

And what did one say to that? Tom sighed, and shook his head. "Let's find you a fire, before you catch your death."

He turned away — more from the woman's great dry sobs than from Skeres's blue-lipped grin — and went to recover Cordaillot, who still lay curled on his side, moaning and groaning. Whether they'd heard the commotion, or seen it from afar, people were beginning to gather, coming from Smithfield and from the fair, peeking among the stalls.

Lord, but he was cold... Tom picked his cloak up from the ice, shook it, and tried to wrap himself in it. It felt like donning a sheet of snow. When a pair of constables made their way through the small crowd, he made himself draw tall, and steady his voice through chattering teeth, though he spoke low enough that only the constables would hear.

"In the Queen's name, this man is under arrest." He pointed at the dazed Frenchman. "I'm taking him..." Where? The long day, the fight, the rescue, and the relief of being away from the breaking ice, it was all beginning to catch up with Tom, making him numb, and tired, and a little dim. Even inspiration, when it struck, felt sluggish. "I'm taking him to Ely House."

Ely House, that was nearby, that was home to the Vice-Chamberlain of the realm: it had the wardsmen draw straighter, and offer to escort this person who was obviously a Queen's man.

Much to the eager delight of the fair-goers, the constables picked up the dazed Cordaillot between them, and in a trice were ready to march him away — with the Minotaur's eager, if shuddering, assistance — and it was then that Tom found Gillot Gurney at his side, gaze dull and hostile.

Oh yes, Bagger. Bagger, whom he'd done naught to save, if only for the hangman.

"A man drowned in the pond," he called to the constables. "His name was Austin Bagger, of..." He stopped short. What ward had Bagger called home? He sought the woman's eye in question, but she turned away. "I don't know. There may have been a hue and cry for him in the Blackfriars, though."

Not that he knew for sure. Oh well, it mattered little enough. Jove, but he was forspent. He made to run a hand down his face, and stopped, for his gloves were encrusted with frozen mud. When he made to move away he nearly walked into someone — and found that somehow he'd managed to forget Gillot Gurney standing rigid at his elbow, thin lipped and shaking, and staring at Cordaillot.

"What had Austin done, that that one should kill him?" she asked, hoarse and raw. "That you wanted him hanged?"

For the first time Tom noticed that she wore no cloak, no pattens, she'd lost her coif, and her hair fell a-tumble down her back.

He'd have given a good deal not to have to deal with her. "Sister Gurney, you said so yourself: no man hides for a week in a hospital because of his good deeds." There was no answer, and he forged ahead. "He took money from the Frenchman to murder at least two men."

The woman nodded stiffly, just once, and stood there at the edge of the dirty ice, hugging herself against the cold, against her bitterness, and her grief, as Tom hastened away after the constables and the prisoner, with the half-frozen Skeres in tow.

There were roaring fires at Ely House, and there was Sir Christopher Hatton, just as Tom had very much hoped, and there were messengers to have Mr. Davison sent for. What he hadn't reckoned on, was that the cursed Cecils should be there as well, father and son.

"We were discussing Her Grace's slowness in this matter of the warrant," the Vice-Chamberlain said rather pointedly.

Standing by one of those roaring fires, his clothes steaming in the welcome warmth, Tom knew this for a dig at Lord Burleigh, rather than explanation for himself. He bent to warm his hands to the flames, most of all to hide his frown. Discussing in the absence of Sir Francis — and, more interestingly, of Davison, who wasn't lying ill at home, and always allied himself with Sir Francis...

So much for Lord Burleigh's supposed friendship. And at once, as though he'd read Tom's less than pleased mind, the Lord Treasurer strolled close.

"Well, now it seems that young Walsingham brought us just what is needed," he said, bright eyes travelling from Hatton to Tom and back.

So very convenient, that knowing gaze said, and it took all of Tom's self-possession to bow as though he'd truly received praise — all the more because, at his father's elbow, Robert Cecil stood narrow-eyed and watchful.

Did Hatton observe the wordless strain? Hard to tell, but Tom always thought the Vice-Chamberlain hid much under his air of fierce jollity.

"Will he accuse that scoundrel Châteauneuf, do you think?" Hatton asked.

All the way from Smithfield to Ely House, and as he waited for the master of the house to be advised of his presence and that of his strange following, Tom had spent his time arraying the story in his mind, what he would tell, and what he wouldn't — his work made that much easier for Perkin and Bagger being dead, and Bonetti unable to speak. Hatton's question was one he'd considered, and had an answer for, although he made pretence of musing over it a while.

"I wish I could say so, Sir," he said, shaking his head. "But I'm not sure. Cordaillot has admitted very little to me."

"But you think that you know what happened." It was never comfortable to hold Lord Burleigh's piercing, knowing gaze — much less with the added weight of young Robert's knowledge.

It was, however, easier to do when one was secure in Sir Francis's favour.

"Yes, Your Lordship, I believe I do." Tom kept his eyes firmly on the father. "What I don't know is how far the Ambassador is involved."

Hatton clapped his hands once. "It may not matter much. I say we hear the Frenchman among us first, and then we'll see about a written confession."

And Lord Burleigh nodded, and the Vice-Chamberlain called for his people to bring in Cordaillot, and they were going ahead there and then — and never mind that Davison hadn't arrived yet.

Oh Jove! Sir Francis's one firm ally in the Privy Council, and they were leaving him out, and it wasn't as though Tom, little more than a courier after all, could do anything to stop them, when Cordaillot was marched in by no less than three men. Two were Hatton's servants, the third was Skeres, in dry and ill-fitting borrowed clothes, so red of cheeks he glowed, after his encounter with Smithfield Pond — and, Tom suspected, with a few tankards of the Vice-Chamberlain's ale.

Cordaillot himself was of a sickly pallor, but for the bruise mottling the side of his face. He held himself erect, though, and had recovered most of his cold, sharp manner. Not all of it, though: there was the slightest quiver in his voice, as he proclaimed himself a servant of His Excellency the Ambassador, and a subject of the King of France.

"And therefore, *Messieurs*, I object to being assaulted under the guise of an arrest!" He glared at Tom who, for his part, could have embraced the man, since each moment lost in such petty squabbles was a moment gained for Davison. Had anyone told Tom he'd ever bless Pierre de Cordaillot... But bless him he did, as the Frenchman went on to demand that His Excellency be advised, and to claim astonishment at such high-handedness from the Lord Treasurer and the Vice-Chamberlain, and to refuse to answer any questions…

"Then answer none!" Hatton snarled at length, whose brow had been growing more and more thunderous. "It will be enough that you listen to what Mr. Walsingham has to say."

He motioned brusquely at Tom, who took his time going to stand before the Frenchman — and, as he did, there was a knock on the door, and Davison walked in.

Thanking the Fates, Tom waited as the councillor greeted his colleagues, ignored young Cecil, raised an eyebrow at Tom himself and, with an air of grim satisfaction, went to sit.

"Please, go ahead," he said, as though nothing had happened. Oh, this would cause ripples in Council — but for now…

Tom turned to Cordaillot.

"*Monsieur* d'Estrapes used to fence at Rocco Bonetti's college," he began. "And you also went there often enough. Arranging things for *Monsieur* de Châteauneuf's guests, escorting them there, paying their fees on the Ambassador's behalf, the way you did for the Master of Gray."

There was a mirthless chuckle from Hatton, and Cordaillot's lips thinned over some answer he didn't make.

"There you made the acquaintance of William Stafford. You and d'Estrapes both conversed with him — but you, mostly, for, like you, Stafford didn't fence. He was only there to watch — and to talk to French secretaries, if he could. So you heard his tale of woe, and a request for help in travelling to France — in exchange for something. Both Stafford and d'Estrapes have confessed that much, though they differ on who first mentioned regicide. Neither of them, it must be said, made much mention of you."

Cordaillot straightened. "Then you see —"

"But then, neither of them knows that you heard Bonetti's English servant boast that he was off to Court with Leicester's Men, that he was never going to scrub a floor again. The Italians were sour enough about it — but you… it must have frightened you: this man who was a servant of Lord Leicester — the Queen's own favourite. Had you caught him eavesdropping on Stafford, too?"

Through clenched jaws, Cordaillot tried to sneer. "I commend you on your power of invention, *Monsieur*," he said.

"The eavesdropping is a guess," Tom admitted. "In truth, I don't know, nor how you found Austin Bagger — but you hired him to follow Perkin at Placentia and kill him. To make it seem like an accident. With Perkin dead, Stafford could continue his murderous plot, in time to save Mary Stuart."

"There was hope while the Scottish Queen was still living," murmured Lord Burleigh, who must have read Moody's confession.

Cordaillot stared at the Lord Treasurer long and hard. "Is it not a Christian's duty, *Monseigneur*," he asked, cold again, "to pray that a life — a sovereign's life — may be spared?"

An icy silence met this — all of them thanking God, most likely, that the Frenchman's argument would never reach the Queen's ear.

It was with some abruptness that Tom resumed.

"To pray, yes. To kill is another matter, isn't it? And all for nothing, for then Stafford lost his courage. Not a day after you'd had a man murdered to protect him, the fool must go and discover it all. I'm sure your Ambassador has ears enough at Court that he heard of it the same day. He must have been furious — and so must have you —"

"His Excellency knew naught of this!" Cordaillot stepped forward, hands fisted and shoulders taut. "Yes, Stafford came to Salisbury Court, he spoke to d'Estrapes, he said he had the means to have your Queen murdered. And d'Estrapes, who lacks a sparrow's wits, went with him to the prison, to speak to some prisoner or other who said he knew how to do the murder. When His Excellency heard of this, oh, he was very, very angry. He berated d'Estrapes for a fool, ordered him back to Paris, and forbade that Stafford should ever set foot at Salisbury Court again. This is how angry he was!"

"But not angry enough to advise us, Her Majesty's Councillors, that a subject of the realm was plotting murder," Davison said sourly.

"Is that a foreign ambassador's duty?" It sounded as though Cordaillot was repeating someone else's words. "Every word that we utter, any step that we take, is looked upon with such suspicion."

Before Davison could explode, Lord Burleigh raised both hands, and hummed in the most understanding manner. "Still," he said. "It could be argued that, if France claims any friendship toward England, a warning would have been in order."

A twist of the mouth. "A difficult point, *Monsieur*," Cordaillot said — again as though speaking another's words. "His Excellency was sending to Paris, asking the King's pleasure on what he should do, but Stafford confessed. His Excellency was greatly relieved — and that's all there is to it."

"Yes, yes," Hatton waved this away. "We've heard the same from d'Estrapes. And perhaps, for all he knows, it's true. But you, *Monsieur* — you and the Ambassador…?"

And this time Cordaillot couldn't help himself. "The Ambassador!" He shook his head and gave a bitter laugh. "To His Excellency Stafford's raving were like the plague! He was afraid he would be blamed, sent away from London to face the

King's wrath." He looked from man to man, and there was a colour of contempt in his speech. "He ordered us all to forget Stafford's ravings, and the man at Newgate. Never once did he think of the *Reine Marie*."

And now this Tom believed. Unlike d'Estrapes, this secretary wasn't protecting his master, who perhaps had seen through Stafford, and perhaps hadn't, and either way had been wary of compromising himself for the sake of Mary Stuart. Cordaillot, on the other hand…

"But you did think of her." Tom stepped forward to loom over the Frenchman. "You thought that, once Her Highness was dead, and Mary Stuart on the throne, none of it would matter. So you stopped Perkin —"

"No!"

"You would have been hailed as a hero in Mary Stuart's England. In Queen Elizabeth's, though, you were a murderer and a plotter —"

"No, I tell you!" Gone was the coldness, replaced by a passion of bitterness.

"Your master, if he knew, would throw you to the wolves to save himself: what could you do, but cover your tracks?"

"You little prying toad!" Oh, the hatred burning in Cordaillot's wide-set eyes! "You lie. You meddle. You slander. You spin inventions so your masters can blame the French, and drag *la Reine Marie* to her fate!"

Tom's breath caught, for this was far too close to the truth for comfort, no matter how blindly Cordaillot was lashing out. And, of all things, it must be Lord Burleigh who intervened, with the barest curl of his knowing smile.

"It seems to me that we've little need for invention, with what you've already done today. You can hardly deny that."

"Now I will say no more, *Monseigneur*, since all I can tell you either already know, or will not believe."

And with that he crossed his arms, and turned away from Burleigh and them all, straight-backed, staring at the grey sky past the window, until Hatton clicked his tongue in disgust.

"Sulking will avail you nothing, Cordaillot. We know what happened, don't we?" This last to Tom.

And this, thank God, was safer ground. "We know that Rocco Bonetti had suspicions, when he learnt of Perkin's death — and he sent word to me."

"And Mr. Cordaillot knew of it?" young Cecil asked — devil pinch him!

The very question Tom had hoped no one would ask, for he had no sure answer, unless... One single glass piece moved in his mind — the piece that had been a man following him to Blackfriars. Not Cormac Faddigan, no...

"I believe that he followed me from this very house, the morning he came to inquire after d'Estrapes. And when he saw I was going to meet Bonetti, he rushed to seek Perkin's murderer again." A glance revealed Cordaillot staring, stiff and blank, at the window. He never stirred as Tom recounted Bagger's assault on poor Bonetti — but for the working of his jaw.

"But Bonetti didn't die, though he was hurt so grievously he couldn't talk."

"And this man knew it?" Lord Burleigh asked, just as his son had, though less dubiously.

"No, my Lord — nor could he send Bagger to finish the work at the college, so he tried it himself, visiting under the guise of a concerned friend. Poor Bonetti was never alone, though, and then Bagger also failed to kill Michael Moody at Newgate."

And see how this startled Cordaillot, how he swung around, and opened his mouth to protest, and then snapped it shut. Could he be innocent of this one thing among all? Could the assault on Moody have been nothing but a prisoners' brawl? And did the councillors need to hear this? Before Tom could decide...

"A most bungling bully to hire!" Hatton exclaimed with a snort.

But then he hadn't seen the man stomp on poor, wounded Rocco. "That — and perhaps he was growing fearful, or too greedy, or loose-tongued. At all accounts, he knew far too much, and had just wits enough to run and hide."

Davison hummed intently. "But not so well or so far that he wasn't found."

"This was part chance and part my fault, I fear." Tom grimaced. "I went to Blackfriars this morning, to ask questions — being more and more convinced that whoever had hired Bagger must have to do with Stafford's plot. There was no talking to Bonetti, who lies dying at the hospital, poor fellow — but I learnt where tidings of Bagger could be had. And," he strode to stand between Cordaillot and the window, forcing the Frenchman to face him. "And *Monsieur* was there. Again, he couldn't finish Bonetti — but he could hide, and overhear about Bagger. How he was heard, and discovered, and how he ran, you've heard."

"Young Walsingham found both Cordaillot and this Bagger at Smithfield Pond," Lord Burleigh explained to Davison. "Cordaillot caused Bagger's death, and would have killed Walsingham, too."

It irked Tom a little, how grimly amused the Lord Treasurer sounded.

"But Bagger managed to tell me that *Monsieur* Cordaillot had hired him to kill Jack Perkin and Rocco Bonetti. Of Moody, I will say, there was no word."

Cordaillot laughed, and threw up his hands. "And you will believe this?" he cried. "You will believe these lies —" He broke off with a grunt when Skeres grabbed him and threw him on the window bench. But even with the Minotaur looming over him, the Frenchman picked himself up and appealed to Burleigh.

"Milord, you must see that it is all a lie!"

There was no laughter left in the Lord Treasurer's narrow gaze. "Are you saying that your man Bagger lied?"

"He was not my man, Milord!"

"Then he lied when he said so? Or is Mr. Walsingham lying when he says that he did?"

This threw Cordaillot. He warily eyed Tom, as he raked his mind, surely, to remember what he had said before…

Hatton didn't give him the chance. "We have our answer, I believe," he said, and then motioned at Skeres and at his own servant. "Take him away. Lock him up well, while we decide what's to be done with him."

As he was grabbed by both arms, Cordaillot stiffened at first — then swallowed, and took a hold of himself, enough to stand tall between his captors. "*Messieurs*, it is not me that you insult here," he said — just too loud in the effort of keeping his voice steady. "His Excellency the Ambassador will have much to say."

With this he suffered himself to be led away.

There was the shortest silence in the wake of the Frenchman's departure, and then Hatton chuckled.

"His Excellency had much to say about one of his men seized — I can't wait to hear what he'll say now that we hold two!"

"Well," Davison wasn't amused at all. "D'Estrapes was a fool who listened to plotters — but this one's twice a murderer. Even Châteauneuf can't have much to say for him."

By the way he raised his white eyebrows, one'd think there wasn't much that Lord Burleigh put beyond the French Ambassador. "Now I don't know how much of this should be made known," he said, sparing a searching glance for Tom. "It's a very grave matter. I believe, Mr. Davison, that Her Highness should be advised of it at once."

So to have Châteauneuf summoned in disgrace before he could barge at Placentia with grievances to air, the Treasurer didn't say. And so that Davison would be thrown to take the brunt of the Queen's certain displeasure...

Heaven be thanked, for it seemed a heathen thing to call on the Fates at such a moment! Keeping his face as blank as he knew, Tom went to lean against the carved mantel-shelf, and let himself exhale, long and slow. Could he hope that it was done? That Cordaillot's murderous actions had proved the danger of Stafford's plot beyond doubt?

He watched as the three councillors took their place at the table — Hatton grim, Davison sombre, Burleigh inscrutable. Firelight limned them in red gold on one side, and through the tall window the glowering afternoon painted them the starkest grey on the other — which seemed terribly fitting as they chose the words that would force a Queen's hand, and seal the already doomed fate of another.

Just as Sir Francis, from his sickbed, had meant that it should be.

"Robert!"

Tom shook off his fancies as the Lord Treasurer called his son, and found that young Cecil had come to kneel by the hearth's other side, poking skew-shouldered at the fire. He straightened as he was called, impassive and ready.

"You'll be Mr. Davison's amanuensis for this, Robert," Lord Burleigh instructed, before giving Tom his most amiable consideration. "And I'm sure young Walsingham will want to ride to Barn Elms with the tidings."

Couched as it was in regard for the absent Mr. Secretary, it was dismissal plain and simple — and far from unexpected, for one who didn't sit on the Council and never would. In fact, it was just this side of impertinence that such a lowly fellow, instead of bowing himself out, should still ask:

"What of Cordaillot, Your Lordship? I had no warrant to apprehend him. If the Ambassador should demand his release…"

The faintest amusement flickered in Lord Burleigh's eyes — so faint Tom couldn't be sure… Still it was Davison who answered.

"The Ambassador won't be in a position to demand much," he said. "We'll see to it that your actions are made fully lawful, though. After all, you caught him killing a man, and he tried to kill you as well."

A stretch of the truth, perhaps — but it would do for long enough.

Hatton chuckled. "Don't fret, lad. We won't let your Frenchman run. I'll keep him under lock and key … unless you'd rather bring him back to Seething Lane with you?"

And never let Sir Francis know that, if only for a heartbeat, his kinsman believed the Vice-Chamberlain in earnest. At the very last moment he managed to smile at the jest. Jove, but he must be tired!

Still smiling, if a little stiffly, he bowed, and thanked the Vice-Chamberlain, and His Lordship, and Mr. Davison. Did Davison see that he was being set up for the Queen's ire? He did, by the grim set of his mouth — but still he could be trusted to see to Sir Francis's interest in this.

And then Tom did take his leave, and bowed himself out.

He was halfway down the stairs, and contemplating the recovery of his horse at St. Bartholomew, when he heard himself called.

On the landing Robert Cecil stood, one hand on the carved railing.

And it was petty, surely, to wait instead of walking up again to meet the hunchback — but Tom did just that, waiting for the man who thought he'd torn his loyalty to shreds.

"Sir Robert?" He made no effort to hide his dislike, either.

It seemed to amuse Cecil greatly — the black-minded lamprey! See how he had the gall to raise that cursed eyebrow.

"You'll have a snowy ride, I fear," he said, affecting to frown at the sky through the mullioned window. "All the more irksome because you're just back from Barn Elms, aren't you?"

Tom just stared at the man in silence.

Not that Lord Burleigh's son would be discomposed — or was he? Had his knowing smile just tightened at the corners?

"I trust you found Mr. Secretary not too ill," he said, voice growing colder.

But no, it would have taken a greater fool than Tom to flatter himself he'd vexed Robert Cecil. It was all a memento of the threat and a demand.

Young Cecil thinks that he can play you like a fiddle... Was it only this morning that Tom had discussed this with Sir Francis? The means to keep the lamprey wondering, and himself out of prison.

He turned away, not quite swallowing a curse — because this was what a man under threat would do, wasn't it? The loathing he didn't have to feign as he said in a harsh whisper: "I found him ill and despondent." A pause that, hopefully, would seem like angry reluctance. "He sees threats in every corner."

"Did he order you to find the Frenchman?"

Because it couldn't be easy, could it? Cecil was bound to ask questions. Tom angrily shook his head. "He fretted about what Bonetti told me of Stafford, and then there was the assault."

Cecil's arched brows quivered. "This matter of Stafford makes Mr. Secretary fretful?"

"When he thinks whose brother Stafford is. But now..." Tom looked up past Cecil's hunched shoulder, towards the room where the Councillors worked. Where they'd heard Cordaillot.

"But now, yes." Of all things in this world, Cecil reached to pat Tom's arm, and spoke just a little louder. "Have a safe ride, Mr. Walsingham. And a safe return."

And the servant that traversed the hall downstairs carrying a couple of stools, what must he have thought them, but the best of friends taking leave of each other?

Oh Lord.

Tom sighed to himself as Cecil hastened back up the stairs. The moment he found himself thrown into Newgate, he'd know he'd failed in this charade.

CHAPTER 12

Davison arrived at noon, clutching a paper case and looking very solemn, and found the house all full of brisk ado. All London was in the same state, the whole of England astir with wild rumours. The Queen of Scots broken out of prison; London sacked and burnt; the Spanish *tercios* landed in Wales...

Tom, who still continued un-imprisoned, left the latest messenger, who had just come galloping in from Cornwall — drenched with rain, and grim with stories of being stayed again and again on the unquiet roads — to escort Davison up to Sir Francis's room.

On the landing, the Councillor stopped to contemplate the coming-and-going of mud-spattered men down in the hall.

"These are strange times that we live in, young Thomas," he said, shaking his head. "How is Mr. Secretary faring?"

How, indeed? Sir Francis's health had wavered since New Year — for the worse and for the better — until he'd felt strong enough to return to London. Or, at least, he'd felt compelled to do so. All the same, he was still keeping his Aventine, he said — like the Romans of old retiring from public things in protest — but this was not to be openly discussed, not even with an ally.

"In somewhat better spirits," was all that Tom said.

When Davison smiled, it occurred to Tom he'd never seen him do it before. It was a very grim smile, twisting the man's whole face askew, and gone in a heartbeat.

"Well, this should raise his spirits higher," he said, patting his case. "Although Her Majesty jested that the blow could kill him."

To the Queen's jests one laughed, in the Queen's presence. Otherwise…

Tom knocked on the study door, and showed in Davison, and made to retreat — when Sir Francis sat up of a sudden, eyes flashing. What had he seen in his visitor's face?

"Stay, Thomas," he ordered, and then shook his head at Davison's frown. "Old friend, my cousin has worked long and hard for this, and will have to work a good deal more. He may as well hear it now."

And this was how Tom knew that Mary Stuart's time had run out.

Without a word, without quite waiting for Davison's half-hearted nod, he took his place behind Sir Francis's chair, cold of a sudden in spite of the great roaring fire.

His eight years in the Service, his blood, his conscience — all of it had been for this, long before he quite understood it. He watched as the parchment was placed before Mr. Secretary.

"Signed this morning, and to be kept a secret," Davison said, throwing the briefest glance Tom's way. "I'm on my way to the Lord Chancellor to have it sealed."

And of course Tom's eight years were nothing to Sir Francis's work of a lifetime. For a long while Mr. Secretary Walsingham stared at the Queen's great signature, all angles and edges, no matter how many flourishes she drew around it.

"Lord be praised," he breathed, so softly that Tom wasn't sure Davison heard it. And then he was all sharpness again, narrowing his eyes at Davison. "To be kept a secret, you say?"

"As much as possible. So far, only my lords Burleigh and Leicester have seen it — beside us."

"She surely sees it can't be kept a secret for long," Sir Francis retorted.

Reckoning by his sigh, Davison must have raised the same argument — and had his ears singed for it.

"Her Majesty forbids a public execution," he said, and raised a hand to forestall Sir Francis's objection. "She forbids quite a few things, Mr. Secretary — among them to ever address her on the subject again." He knitted his brows in recollection. "She says she has done all that law and reason could require of her."

There was impatience and weariness in equal parts in Sir Francis's huff. "As long as she doesn't change her mind," he said, and then stiffened when Davison dropped his gaze.

This new silence was different — taut and brittle.

Sir Francis stared very hard at his colleague as, outside, the rain hissed, relentless and angry.

When Davison looked up again, his eyes were troubled.

"Her Highness is very unhappy to have this matter on her conscience," he said in a low rumble. Again, he eyed Tom, and sighed when Sir Francis showed no inclination to dismiss his kinsman. "And most displeased with Paulet."

Sir Amias Paulet was Mary Stuart's keeper. Her gaoler, the Catholics said — and for once, by all accounts, they may not be far off the mark. But what could such a zealous man have done now to displease the Queen?

"Because he won't ease her burden," Sir Francis murmured, because he knew his sovereign very well.

So unsurprised he sounded, that it was a few heartbeats before his meaning took shape in Tom's mind. *Ease her burden...*

And, if it hadn't been plain enough, there was Davison's bleak answer: "Her Highness wishes us to write to Sir Amias."

Tom's jaw fell slack. *To ease her burden.* He swallowed hard, and both Sir Francis and Davison had the mercy to ignore him.

Oh Lord — but he was a fool! Only a fool would be angry at his Queen for this. For accepting daily in sacrifice the souls of men who toiled and risked and sinned for her sake and that of England, and yet refusing to stain her own. Only a fool would call in his mind Elizabeth Tudor a shrewd, cunning, capricious old woman who expected others to sin in her place.

To see Sir Francis nod, one would have thought he was discussing the preparations for a hunt. "I'd advise that you go to the Lord Chancellor now, Mr. Davison. Once the warrant is sealed, you'll be so good to come back here, and we'll write that letter."

Had Davison feared to be left alone to deal with this? There was a command from the Queen — but Sir Francis could have pled ill health and stepped out of it. That he did not, poor Davison seemed grimly thankful, as he took his leave.

In the most awkward silence, Tom saw the Councillor to the door, and then joined his cousin again. Perhaps he'd learnt through the years to keep himself in check, or perhaps these past months had worn Sir Francis's patience thin, for he didn't wait for the questions.

"Yes, Thomas?" he asked.

"Paulet…"

"Paulet will refuse, being an honourable man. Her Highness will rage a good deal, but with the warrant sealed, it matters little."

"Will he suffer for it?"

"Not overly, for Her Highness can't very well admit what she asked him to do. There will be displeasure, though."

To ease her burden… It stung Tom's stomach like vinegar. "But can she truly believe that, were Sir Amias to obey her order, she'd be freed of blame? It is no sin at all to execute an enemy who's worked to harm England for so long. But pushing another to murder a helpless prisoner outside the law…" He stopped short, hearing the heat in his voice. "Crave pardon, Sir — I…"

There was no reproach, no impatience in the dark grey gaze — so much like Frances's. "I've always thought you'd make a good lawyer, Thomas — but a prince's conscience has different workings. Consider this: what troubles Her Highness more, to sin *per se*, or to sanction the death of another crowned Queen? Either way, be sure that she'll find someone to blame. Myself perhaps, or more likely poor Mr. Davison."

"But, Sir…"

Sir Francis's eyes strayed to the table where the inlaid case sat, and the Queen's gift — the golden chain that had journeyed from Barn Elms together with Sir Francis, and the *Histories* of Polybius.

"At the same time, sovereigns are men under their resplendent mantles, Thomas. Or women. The mortal vessels into which God himself pours the fire of Royal power — and this is what we serve as best we can: that fire, and God's own will. That we can be burnt doing it, is in the nature of things."

Burnt, not unlike those who worked against that same fire. Father Ballard, Mary Stuart herself, Cordaillot — unless Cordaillot was to benefit from the rueful goodwill that, once the Scot Queen was dead, was planned to restore Châteauneuf and D'Estrapes to freedom with many apologies. But then, they all believed they were serving Divine Will in turn. It was those who had no such compunctions — like the Scots envoys, and Stafford, and Archibald Douglas — who served themselves, and seldom seemed to be burnt.

In the end, there was no answer for Sir Francis — except for one.

"If you've no need of me now, Sir, I'd better go and see to the messengers," Tom said, holding his cousin's gaze. "I'll come and write for you when Mr. Davison is back."

I'll write that letter under your dictation. I won't desert you. I won't hide. I'll follow you, and shoulder my part of the burning. None of this he said, but Sir Francis must have heard it all the same, because he nodded and, of all things, smiled.

Didn't they burn men inside brazen idols in Hannibal's Carthage? Tom shook off the notion as he hastened downstairs, to see to the messengers. These unprofitable — and quite possibly traitorous — musings, he'd keep for his own leisure. For his sleepless nights. He was of those who did what must be done. Of those who served not an ungrateful Queen, but that fire of Royal power.

Or was he? Tom stopped short, struck by the sudden thought.

Was he, really?

No, in honest truth perhaps he wasn't. In honest truth, for all his squeamish conscience, he lacked that purity of purpose. The one he served was the great man who, at the cost of his own soul, kept that fire burning in the vessel that was Elizabeth Tudor. He served that clear-eyed, selfless, unbending courage he wished he could possess. Surely there were worse, and pettier, and meaner aspirations in this world?

He shook his head at himself, and resumed his descent.

Yes, he decided, as he beckoned to Skeres who awaited at the stairs' foot, and plunged in the whirl of true and false havoc in the scriveners' room: he had, after all ... how had Marley put it in his play?

He had an aspiring mind.

HISTORICAL NOTES

[A] practice betwixt the French Ambassador and a lewd young miscontented person named William Stafford, and one Moody, a prisoner in Newgate, a mischievous resolute person, how her Majesty's life should be taken away.

Lord Burleigh, 17 February 1586/87 (HT.iii.224)

In the very early days of 1587 (still January 1586 in the slightly maddening notion of Elizabethan time-keeping), yet another Catholic plot came to the surface in the middle of festivities: William Stafford confessed to Mr. Secretary Walsingham first, and then several other Privy Councillors, that he'd meant to murder Queen Elizabeth, and put Mary Stuart on the throne, with the full approval of Guillaume de Châteauneuf, the French Ambassador in London.

The thing caused, understandably, a considerable stir, all the worse because William Stafford was not any penniless young discontent. In spite of his family's well-known Catholic leanings, his mother had some influence at Court and with the Queen herself, and his brother was the Queen's Ambassador in Paris, a Cecil man, and a thorn in Sir Francis Walsingham's side. That young William should go and confess to Mr. Secretary, of all men, was perhaps a little strange. All else apart, Sir Francis was not even at Court, held at his house of Barn Elms by a combination of ill health, familial grief, and dissension with the Queen... Nonetheless, it was to him that Stafford went with his sudden change of heart. Sir Francis, apparently, did little more than hand the man to his colleagues: the repentant aspiring regicide was promptly imprisoned at the

Tower, and so was Châteauneuf's secretary Léonard d'Estrapes (or des Trappes), caught while he tried to flee to France. The French Ambassador reacted with great indignation — but, while firmly laying the whole regicidal scheme at Stafford's door, he could not deny that he knew of it, and his reasons for not informing the English government sounded embarrassingly weak. It was not long before he was put under house arrest, and his correspondence stopped.

Queen Elizabeth was not amused. Ever since October, when Mary Stuart had been convicted and sentenced to death, she had been dithering over her cousin's execution. It was the unavoidable next step, but (much to Sir Francis's exasperation) Elizabeth was loath to have on her conscience the death of her troublesome cousin and fellow-queen. Now this piece of evidence that Mary was still a dangerous beacon for all sorts of conspirators, home and abroad, was just what it took to alarm Elizabeth into action. She still did it with the worst grace — and her attempt to have Sir Amias Paulet murder Mary is as chilling as it is fascinating — but in the end, on the 1st of February, the death warrant was drawn and signed, and there was no going back. A week later, Mary Stuart was beheaded at Fotheringay.

And that would have been that — except for the aftermath of the Stafford Plot itself, or rather the lack thereof. Nothing much happened to William Stafford who, in time, was released from prison and suffered to lead an uneventful life. D'Estrapes and Châteauneuf regained their freedom soon enough, together with an apology from Sir Francis Walsingham himself: perhaps the Council — particularly Davison — had been a tad hasty to trust Stafford's word... The way it all sizzled out — except for Mary Stuart's death, of course — has led a number of historians to doubt the authenticity of the plot. Isn't it possible that young Stafford (who, in a letter, had proclaimed himself eager to repay his unspecified great debt to Mr. Secretary) might have been under orders to feign a plot, and to involve Châteauneuf, to both force the Queen's hand, and minimize any possible French interference?

Well, it is. Sir Francis had worked very hard to rid England of the Queen of Scots, and may well have run out of patience with Elizabeth's qualms. While there is no certain proof that he crafted a faux conspiracy to force his sovereign's hand, I have no particular trouble believing it. I chose it at my central storyline for this book, because it makes for a fascinating tale.

Of all the people involved in it, only Jack Perkin and a couple of suspects are entirely fictional. All the rest are real, and their actions as described in the book are (more or less closely) based off the contemporary sources on the plot: William Stafford, Michael Moody, Ambassador Châteauneuf, d'Estrapes, Cordaillot, the Scots envoys, Archibald Douglas, Sir Christopher Hatton, Sir Walter Mildmay, Lord Burleigh, Sir John Popham, and poor William Davison, who ended up as the scapegoat for it all, and spent time in the Tower.

Sarah White, her daughter Janet, and Elias Werner are fictional, and Rocco Bonetti's involvement in the matter is entirely my invention, but Bonetti, his high-born pupils, and "his boy" Gerolamo/Jeronimo are historical, and it's true that poor Rocco died, early in 1587, of the wounds inflicted on him by a nasty piece of work named Austin Bagger. George Silver, who tells the tale, blames (not very sorrowfully) the fact on the keen rivalry between the Italian and English fencing schools, and in truth, people like William Joyner, Isaac Kennard, William Mucklowe, and his pupil Horne (whose names I found in *The Noble Science*, Herbert Berry's transcription of Sloane Ms. 2530) would have little reason to love the self-important and wildly successful Italian. All I did was to tie the fencing rivalry together with the Stafford Plot.

It is also true that Will Kempe and Leicester's Men were playing and tumbling at Court at the time, and that Kempe had carried (and miscarried) letters for his master — at a time when the alliance between Lord Leicester and Secretary Walsingham was beginning to fray at the edges. The trust had been waning for some time, but it all soured after Philip Sidney's death, when Frances did miscarry a baby girl.

Finally, while Tom's debts are only too real, there's not the slightest hint that he was ever accosted by Robert Cecil on the matter, nor that Audrey Shelton was ever supposed to marry Edmund Walsingham. Nor is there anything to suggest that Tom was at all involved in the Stafford Plot — but it seems to me that it would have made a good deal of sense for Sir Francis, in his difficult moment, to rely on his trusted young kinsman.

A NOTE TO THE READER

Dear Reader,

Thank you for reading *A Snare of Deceit*. I hope you enjoyed it. You'll have noticed there's a certain amount of fencing in this book — both in play and deadly earnest. If you read the second book in the series, *A Treasonous Path*, then you may remember the Italian Rocco Bonetti, fencing master and occasional intelligencer. Back then he was the only Master in sight, and his career only played a marginal role; this time he has been joined by several of his colleagues (although he would shudder to hear me call them so) — and the rival fencing schools in London are rather integral to the plot. A good deal of research was involved, and I have a little story to tell about it.

Just as I was working on my final draft, the historic Accademia Campogalliani started work on the production of a play of mine about James Crichton of Cluny, the real Admirable Crichton (as opposed to Barrie's resourceful butler): Crichton, a young Scottish adventurer of good birth and many talents, arrived in Mantua in early 1582, and enjoyed a meteoric success. Then, in the course of five short months, came to grief, as meteors do — in the sort of way that, when it's brought to the stage, requires some serious swordplay.

Enter Fausto Lusetti, a modern-day Provost-at-Arms specialising in historical fencing, and his Free-Scholar, Giulia Pasini. When I heard from my friend Barbara (stage-manager extraordinaire) that these two had been brought on board to coach our two leading men, I jumped at the chance — and begged for half an hour with Fausto and Giulia. Permission being granted, I gate-crashed the very next rehearsals, and met the fencers. It turned out that Fausto had read my Crichton novel years ago, and was quite happy to help me with *A Snare of Deceit*. So I spent a happy hour with him and Giulia, plying them with questions, taking copious notes, seeking advice about the various fencing scenes, and sketching stick-figures as they demonstrated for me the Italian and the English styles in the foyer of the Teatrino d'Arco. In truth it was rather longer than an hour, and rather more than happy: what a joy to see my research come to life like this, to see put into practice what I'd previously only read about, to admire the skill and elegance of these extremely knowledgeable, generous people, who never tired of answering questions and offering suggestions! Then I drove home with pages and pages of notes, and spent a day rewriting several scenes, with the advantage of having actually *seen* how Tom, Bonetti, young Gerolamo, Kennard, Bagger, Cordaillot and the others would have fenced some four centuries ago.

It was an unexpected and thoroughly fascinating aspect of the research that went into *A Snare of Deceit* — and I hope I did justice to Fausto and Giulia's bravura in my story.

What do you say, dear Reader? Did you enjoy the fencing in the book?

I'd love to hear from you — about this or Tom's adventures generally —through my **website** or **via Twitter** — where I tweet under the handle **@laClarina**. Meanwhile, if you enjoyed *A Snare of Deceit*, I would truly appreciate it if you'd drop by **Amazon** and **Goodreads** to post a review, and let other readers know that you enjoyed this novel.

Thank you, and we'll meet again in the next Tom Walsingham book!

C. P. Giuliani

Sapere Books is an exciting new publisher of brilliant fiction and popular history.

To find out more about our latest releases and our monthly bargain books visit our website:
saperebooks.com

Printed in Great Britain
by Amazon

44534581R00165